I0746952

or really impressed. This service is reserved for emergencies, sir, not fairy tales.'

"Readers interested in a blend of comedy, thriller, and medical mystery will find *Pleasuria: Take As Directed* just the ticket for an involving, different story that creates a compelling tale that's hard to put down and satisfyingly fun."

—MIDWEST BOOK REVIEW

"Pleasuria is a 'who done it' murder-mystery that you don't want to have solved. Sprinkled with enough levity to effortlessly transition from tragedy to fortune, Jessop has found our pleasure center and we are begging him for more. Take only as directed!"

—BENJAMIN H. BERKLEY, author In Defense Of Guilt and
Against My Will

"A very funny novel from John J Jessop. Who wouldn't want to give up a stable but boring job to become a private investigator! The quirks, antics and aspirations of a middle-aged man in the throes of a mid-life crisis are farcical at times but all the better for it. The Red-Rocket is pure class. I thoroughly enjoyed this book and look forward to more from John."

—HEIKE PHELAN, author of Child Convict

Pleasuria:
Take as Directed

by John J Jessop

ISBN: 978-1-7358178-3-5

This is a work of fiction. The characters are both actual and fictitious. With the exception of verified historical events and persons, all incidents, descriptions, dialogue and opinions expressed are the products of the author's imagination and are not to be construed as real.

Published by:

JJJESSOP LLC

PLEASURIA

TAKE AS DIRECTED

JOHN J JESSOP

DEDICATION

To my beautiful baby sister, one of the strongest women I have ever known, who grew into a loving mother, awesome human being, and best friend; and for those late-night talks where we were able to somehow turn tragic memories into laughter.

CHAPTER 1

CureStuff Pharmaceuticals was a biotech company located in Research Triangle Park, North Carolina, that developed treatments for depression, restless leg syndrome and erectile dysfunction. Dr. Wendy Thompkins, senior vice president of clinical trials, sat in the boardroom, struggling to stay awake as Dr. Richard Littlething, the five-foot-six-inch troll who was president and CEO of CureStuff, droned on to senior management about the company's quarterly report. Wendy was a fifty-year-old physician who maintained the strict image of a successful executive, her posture permanently erect and her wardrobe a tailored, dark-blue pants suit. Tall and slender, with the long, athletic legs of a runner, she kept her red hair short and relaxed in natural waves. She had blue eyes, a smooth complexion, full lips and a small mouth that seldom held a smile, all of which remained free of makeup.

Wendy ran the clinical trial for their new blockbuster drug for depression and was waiting for her turn to report on the study progress. She perked up when she heard Dick Littlething say, "We at CureStuff are sitting on a new drug for depression that has the potential to make millions. If the ongoing clinical trial shows that the drug works, we'll be rich beyond our wildest dreams. Failure could mean bankruptcy and massive layoffs. I don't know about the rest of you, but I just bought a forty-foot boat and a new Mercedes for my ex-wife, and I can't afford to be looking for a job right now."

Dick turned to Wendy and said, "Now, Dr. Thompkins will give us a progress report on our very important clinical trial."

Wendy looked startled and leaned forward in her chair, grabbed the table with both hands and whispered, "Oh my God! That feels so good. What's happening?"

Dr. Lance Harden, SVP for research and Wendy's current lover, glanced in her direction from his seat next to her. Her eyes were glossed over, accompanied by a bewildered smile. Realizing there was something wrong, he tried to cover for her by interrupting. "I don't think that we have anything to worry about, Dick. As you all know, I developed the drug in my laboratory, and it showed great promise in the studies in depressed rats. And those rats were really depressed. We forced them to watch CNN 24/7. With a steady dose of our drug, the rats were quite cheerful by the end of the study."

Dr. Tanya Grayson, VP of the toxicology group and Wendy's best friend from their time together at the University of North Carolina, spoke up. "That's just what we need, Lance, a bunch of happy rats. Studies have shown that drugs that work well in humans generally bring in a lot more money than drugs that work well in rats."

All eyes turned to Wendy again, expecting her to speak. Instead, she leaned forward further in her seat, her body stiffened; she wore a far-off stare. "Ooooh, that's nice; that feels really good. Don't stop."

Lance turned and whispered, "Wen, what's the matter? You look a little strange. Are you okay?"

Wendy's nipples were erect, and she felt a strange wave of heat flow down her belly and a tingling between her legs. She had an uncontrollable urge to squeeze her thighs together to enhance the delightful sensation.

She broke out into a hot sweat, began to moan softly, and whispered, "Ooooh, yes, don't stop, please, please."

The senior managers stared as she moaned louder. Lance was particularly attentive; he had heard these sounds from her before, but in the privacy of his bedroom. He turned and whispered to her again, more forcefully, "Wendy, are you okay? Is something the matter? You seem to be moaning, and not in a good way—at least not for here."

Without realizing it, Wendy had grabbed the edge of the oak table with both hands to steady herself for the impending explosion of pleasure, too far gone to hear Lance. She thought, *What the hell is happening? I have to stop, focus, be professional. Give this stupid report. But oh God, that feels so good. I'm almost there.*

Lance was getting increasingly concerned as Wendy moaned again, louder this time, and said softly, "Ooooh my God! That's incredible. That's soooo good!"

Lance smiled, shrugged, placing both of his hands on the top of the conference table. He did his best to send the telepathic message, *It's not me. Nothing going on here. See, my hands are in plain sight.*

Dick, preoccupied with trying to think of a catchy response to Lance and Tanya's comments, noticed Wendy's excited state. "Dr. Thompkins. It's time for your report. Are you okay? You appear to be aroused, odd for a company meeting. Is it something I said? While it's quite flattering, I've never seen my quarterly reports have this effect on anyone."

Dick saw her hands clinging to the table, unavailable for self-stimulation. When she didn't respond, he suspected she was mocking him; it wouldn't have been the first time one of his female colleagues had done so. He said more sternly, "This is not appropriate behavior for a business meeting. But if it must continue, perhaps you could share your secret with the rest of us."

When she still didn't respond, he started to walk around the table towards her. He noticed that Lance, seated next to her, had placed his hands on top of the table in front of him. Dick wondered if this was some sort of magic trick. He was tempted to get down on one knee and look under the table to see if there was anything else that might be interacting with Wendy to place her in such a state, but that wouldn't have been very professional. Stopping a few feet from her, he said in a much louder voice, "Earth to Wendy. Are you okay? Is there anything I can do?" His lips twitched into a smile at the thought.

Panting, Wendy was very near climax and said in a shaky, far-off voice, "It's okay Dick. I'll be fine, in another minute or two."

Lance had seen this before—as a participant. *Damn, she never gets that excited with me. What have I been doing wrong?* Without realizing it, he mumbled out loud, "Oh Lord, here it comes." He winced, purposefully sat on his hands and looked away.

Finally, Wendy let go; her entire body shook, her muscles contracted and she let out a muffled scream as the waves of sexual bliss flowed through her loins. "*Aaaaahh! Oh God, Oh God. That's sooooo good!*"

Lucy Chang, VP, Regulatory, said cheerfully, "Oh my! That looks amazing. I'd like some of that. Hopefully, it was something in the coffee; I had two cups this morning." She seemed to concentrate and looked expectantly down at her lap.

Lance said quietly in Wendy's direction, jealousy in his voice, "Damn, woman. You've never gone off like that when we're together. What'd you do?"

Wendy collapsed onto the table, resting her head on her arms as she tried to collect herself, regain her composure and her strength. The boardroom was silent as the other senior managers sat in awe at what they had just witnessed. After a couple of minutes, Wendy raised her head abruptly, red with embarrassment, an uncontrollable smile returning to her face, and thought, *Oh my God. Not again!* To the room she said, "Sorry everyone, I don't understand what's happening to me." With that, she jumped up from her chair and ran out of the room, headed for her office.

Perplexed, Dick Littlething and the other senior managers remained still for a few minutes, trying to process what they had just witnessed. None of them had ever seen anything like this in a company meeting. Dick finally said, "Wasn't that something? I think I had better go after Dr. Thompkins and make sure that she's all right. I can't decide if I'm worried about her or just a little jealous. But first, onto more important matters."

For the next ten minutes, the chief executive finished his quarterly report, and no one seemed to care. Once finished, he walked out of the room, with Lance and Tanya close behind.

They found Wendy lying on the floor, her administrative assistant, Barbara Johnson, standing over her looking very concerned. Littlething asked, "What the hell happened? Wendy ran out of the boardroom after having some sort of fit, or seizure, or orgasm?" He looked at Lance and Tanya, and they just shrugged. "Is she all right?"

This seemed a strange question, considering she was on the floor of her office, barely conscious, her breathing labored and shallow.

Barbara, obviously dazed, confused, and terrified for her boss, said excitedly, "I don't know what happened. Dr. Thompkins came running by my desk and into her office, sat in her chair and started making strange moaning sounds. She was too distracted to close her door, so I could see and hear everything. I thought she was having some sort of fit, or maybe she'd been possessed. I asked her through the open door if she was okay. When she didn't answer, I got up the courage to go inside. I found her sitting at her desk, eyes glazed over, clutching the arms of her chair. And she was moaning as though she were about to . . . well . . . you know." She whispered this last part, obviously embarrassed.

Dick finished the sentence for her, "Have an orgasm? We're all adults here. I assume we know what an orgasm is. She already went off once, during the business meeting of all things. Very distracting and inconsiderate. Interrupted my quarterly report."

Barbara Johnson continued, tearful, "I tried to talk to her, to ask if there was anything I could do, but she just ignored me. Her moaning got louder and louder, and then it seemed that she did, in fact, have a . . . well . . . you know . . . a happy ending. A very happy one based on the way she screamed and her entire body shuddered." She looked around again and sheepishly resumed. "After a minute or two, it started all over again. This time the moaning was more intense and the scream even louder. I couldn't believe it. Then a third round, even stronger than the first two. It was like the Energizer bunny, she kept going and going. Then she just collapsed and fell off of her chair onto the floor."

"My God. How many happy endings does that make? Three? Four?" Dick asked. "And in the span of ten minutes? Now I'm more than a little jealous. I have no idea what could have caused such a thing. It wasn't anything in the air or water, because no one else in the room reacted like that. I certainly never felt anything." He sounded disappointed. "I thought at first it might be Harden up to no good; he was sitting next to her, but his hands were on the table and his feet on the floor best I could tell."

To Lance he said, "You and Wendy are together, right? Is it normal for her to go off multiple times like that?" Lance just nodded, smiled, and shrugged, not willing to admit that he had never gotten a response like this from her.

Barbara continued, her voice agitated and filled with concern for her boss. "I don't know about that, but she doesn't look good. I felt for a pulse, and I even placed a mirror under her nose and mouth like they do in the movies. She still appears to be breathing, but only barely. I'm no doctor, but my guess is that whatever it is, she needs help. I dialed 911 and the ambulance is on the way. Hopefully the paramedics will get here soon."

Lance, worried about her and a little sensitive about the fact that he had never been able to give her an orgasm of this magnitude or repetition—in fact, no repetition at all—said, "She's in bad shape alright. I don't know what the hell happened to her, but I plan to get to the bottom of this. It just isn't normal. It would be terrible if she died from too much pleasure. Is that even possible?"

Dick said, "I can't imagine what caused her marathon of orgasms. But, whatever it was, I'd like to get a little for myself."

Tanya, disregarding the fact that he was her boss, said, "Dick, you're an idiot. Lance is right. She looks like she might not make it."

The phone on Wendy's desk rang. Barbara answered. "The ambulance is here? Yes, we're on the third floor, Dr. Wendy Thompkins' office. Send them up, now. Please hurry!"

CHAPTER 2

Dr. Jason Longfellow worked as a drug reviewer for the US Food and Drug Administration. He was forty-five, tall, and slender from routine exercise. Second-generation Dutch, he had blue eyes, straight, sandy-brown hair with a smattering of gray, and a sculpted chin. His prominent nose was crooked from having been broken once as a child, but his sharp smile and glowing white teeth provided enough of a distraction that most people didn't notice. To his mind, he resembled Ichabod Crane of *The Legend of Sleepy Hollow*, but women found his combination of intelligence, clumsy charm and innocence to be attractive.

Jason was a good man, but he had his issues—difficulties dealing with stress, indecisiveness, a lack of understanding of the female gender, and a whopping midlife crisis. He was neurotic, OCD, and an introvert, preferring his own company to the point where he often carried on long conversations with himself, sometimes in his head, but often mumbling aloud. He lived a very stressful life—a government job involving review of highly-technical documents, a long, daily, nerve-wracking commute from Northern Virginia to Maryland on the Washington Beltway, the difficulties of marriage to a strong-willed woman and raising a family with three young daughters, each of whom had arrived with her own set of trying circumstances.

Chelsea, Jason's wife of twenty years, was of Swedish descent, a natural blonde with clear blue eyes, a perfectly formed nose, and smooth, unblemished skin. Jason had first fallen in love with her full, beckoning lips and slight, dimpled chin. Or maybe it was her body; he was a man after all. A slender woman at five-nine, she had well-proportioned and balanced curves, peaking in a tiny waist clearly defined against her perfectly rounded hips and buttocks. Her long, slender, sinewy legs didn't hurt. Maintaining this level of fitness and allure had come naturally to Chelsea in her twenties, but by her mid-forties it required that she faithfully work out five days a week, usually early morning before work. She didn't get much sleep, but she wore her exhaustion extremely well.

Jason and Chelsea had met at Georgetown University Medical School when he was a graduate student in the pharmacology department and she was in the nursing program. He was amazed when this gorgeous woman with long blonde hair agreed to marry him. She was strong and independent, traits that Jason admired in her—most of the time. She had started out as an intensive care nurse, but after a couple of years she had developed night terrors as the horrible tragedies followed her into her dreams, and she had moved into hospital administration.

It was a typical Saturday morning not long after Jason's forty-fifth birthday. Chelsea had made breakfast and the children were fighting in the other room when Jason lost it over morning coffee.

He told Chelsea, exasperated, "I've been at the FDA doing the same job for twenty years and I'm bored to death. When you add in my twenty-four-mile, two-hour commute to work every day and the adorable little monsters that we call our children, I'm aging at a disturbing pace."

Jason told his wife how he loved spending time with her and the girls, and how concerned he was that they were growing up so fast.

"Lizzy's already thirteen, Lilly's eleven and Lucy is five. It's impossible to communicate with the teenager, and Lilly isn't much better. They're great kids, but you have to admit they're a handful, and I'm becoming way too friendly with gin martinis with olives."

His midlife crisis was in full bloom as he spoke of how he missed being able to just jump into the car and drive wherever he wanted, whenever he wanted. He felt trapped in a deep rut, with no way out. He complained of being too tall, at six-seven, to fit into speedy sedans or sports cars. "Damned car manufacturers. I should sue them for size discrimination. Maybe I should get a motorcycle, a Harley, hop on it and head out West. I'd only be gone for a few weeks. What do you think, Chelse?"

Chelsea just gave him her best disapproving stare, shook her head. "What do I think? I think you've lost your marbles. We have three daughters, and I didn't do that all by myself. You don't have time for a freakin' midlife crisis. You can't just hop on a motorcycle and ride off into the sunset, although you seldom shave on weekends and always look like you need a haircut with your hair hanging down over your ears, so I guess you do look kind of like a crazed member of a biker gang. And if you do ride off on a Harley, I'll ride off in my much larger Ford Expedition, find you, run you over, and drag your ass back home. You are not leaving me here alone to raise our little angels."

"Yikes. You wouldn't destroy a perfectly good motorcycle just because I took off for a couple of months, would you?"

"It's not the motorcycle you should be worried about, Jason. It's needing to remove the front bumper of my Expedition from your spleen that should concern you." With that, she smiled and headed upstairs for a bath, thinking, *Ah, a blissful soak in a tub filled with hot water and sweet-smelling bubbles, guaranteed to relieve the stress of living with a crazy person. I'll have a glass of wine with that.*

Jason was eating toast with a bowl of his favorite cereal, Cheerios. When she left him alone in the kitchen, he started counting the Os swimming in the sweetened milk. He mumbled, "One, two, three, she won't run over me. Four, five, six, my life I need to fix. Seven, eight, nine . . . oh screw it. I need to do something exciting, change things up, maybe get the hell out of Dodge for a while. I long for the good old days, just me and Chelse, still in school, small apartment, no kids, wild and free. I'm going crazy. I need to have some fun, shake things up."

• • •

Nothing ever seemed to come easy for Jason, and building a family was no exception. While they were still in school, Chelsea had agreed to put off having children until Jason had finished his doctorate and established himself at the FDA. He actually hoped for a much longer reprieve from parenting, but when they were in their early thirties, Chelsea's biological alarm had sounded and they'd begun trying. Jason enjoyed the trying, a lot, but she just wasn't getting pregnant.

"We should see a doctor," she had told Jason one Saturday morning, after several months of negative pregnancy tests. "I want a baby, and this isn't working. We need to get checked out to see if our plumbing is okay."

"So when's our appointment?" he asked, knowing that when she said *should*, the appointment was already made. "I doubt there's anything wrong. I've heard people at work say it can take up to six months to get pregnant, sometimes longer depending on your age."

"We have an appointment with Dr. Gleason at the clinic near my office, Monday morning at nine. Dr. Gleason told me on the phone that they'll need a sperm sample. Can you handle that?"

"Sure. Happy to oblige. How many samples do they need? Maybe I should buy porno for the occasion. Or maybe you could do that striptease routine you did on our honeymoon."

Chelsea was not amused. "If you bring any porn into this house, you'd better be ready to have it surgically removed from where the sun don't shine. You are much man, and I'm sure you can use your imagination for some bizarre fantasy to get you going."

"It's not going to be easy now that you've placed that delightful surgical image in my head. But I'll manage somehow. We men are quite clever. I always hold back a fantasy or two for such occasions."

Monday morning rolled around, and Jason found himself at the clinic being poked and prodded by Dr. Gleason, who, to Jason's embarrassment, turned out to be a lovely young female fertility specialist. Jason thought, careful not to mumble out loud, *Here I am, with an attractive young woman handling my junk, and I'm not even enjoying it.*

After his examination, Dr. Gleason said, "Okay, Jason. Everything's where it should be."

He said, nervously, "Well, that's good to hear. I was worried that something might have fallen off."

She chuckled. She knew how embarrassing this was for most men, and she enjoyed watching them squirm. "Now that we know you're intact, go on up the hall and give us a sperm sample while I examine your wife. There are special magazines in the rooms if you need help getting started. In my experience, most men are well practiced."

"No problem, Doc. How much sperm do you need? A pint? A quart?"

She laughed. "Gee, like I've never heard that one before. No need for you to wear things out. You need to save as much as possible to get your wife pregnant. Just a small sample will do."

He found several magazines with fold-out pages. He settled on a Hawaiian model with long, flowing, straight black hair and bronze skin. *Might as well go exotic,* he thought. When he had finished, he said to the sperm sample, "I just know that there are plenty of you guys and you are Olympic swimmers. The problem can't be with us. We are manly men." The sperm didn't answer, which Jason thought was probably a good thing.

When he came out of the room to deliver the sample to Dr. Gleason, Chelsea was waiting. "The doctor had to move on to her next patient. She said that you set the record for longest time in the sample room. I think she plans to give you a trophy on our next visit. I'd ask what took you so long, but I'm not sure I want to know. Give the sample to the nurse at the desk, and let's get out of here. And I see that magazine sticking out of your back pocket. Please leave it on the table. Jesus, I can't take you anywhere."

• • •

They met with Dr. Gleason again the following week, after all the test results were in. Sitting in the doctor's office with Chelsea, Jason said to Dr. Gleason, "So, I'm guessing it's not my guys. I'm confident my sperm count is high and my guys swam the race in record time. So what's the problem, Doc?"

Chelsea gave him the death stare out of the corner of her eye. "Forgive my husband. He can be an idiot sometimes . . . actually, frequently. So, what is the problem? Why can't we get pregnant?"

Dr. Gleason gave them a sad look, and said, "The good news is that Chelsea is fine."

Chelsea, smiling tentatively, said, "And there is bad news?"

Jason grimaced, and felt a little dizzy. *Not me. Not me. Please, not me.*

Dr. Gleason sighed, and said, "Jason, your sperm count is low, and the little guys are slow swimmers. In fact, I'm not sure they know how to swim at all."

He frowned, and said weakly, "Don't sugarcoat it, Doc. How bad is it? If my guys were sea creatures, would they be more like sea bass or dolphins?"

She answered, a note of sympathy in her voice, "Jason, if we're using a sea creature analogy, I'm sorry to say it would be more like coral."

"But coral don't swim. They just hang around on the bottom of the ocean."

The doctor gave a weak smile, shrugged. "Exactly. I'm sorry to say that it is unlikely the two of you will be able to have children of your own."

Jason, still in denial, said, "That's not possible. I work out every day. I'm healthy as a horse. I'm a manly man. I figured my sperm would be world champions. This can't be right. Do the test again. I'll go home, work out, get plenty of sleep tonight, and give you more sperm tomorrow. Maybe I just didn't get enough sleep, and the little guys were tired. Is there anything I can do? What if I start eating raw meat, raw steak, would that help? What about oysters? Tabasco sauce? I could eat lots of tacos with tabasco sauce and hot chili peppers. Maybe that would get the guys going." He put his face in his hands. "Oh God. It can't be me."

"Calm down, Jason. It's okay," the doctor said. "This is not uncommon. Normally, when a man has this problem, there are ways he can change his diet that might help. But, in your case, your guys are—how can I say this—dead on arrival. If anything, they appear to be swimming backwards, like they're running away from something. No amount of raw meat, oysters, tabasco sauce, or chili peppers is going to help. Studies have shown that when a man's sperm are DOA, it's not likely that his wife will get pregnant. However, there are other alternatives to having children naturally, one of which is adoption. There is also surrogacy, or we could try *in vitro* fertilization, although that's quite expensive and can take several tries, with no guarantees."

• • •

Jason left the doctor's office mortified and drove home in silence. Something felt dead inside. Something *was* dead inside. He knew Chelsea was hurting, her biological clock on constant alarm, and he did what he could to console her, signaling a willingness to explore options. They both went back to work, and he kept very busy to avoid thinking about the bad news. However, Chelsea was not someone to sit on her hands and brood.

After meeting with Dr. Gleason, Chelsea thought, *I REALLY want a family. It's time. We talked about adoption, but I'm afraid Jason might not be ready yet. Maybe I should check it out first, and then bring him my research when I'm done. I don't want to upset him.* So, she researched the adoption process on her own, using her annual leave to meet with an adoption lawyer in Vienna, Virginia, with connections to Central and South America.

On a Saturday morning, three weeks after their traumatic doctor visit, Chelsea got up bright and early and fixed Jason a nice big breakfast with all his favorites—bacon, fried eggs over easy, biscuits, hash browns, pancakes, and black coffee. They usually slept in on the weekend and breakfast was limited to coffee and toast. This morning his wife actually made pancakes, from scratch.

As Jason sipped coffee and shrugged off the haze of a foggy brain, he poured syrup on his plate.

"Jason, I need to tell you something," his wife blurted excitedly. "I met with an adoption lawyer, and there is a baby girl in El Salvador waiting for us to come pick her up. If you are okay with this, I have to leave Monday morning, because there are two other couples that are also interested in her. According to the lawyer, we're next in line, but we need to act immediately. I've already bought the airline ticket and made the hotel reservations, and I can go alone since you don't have time to take leave from work. According to our lawyer, I can do this by myself, and all you have to do is sign the papers when I get back with the baby, and the thirty-thousand- dollar check to cover the lawyer, airline tickets, hotel, and all the in-country legal and adoption fees. I hope you are good with this. I wanted to surprise you. So, *surprise!*"

Jason had just shoved a fork full of pancakes into his mouth and was washing it down with hot coffee when she hit him with her news flash. He started choking and hot coffee spewed from his nose. He took a drink of water, which helped with the choking but did nothing to bring down his blood pressure, which had just gone off the charts.

"Say what? Adopt a baby? El Salvador? Monday morning?" He was vigorously shaking his head back and forth in disbelief at what he had just heard, his mind having difficulty processing his wife's words, trying desperately to make it go away. "When . . . what have you done? We haven't discussed this lately . . . new baby? I have to be at work on Monday."

"Jason, I really want this. I need it. It's time for us to start our family, and this opportunity came up as soon as I reached out to someone about adoption. I didn't tell you about it at first, because I was terrified that you weren't ready, and I just couldn't deal with that possibility. So there it is. Are you with me? I checked, and my passport is valid. I'll go get our first child, a baby girl."

She asked, "What do you think?" But Jason knew there really wasn't anything to discuss. This was a done deal.

On Monday morning he drove his wife to the airport and watched her board an old passenger jet with the name *TACA AIRLINES* painted on the side along with a giant picture of a colorful parrot.

"What can go wrong?" he mumbled to himself, hearing the fear in his own voice as he watched the large parrot ascend into the sky. "She's flying to Central America on an obsolete passenger jet to adopt a baby from a war-torn country. Nothing to worry about. Nothing at all."

Much to his surprise, two days later, Jason got a call from Chelsea. "They already gave me the baby. She's beautiful and I've been caring for her in my room at the Hilton San Salvador. It's crazy. Be home in a couple days."

· · ·

Upon baby Lizzy's arrival, Jason returned to his job at the FDA and Chelsea had taken a month off for maternity leave. They hired a nanny when Chelsea started working again, and life for Jason seemed to be leveling out. Caring for the baby at night was tough, but he liked seeing his wife happy. *I can handle one kid,* he thought. Not Chelsea. Her biological clock alarm was still blaring.

Two months after the trip to Central America, early on a Saturday morning after a long night of baby screaming, Jason was in the nursery trying to rock Lizzy to sleep. He was exhausted, and he thought he might be hallucinating when he smelled fresh coffee, frying bacon, eggs, potatoes, and toast. He was hungry, and at first he smiled. Then it hit him, and he thought, *Oh no. Not another big breakfast.*

"Good morning, dear. What have you done?"

Chelsea waited until he had his first cup of coffee before she said, "Honey, I've been thinking."

"That's never a good thing."

She let the sarcasm slide. "I heard on the news that studies have shown that single children often grow up unable to cope with life. So last week I placed our name on an adoption list at an agency in Washington, DC. I thought we'd do a US adoption this time. One of their adoption counselors told me that it would be five to seven years—at the earliest—before we would be able to adopt a child from the US. Lizzy will have to wait a while for a sibling to play with. Foreign adoptions are a lot quicker but also much more expensive."

He sighed and thought, *Whew, that's not so bad. Five to seven years is a long time. I guess I dodged a bullet. I'll just enjoy this bountiful breakfast, and then catch a nap.*

"That's fine, Chelse. I'm glad you did it. Five to seven years is just about right. By then we should be pretty good at this parenting thing, and that'll give us plenty of time to get the house ready for another baby. Just for the record, I read somewhere that studies have shown that in families with more than two children, there's a 75 percent chance that at least one of the parents will go skydiving without a parachute. So, I vote that we stop with two."

• • •

Over the next year and a half they did begin to get the hang of the parenting thing. Chelsea was back at work, Lizzy was sleeping through the night and giggling through the days, and peace and happiness prevailed. So when Jason came home from work on a Friday and caught a whiff of steak and macaroni and cheese, his guard was down. His first thought was that this was a nice surprise, and he was hungry. Chelsea met him in the kitchen, gave him a big hug.

"Welcome home, dear. I hope you had a good day. I have a nice dinner waiting for my man after a hard day at the office." When he heard this, along with the smell of that delicious food, all kinds of alarms sounded, followed by a huge anxiety attack.

Chelsea led him into the dining room, and there was a veritable feast laid out on the table; steak, loaded baked potato, blue cheese wedge salad, homemade macaroni and cheese, biscuits, the works, and an ice-cold Molson Golden ale. He knew he was in trouble, because in their entire marriage she had never cooked on a Friday night. They both worked, and by Friday night they were barely able to answer the door when the pizza arrived. When he saw the table, he said, "Woman, what did you do now? You even made biscuits, from scratch. You never make biscuits. I hope you have a lot of that beer, 'cause I'm guessing I'm gonna need it."

Chelsea just laughed, gave him another big hug and kiss.

"Oh, Jason, I have some wonderful news! The adoption agency called today, and told me that they have a baby for us. We are to pick her up first thing Monday morning!"

Jason had just started chugging the remainder of his beer when she began talking. When he heard the words coming out of her mouth, the ice cold Molson's came out of his nose. He began to sputter, "Baby . . . Monday morning . . . two-day pregnancy? . . . What happened to five to seven years? Are you kidding me? Please tell me you're kidding." With that, his eyes rolled back into his head, and he slid slowly off of the chair and onto the floor, momentarily unconscious.

When he came to and got off the floor, he said, "Sorry, honey, I must be really tired. I seem to have taken a brief nap. I'm not sure that we're ready for another baby. Lizzy's only eighteen months old. We finally have a satisfactory daycare thing set up for her, and I don't know how a new baby will fit in. We don't have a nursery anymore, and you are working again. Is this really the right time?"

She responded, her words well-rehearsed. "Jason, I have things under control. I've already called all our friends, and four couples are showing up bright and early tomorrow morning to help out. They're bringing baby blankets, diapers, formula, bottles, and all the trimmings. We kept Lizzy's crib, and we just need to get it down from the attic. This is a four-bedroom house, and we can set up the room next to our master bedroom as the nursery. With our friends' help, we'll easily be ready for the new baby by Monday morning."

Monday morning, after a breakfast of toast and coffee, a totally exhausted Jason and Chelsea drove to downtown Washington, where they picked up Lilly Beth Longfellow. On the way home in the car, Jason said, "Chelsea, honey, we're thirty-four, we agreed on two children, and Lilly makes two. The first involved a flight to Central America on a giant parrot, and this one came to us via a two-day pregnancy. If we survive this, can I please get you to agree that we have completed our family?"

Chelsea's response surprised Jason. "Yes, dear. If you want, when we get home you can write it down and I'll sign the agreement."

• • •

Once again, they settled into a nice, comfortable routine. Chelsea stayed home with baby Lilly for three months, at which time they managed to find a new daycare provider, Connie Harper, willing to commit to both Lizzy and Lilly. She was expensive, but worth it. Jason did his best to spend as much time with the children as possible, and it was his job to read to Lizzy and then to give Lilly her last bottle of the night before tucking her into her crib. As they grew older, the kids seemed well adjusted and Chelsea appeared to be happy.

When Lizzy was eight and Lilly was six, Jason and Chelsea took the family on a two-week vacation. They rented a house on a large lake in North Carolina that came with a twenty-two-foot ski boat. The girls had a great time swimming, tubing, and learning to water ski; they had special wooden beginner's skis, call Snoopy skis, that were tied together and so buoyant that Lilly, the smaller of the two girls, could stand on top of the water. On their final weekend, they ran out of food, so Jason went to the grocery store. When he got back to the house, he found the girls crying hysterically, and Chelsea trying to calm them.

"What happened?" he asked when he walked through the front door. "Why is everyone so upset?"

Lizzy, sobbing, said, "While you were gone Mommy threw up a bunch and then went to sleep, and we couldn't wake her up."

Lilly cried, "Mommy fell down on the floor, and she wouldn't get up. We thought she died!"

Chelsea said calmly, "Everything's fine. I felt nauseous, and I threw up a couple of times. I guess I got so weak that I either passed out or fell asleep for a while. Maybe I'm coming down with the flu."

Jason felt her head for a fever. "We're going home tomorrow. If you aren't feeling any better, you should go to the doctor and get checked out."

The next Monday morning, Chelsea called Jason at work, "I still don't feel quite right. I made an appointment to see the doctor this afternoon." At four o'clock Jason pulled his Toyota 4Runner into the garage and went into the house to relieve Connie of her daycare duties.

When he got home, Lizzy said, "Please read to us, Daddy. We'll sit on your lap."

Lilly added, "Yeah, Daddy. Read us *Hop on Pop*. Please, please, please."

He had read *Hop on Pop* so many times he could repeat it by heart. It made him a little crazy to read them their favorite books over and over, but he loved them and he figured a little more crazy wouldn't kill him.

When Chelsea called at five o'clock, he answered on the first ring; he'd been worried that the doctor might find something seriously wrong with her.

"Hello, honey. What did the doctor say? Is everything all right? . . . Chelsea, talk to me. What did the doctor say?"

"Jason, you need to sit down, honey, before I tell you what I have to tell you. You know when I threw up and passed out during our vacation in North Carolina? I didn't say anything to you, but it really didn't feel like the flu. I didn't want to worry you, but I was afraid that there was something else wrong, perhaps seriously wrong."

"Oh my God, what is it? Brain tumor? Epilepsy? What?"

"I'm pregnant."

His mind frantically searched for other things that she might have said that would sound like *I'm pregnant.* He thought, *Maybe she said*

"I've got a pimple," or "I'm panicked," or "I'm present," or maybe even a weather report, "It's precipitating." Perhaps she said something else. ANYTHING else!

"Pregnant? I'm forty. Too old for more children—a new baby, no sleep. In my sixties when baby goes to college; no early retirement. Someone help me!"

Jason dropped the phone and fainted, his head falling forward onto his chest. He was out for less than a minute. He came to still sitting in the chair and took the phone from Lizzy, who had been talking to her mom.

"Sorry, hon, I took another brief nap, but I'm back. Did you happen to tell your doctor what we were told twenty years ago, about how we could never get pregnant? How my guys were DOA? What did he say to that?"

Chelsea chuckle. "Yes dear, you better believe I told him what his colleagues told us. And he told me that studies have shown that sometimes a man's sperm get livelier as he ages, resulting in pregnancy later in life. The doc asked me if you've changed your diet, eating more meat, chili peppers or tabasco sauce. Apparently, studies have now shown that eating these things also helps increase sperm motility."

• • •

Jason didn't sleep for the first three nights after that call. On the fourth evening, he came home from work in a daze. Chelsea met him at the door, saw that the right front bumper of his car had been demolished.

"Jason, what the hell happened? Are you all right?"

"It wasn't my fault." he said. "One of those damned trees around the corner on Elm Street jumped out in front of my car. Or maybe I fell asleep and ran off the road. I don't know. Anyhow, it was an empty lot, and no one was hurt. It sure as hell woke me up. My poor 4Runner—it was still drivable, so here I am. Help me."

Eight months later, Lucy Lee Longfellow was born, the third and last of the Longfellow daughters. She was beautiful, and became one of Jason and Chelsea's greatest blessings in spite of her surprising and somewhat late arrival on the scene. When he found out that this third child was also a girl, his first thought was, *Three daughters, three beautiful daughters, what a lucky man I am*. Then visions of a world full of danger, puberty, teenage girls, teenage boys, teenage pregnancy, college parties, and tuition skimmed the surface of his mind, and his happy thoughts were immediately followed by a more ominous one.

Oh my God, three daughters. I'm a dead man.

CHAPTER 3

Jason had been working as a drug reviewer for the FDA for twenty years. He loved his wife and daughters, but he was bored. Over Saturday morning coffee, a couple of weeks after their discussion of his midlife crisis and buying a motorcycle, he tried to bring up this problem with Chelsea again.

"When I started with the FDA, it was exciting and interesting reviewing drug applications from companies all over the world. But at this point every new application looks the same. I'm going to go insane if I look at one more. The walls of my office feel like they're closing in on me. There must be something else I could be doing with my life. I know I have to keep working to support our family, but I need a change."

"Jason, you have responsibilities—a wife and three children. You can't change careers at this point, and you can't just drive off on a freakin' motorcycle. We've already had this conversation. Grow up and tough it out."

"You know, Chelse, I've always loved murder mysteries—reading them, watching them on TV and at the movies, especially the hard-boiled detective stories with characters like Mike Hammer, Sam Spade,

Philip Marlowe, and Robert B. Parker's Spenser and Jesse Stone. My all-time favorite TV show was *Murder She Wrote*, where week after week the venerable Jessica Fletcher solved murder after bizarre murder. You know, you're lucky, Chelse. If Mrs. Fletcher had come along first, I'd have probably married her."

"That's great, if you like wrinkled old women. How old is Angela Lansbury now? A hundred? If Brad Pitt had come along before you, I'd have had sex with him first. But I met you instead, and here we are."

Chelsea was getting more and more concerned with this crisis Jason seemed to be having. She didn't know where it was going, but it probably wasn't to a good place. He was a little OCD, and once he got hold of something he usually wouldn't let it go.

Jason bought the DVD box set of *Murder She Wrote* and watched all the episodes over and over. His passion for murder mysteries, and especially Mrs. Fletcher, was wearing thin on Chelsea, and she became especially concerned when one morning, a few weeks into his unraveling, she found him in the kitchen trying to find a sharp knife to slice a loaf of bread.

"Chelse, I can't find the butcher knife. I'll bet someone stole it and is planning to murder us. I need to ask myself, 'What would Jessica do?' She'd be able to figure it out." After that morning, his catch phrase became "WWJD?" When a serious mystery happened, like losing his cell phone or the mail carrier delivering other peoples' mail to the Longfellow residence, he'd say aloud, "WWJD?"

Then he started seeing imaginary murders everywhere. At the grocery store, there was a guy napping in his car in the parking lot while his wife ran inside. Jason told Chelsea, "I'll bet that guy's dead. His wife probably killed him and left him there."

Chelsea shot him the death stare. "Sounds like a great idea to me. I'm looking forward to seeing if she gets away with it."

Then there was the neighbor that hadn't picked up his newspaper from the front porch for a couple of days. Jason had said to Chelsea, "I'll bet someone broke in and murdered Mr. Sully. His body's probably rotting in his living room as we speak. Maybe I should go knock on his door, just to make sure."

"Jason, I know for a fact that he's visiting his daughter in Pittsburgh. What is wrong with you? I'm beginning to think that I really do need to call the guys with the net."

"Are you sure? Maybe that's just what his daughter wants everyone to think. She might have killed him for his money."

Then there was the buxom redhead across the street that missed her usual Saturday afternoon jog. Jason noticed because he always managed to be near the front window about the time she headed out. She usually wore spandex pants and a low-cut blouse, and he enjoyed watching her bounce up the street.

He said to Chelsea, "I haven't seen Vicky, er . . . Mrs. Dawson out for her run this afternoon. I hope her husband didn't murder her in the night. Maybe he caught her with another man." Jason said this with a little too much twinkle in his eye.

"If I catch you gawking at Mrs. Dawson in one of her jogging outfits again, I might just kill you in your sleep. Then you can investigate your own murder."

Jason started to point out that he couldn't possibly investigate his own murder, but he realized the absurdity and just let it go. He said, pouting, "Well, she never misses her Saturday afternoon run. It's certainly possible that something bad has happened to her. I'm just a concerned neighbor."

Soon Jason started talking about becoming a private eye. The real kicker was when he signed up for online classes to get his private investigator's license. When Chelsea found out, she snapped.

"Jason, you've got to be kidding. You already have a job. You're commuting, raising a family, helping with the chores. When in the hell are you going to have time to finish the classes, let alone investigate imaginary murders? And you better not say you'll do less around the house."

• • •

On a Sunday, a couple of months later, Chelsea tried her best to talk Jason out of this insanity.

"Jason, when you started talking about getting your PI license, I thought you were kidding, just teasing me because I give you such a hard time about watching *Murder She Wrote*. But you're almost finished with the required sixty hours for an online detective course. What are your plans from here? We need your government salary, and you have no experience with law enforcement. Aren't most private investigators ex-cops with real-life experience investigating crimes and arresting criminals? Don't you need a firearm? You know how I feel about guns. I need to understand your intentions. Are you just doing this as a hobby? Do you plan to work as a private investigator on the side, or are you actually planning to quit the government and work full-time as a private snoop? What the hell are you doing? You are driving me crazy!" The longer she talked, the more upset she got, and the louder she became.

Jason remained surprisingly calm as he answered. "Don't worry, dear. Everything will be okay. I don't plan to quit my day job. I'll finish my sixty hours of private investigator's training online, apply for my official license, get a business license, and probably do the required firearms training for a concealed carry permit. But no worries. I only plan on doing PI work on the side, taking cases that I can do on weekends for fun, for some variety in my life. Most PIs don't deal with anything serious anyhow; the cases generally involve tailing spouses for proof of an affair, or helping someone find a long-lost family member. I might actually be able to pick up some extra cash on the side."

Chelsea could hardly believe her ears. She knew Jason very well, and he was not one to do a half-assed job at anything.

"Are you nuts? You've never done anything *part-time* in your life. You are an obsessive-compulsive workaholic. Jason, we need your government salary to pay the mortgage and for the essentials—you know, food, clothing, shelter. You can't go off half-cocked pretending that you are fucking Sherlock Holmes and forget to provide for your family. You are a grown-ass man with a wife and three daughters to support. If this is part of your midlife crisis, why don't you just have an affair or buy a sports car like most men your age? I wouldn't like it, but at least I could understand it. But a PI? That's crazy. If you do this, maybe I'll change careers too. Hospital administration is boring as hell. Maybe I'll just decide to become a stripper or pole dancer. I've heard there are a couple of places up in Maryland looking for exotic dancers; what do they call them now, gentlemen's clubs? You can be Sherlock Holmes, or maybe you'd like to borrow one of my dresses and turn into Jessica Fletcher, your heroine, and I'll start stripping for a living. How about that?"

Jason, still unusually calm and seemingly committed to his decision, said, "Honey, why is it so crazy to want something new and different with my life? I'm tired of sitting in that office day after day, looking at the same data over and over. I want some excitement. I've been trained as a scientist, and Sherlock Holmes used the scientific method to solve crimes. I might make a good detective, although I'll give you the fact that I'm not likely to become another Jessica Fletcher. I'm too tall and my legs are too hairy to look good in a dress." He smiled, trying to lighten the mood, but he was glad they were not in the kitchen where Chelsea had easy access to a frying pan or kitchen knives; she was not looking all that friendly at the moment.

• • •

Jason finished up his sixty hours of online training, obtained a business license, bought himself a 9 mm Glock pistol, got a concealed carry permit, and set up a website advertising himself for hire as a private investigator. On his website he branded himself as *The Effective Detective,* but his wife cleverly pointed out to him that it should say "The Defective Detective." She was not a happy camper.

CHAPTER 4

The stress of Jason's daily commute from Herndon, Virginia, to Maryland, working full-time, and raising three daughters was killing him, and getting his PI license hadn't done anything to ease his midlife crisis. To get relief from one of his problems, he decided that he needed to carpool, so he put up a sign on a bulletin board at work and the very next day was contacted by Dr. Joanne Shipley, who wanted to meet him in person to discuss a possible arrangement. They met for lunch at the cafeteria.

Dr. Shipley was in her mid-thirties, tall at five-eight, and athletic, with slender arms and the long, muscular legs of a runner. She had long, straight brown hair ending at her shoulders, and a face with the standard beauty worthy of a Maybelline commercial—big brown eyes, a little button nose, and perfectly applied makeup with dark-red lipstick. She wore a dark, tailored women's business suit that said, "I'm a serious professional. Don't give me any grief."

She had come to the government from a job with a drug company, which explained her meticulous appearance. Those on government salaries tended toward the frumpy department-store look. As it turned out, Dr. Shipley's office was on the same floor of the sprawling government building as Jason's, and she only lived four blocks from him in Northern Virginia.

"So, I'm surprised we haven't run into each other before, since your office is just up the hall from mine. Are you new to the FDA?"

She looked up from her salad and said, reluctantly, "I've only been here for a few weeks. I'm kind of an introvert, and I prefer to stay in my office and work."

He could see that while her appearance gave the impression of a confident professional, she was painfully shy. He tried again. "Well, as I said on the phone, I'm looking for someone to carpool to work with. Would you be interested?"

She paused for a few moments, thinking, *Some of the men at my last job were overly aggressive. Honestly, I probably could have filed for sexual harassment a couple of times. This guy seems nice enough, though, and he doesn't have any obvious disgusting habits.*

"Are you married, Jason?"

"Yes."

"Happily?"

"Yes."

"In that case, yes. I'm interested. We live close to each other, and you don't look like a serial killer, so I guess it would be all right." She blushed a little as she said it.

He responded, "Well, I don't know what a serial killer looks like, but I'm not particularly difficult to get along with. My wife and three daughters trained me well."

"Three daughters. That must be interesting. I have three sisters. We never got along very well, and it made our father crazy." She was now smiling. "I'm married, too. My husband's name is Tom, and he just started working for the Environmental Protection Agency. We have twin boys, age ten. We recently moved here from Chapel Hill, North Carolina."

"Twin boys. Wow, that must be a handful. I only have experience with daughters, although I've heard boys are more physical with their fights and break things more often. But I can't imagine that they are any worse than my older two. Lizzy and Lilly are thirteen and eleven, and they fight all the time. They also break stuff, but the worst is the back talk, especially the teenager. There are entire weeks when I want to run away, but I know that my wife would just find me and drag me home."

Joanne smiled. "Oh, Jason, it can't be all that bad. I'll bet they are little angels. I still want a girl, but we just started new jobs and Tom wants to wait a while before we add to the family." In spite of her shyness, she seemed to be getting more comfortable with Jason.

"So, I need to get back to work. How about the carpooling?" Jason asked. "We could start on Monday morning."

Joanne thought for a moment, and then said, "Sure, let's give it a try. Who's going to drive the first day?"

"I'll pick you up at five thirty on Monday. I'll drive the first week, and we can go from there."

Jason told Chelsea that he was going to start carpooling to work, but he failed to mention that he was riding with an attractive brunette. The following Monday morning he picked Dr. Joanne Shipley up in front of her house and aimed his car towards the Dulles Toll Road on his way to I-495 and on to Maryland. Joanne had barely said a word, but by the time they passed through the toll booth and were headed toward the exit for I-495 North, she seemed to perk up some. In fact, to Jason's surprise, she became quite chatty.

"How was your weekend? Did you do anything fun? How is your sex life with your wife?"

Having had just one cup of coffee, Jason was still not entirely awake, and he barely heard what she said. He didn't process her last question at all. He just nodded in response and said, "My weekend was fine. Just the usual stuff, hauling the kids around to their endless events, soccer, birthday parties, you know. You said you had young sons?"

"We left the boys with my mother over the weekend, and my husband and I had sex in our hot tub, in the kitchen, the dining room, well, pretty much every room of the house. We even did it in his Lexus, parked in the garage. I just couldn't get enough. It was a great weekend, and I'm still in the mood this morning." She looked at Jason like he was a piece of steak and she was hungry.

All at once he was wide awake and paying attention. He turned and saw the look on her face. He noticed that she had begun to unbutton the top button of her blouse. *What in the hell?* He turned to look at her.

"You know, my husband will be at work this morning. You could turn this car around and we could go back to my place to get to know each other better. We really should know each other a lot better if we're going to be carpooling every day."

Jason was flabbergasted. This quiet, shy woman was turning into a sex-starved animal before his eyes.

"Joanne . . . Dr. Shipley, are you okay? I don't understand what's happening."

She reached across the console, placed her left hand on his crotch and rubbed gently.

He said, "Well, that's nice . . . I mean . . . what the hell are you doing? What's the matter with you?"

She never even flinched. Instead, she unbuttoned two more buttons on her blouse with her free hand, revealing a black, lacy bra, nipples at full salute. Her breasts were overflowing, pressed together like two supple grapefruits into such overwhelming cleavage that it could've distracted a man from even the most dangerous of situations, like the heavy traffic on the Washington Beltway.

"Do you like what you see?" she asked, pulling at her bra with her free hand until her nipples threatened to break free of their lacy confinement.

She began to rub harder and gently squeeze with her left hand. At that point Jason reflexively pulled the steering wheel to the right and accidentally changed lanes, almost running a brand-new Corvette convertible off the highway. Horns blared, middle fingers were exchanged and Jason regained control of his car, and himself. Struggling mightily to focus on the traffic instead of supple fruit, he said, "Dr. Shipley, I don't know what's come over you, but I am going to turn this car around and take you home. Are you drunk? Did you put something strange in your coffee this morning?" He took hold of her left hand, removed it from his crotch, put it back, but then finally removed it again and pushed it away, and took the next exit off of I-495. He followed the exit ramp and re-entered I-495 headed in the opposite direction, back toward Virginia and home.

When he turned to look at Joanne again, she was no longer paying any attention to him at all. She was smiling ear to ear, her brown eyes glossed over, and she was starting to moan gently. The moaning continued to increase and she began to squeeze her legs together and gently massage her breasts with both hands, her eyes now closed and a strange look of anticipation on her face.

"Oh, God. That's unbelievable. I don't want this to ever stop. Oh, Tom. Oh, Jason. Oh, Brad." He had the distinct impression that she was in the throes of passion, headed for an orgasm, and she didn't appear to be particular about whose name was associated with the event.

Jason grumbled to himself, "Chelsea mentioned Brad Pitt recently too. Do all women fantasize about having sex with him?"

Joanne's moaning got louder, until she began to scream, "*Aaaaahh! Oh my God. Oh God! Aaaaahh!*" It was pretty clear to Jason that she was indeed having an orgasm. He had helped Chelsea to experience the same on many occasions during their years of marriage, but he had never seen anyone spontaneously reach that point. Her hands were now lying still in her lap, not touching anything of an erotic nature.

Jason looked to his right, and saw an old man in a blue Mercedes SUV driving alongside them, staring in at Joanne. He was grinning, intent on watching for as long traffic would allow. Joanne's blouse was half opened, ample cleavage there for all to see, and it must have been obvious to the stranger that something exciting was going on in Jason's 4Runner. The man actually gave Jason the thumbs-up. Meanwhile, Joanne continued the cycle of moaning and screaming, as wave after wave of happy endings washed over her.

Jason had no idea what was going on, and when the fourth or fifth orgasm ended—he had lost count—and she clearly began the climb to another one, he changed his mind and said, "Joanne, I don't know what's happening to you, but it seems to be out of control. I'm taking you to the Inova Fairfax Hospital Emergency Room in Falls Church, where hopefully someone can help you."

Jason parked and escorted Joanne into the ER, still trembling and moaning quietly. Anxiety grasped Jason as he realized, *This might not have been such a good idea. Chelsea works here, in the administrative building next door, and I neglected to share that my carpooler is an attractive brunette. Perhaps this is a mistake.*

The odor of rubbing alcohol, sickness and sweat, along with a blast of cold air from the AC, hit him as he walked through the automatic door, Joanne Shipley in tow. He hated hospitals. He told the nurse at the desk, "My name is Dr. Jason Longfellow. My friend and carpooler here, Dr. Joanne Shipley, appears to be having some sort of excessive sexual response to an unknown stimulus, and she seems to be experiencing spontaneous . . . well . . . happy . . . you know . . . endings . . . orgasms. I wasn't sure how to handle the situation, so I brought her here. Can you please help?"

At first the ER nurse thought that this must be some kind of sick joke. But before she could say anything, Joanne let out a loud moan and muffled scream that could only be interpreted as someone experiencing what Jason had described. Nurse Jones said, "Hmmm. I've never seen anything quite like this. We need to get her to a private room as soon as possible; she's upsetting the other patients. I'll get a wheelchair and take her back to one of the examination rooms." She called one of the orderlies to bring a wheelchair, stat.

A male orderly arrived almost immediately with the wheelchair, and the nurse helped Joanne to sit. Before moving her, the nurse said, "Did you say your name was Longfellow? Are you by any chance related to Nurse Chelsea Longfellow in our administrative office?"

Jason considered denying any knowledge of a Chelsea Longfellow, but his mouth, seemingly on its own, said, "Yes, Chelsea is my wife."

"Wow. That's quite a coincidence." An evil smile on her face, the nurse then said, "I'll give her a call to let her know her husband's in my ER. She'll probably want to hop on over here from the admin building to see you." With that, she rolled Joanne through the doors to the private examination rooms.

Since he was not family, Jason wasn't welcome, nor did he have any desire to accompany Joanne to the examination room. He was trapped. He thought about fleeing but realized that would just make it look worse when Chelsea showed up. *Oh boy, I'm screwed!*

He took a seat in the waiting room to await his fate. Ten minutes later Chelsea walked through the automatic doors of the ER, immediately found her target and launched herself in his direction. Before he could stand to greet her, he saw the anger and confusion in her eyes.

"Jason. What the hell is going on? Kathy called me and said you were here in the ER. You brought in your carpooler, who, by the way, happens to be an attractive brunette, but we'll get to that in a minute, and she is having some kind of attack of 'spontaneous' sexual release? What the fuck is going on? What did you do? This is a helluva way to start the week."

Chelsea obviously wanted an explanation, and Jason was at a loss for words. Nurse Jones had apparently told Chelsea everything, and she was not happy. He was taken aback that his wife immediately jumped to the conclusion that he had anything to do with this sexual malady inflicted upon his carpooler. He said, hurt in his voice, "Honey, I honestly don't know what the hell happened. I picked Joanne up at her house, just like we planned. She got into my car, and I started driving to work. When I first met her the other day, she seemed very shy and quiet, and she was that way when we started out this morning. But then something changed. She started talking about her sex life, she seemed to get turned on by I don't know what, she started rubbing my crotch, and next thing I know she's moaning and climaxing all by herself in the passenger seat of my 4Runner. I assure you that I had both hands on the wheel. I didn't do anything wrong. I don't know what's wrong with her. I tried to talk to her, but she just kept having orgasm after orgasm. I didn't know what to do, so I brought her here. I hope it's not some kind of disease, a virus or something. God, what if it's contagious? I was in the car with her and I touched her when I helped her into the ER."

By the look on her face and steam coming out of her ears, Chelsea was about to punch his lights out. She said, "So, it's 'Joanne'?"

Nurse Jones returned. She approached them and said, "Hey, Chelsea. Good to see you. I see you found your husband." To Jason she said, "I just came from the examination room, and the doctor gave your carpooler a strong sedative. She seems to have calmed down, and her spontaneous 'condition' seems to have let up. She's resting comfortably. We'll need for you to fill out some forms in the ER for her. She told us that her purse is in your car, and her insurance card and driver's license are in her wallet. She gives you permission to take the necessary information from her purse to fill out the forms."

Before he could answer, Chelsea said to Jason, "I highly recommend that you contact her husband and get him down here to fill out the forms. More importantly, he needs to know what's happening with his wife. I don't think it's appropriate for you to be going through her purse. If you want, I'm happy to wait here with you. I think I'd enjoy hearing you explain to him what happened with your carpooler—you know, his wife. With any luck, he'll be a big sonofabitch with a bigger temper. But that's your problem. That's in addition to the problem you're going to have when you get home tonight. So, do you want me to stay with you until he gets here?"

Jason just frowned and shrugged. *Chelsea no longer looks like she wants to punch me. I'm guessing that's because she expects Joanne's husband to take care of that.*

CHAPTER 5

To Jason's relief, Joanne Shipley's husband, Dr. Tom Shipley, did not turn out to be a big sonofabitch with a mean disposition. He was, in fact, a mild-mannered environmental scientist working for the EPA. He could have passed for a nerdy, liberal college professor, medium height, slender, short brown hair, blue eyes, and wide-rimmed glasses, wearing a light-blue cotton shirt with button-down collar, blue jeans, and neatly tied tennis shoes. He had arrived at the hospital ER, asked the desk nurse about his wife, and was immediately taken back to see her.

When Tom Shipley returned to the waiting room twenty minutes later, he introduced himself to Jason.

"I just saw Joanne. I assume you're Jason Longfellow, her carpooler? I wanted to introduce myself. I'm Tom Shipley, Joanne's husband. Pleased to meet you." He put out his hand, and Jason flinched before taking it, still half expecting a punch in the jaw.

Jason finally shook. "Pleased to meet you, Tom. How's Joanne doing?"

"She seems fine, although I must say, I'm a little confused at what happened, even after both she and the nurse explained it to me. The nurse said my wife had some kind of attack in your SUV on the way to work, where she suffered repeated orgasms?"

Jason nodded. *Well, he's very direct. I guess that's good, and he hasn't tried to break my face yet. Even better.*

Tom continued, "Joanne corroborated that story, and explained that you had nothing to do with it. Apparently, she had some sort of fit where she became aroused, and had several spontaneous orgasms. I didn't know that was possible. It's the strangest thing I've ever heard, but I've been married to her for ten years and she has never lied to me. She seems to think that someone might have slipped her something that caused this, but that doesn't make any sense because all she'd had was coffee and a little breakfast at home. I don't know what to think."

His voice was surprisingly calm, especially after hearing that such a strange thing had happened to his wife. He didn't appear to blame Jason. It seemed that Tom Shipley might actually have some idea as to what was going on.

"Yeah. I have no idea what happened. I had only spoken to your wife once before at the office cafeteria. I barely knew her or anything about her. She was shy and didn't say much. This was our first day of carpooling. I picked her up early this morning and was driving to work, when all of a sudden she started moaning. It was the strangest thing I've ever seen, or heard. I tried to talk to her, but she was unresponsive, so I brought her here." He left out the part about blouse unbuttoning and crotch rubbing. The guy seemed reasonably calm, but Jason saw no reason to poke the bear.

Chelsea was still there when Tom Shipley showed up, and she was disappointed with his reaction to the news; she had her mind set on seeing Jason punished for whatever had gone on with his pretty brunette carpooler.

"Hi, I'm Chelsea Longfellow, Jason's wife. I must say, you seem shockingly calm, considering what happened. Personally, I was concerned to hear that—as Jason tells it—his driving your wife to work somehow brought her to multiple orgasms. It might just be me, but that sounds a little unusual, and suspicious." Things were not going as she expected, so she poked the bear on Jason's behalf.

"I agree, it's very suspicious," Tom said.

Chelsea thought, *Oh boy. Here it comes. Look out, Jason. This guy's finally going to blow.*

But, to her surprise, Tom said to Jason, "Dr. Longfellow, can we please go to the cafeteria, get some coffee, and talk in private?"

"Please, call me Jason, and yes, by all means, let's get some coffee. This has been a helluva confusing morning, and I would really appreciate anything that you can tell me to shed light on what happened."

Chelsea just shrugged. "Well, if you two guys want some alone time, I'll head on back to work."

Jason gave her a kiss on the forehead and said, relieved, "Okay, Chelse. I'll see you tonight."

The cafeteria appeared upscale, filled with the smells of pizza, hamburgers, and french fries, as well as meat loaf, fish, steaks, and fresh-baked bread. Jason saw various stations that served hot and cold sandwiches, hot entrees of all kinds, pizza, salads, a station for Oriental cuisine, an entire aisle dedicated to various vegetables, and an impressive dessert station. Tom bought two cups of coffee and they took a seat at a table off in the corner of the room where they could speak in private.

Tom paused for a while, trying to figure out how to start the conversation. Jason took a drink of coffee, made a displeased face, and said, "Yikes. Tastes like a combination of battery acid and lubricating oil, thick, bitter, and hard to swallow. I guess they make it strong to keep the orderlies awake. I understand they work forty-eight-hour shifts."

Finally, Tom said, "Joanne told me what happened. She's normally very shy, and she's extremely embarrassed, and baffled. She told me that she had no control over her actions. She's convinced she would have died if the doctor hadn't given her a heavy sedative, which somehow counteracted her symptoms. She asked me to thank you for getting her to the ER so fast."

"I'm glad she's okay. It was clear that she needed help, and bringing her here was the only think I could think to do."

"She believes that whatever happened was chemically induced, and it wore off while she was under sedation. Neither of us can figure out how she ingested anything that might have affected her that way. All she had this morning was a cup of coffee and a bagel with cream cheese at home, and she took the same meds that she takes every morning. She did nothing out of the ordinary." He paused, as if trying to decide whether to continue or not, and then said, "She told me that you're aware we moved here from Chapel Hill recently. She used to work for CureStuff Pharmaceuticals, a company in Research Triangle Park, and I know for a fact that there was something strange going on there before we left Chapel Hill. She kept denying that there was anything wrong at work, but I know something was upsetting her. I was glad when we decided to move up here because it got her away from that company. I'm not saying that CureStuff necessarily had anything to do with this; all I'm saying is that she worked there, and something was not right. She tells me you're a drug reviewer for the FDA, so you know the pressures that exist in the pharmaceutical industry—all the deadlines, the rush to get things done. Back then, I just figured that something like that was upsetting her."

Jason thought it odd that Tom didn't seem all that surprised about what happened to his wife, considering the extremely bizarre nature of the incident. Jason thought, *Maybe I should look into this CureStuff Pharmaceuticals.* The name seemed familiar to him.

Jason finally got to his office around one o'clock. He poured himself another cup of coffee and sat down at his computer, where he searched the internet for CureStuff Pharmaceuticals. He discovered that it was, in fact, a small drug company located in Research Triangle Park, a business park between Raleigh and Chapel Hill, North Carolina. According to their website, CureStuff specialized in drugs and biologics that affected the brain. They were currently working on antidepressant monoclonal antibodies, which targeted brain receptors in the amygdala, a part of the brain that contained one of the main pleasure centers.

Jason was surprised by what he found, and he began to mumble as he processed the information. "So, they manufacture monoclonal antibodies."

Let's see. A monoclonal is a type of protein similar to the antibodies made by the human body to fight infection and designed to act like a drug. Monoclonal antibodies are known for their specificity; they can be designed to stimulate specific cells, such as a specific cell population in the brain, decreasing the likelihood of undesirable side effects. Monoclonal antibodies are currently used to treat cancer by targeting cancer cells without affecting healthy cells. This is interesting stuff.

"But this doesn't make a lot of sense. Monoclonal antibodies have to be given intravenously, and they don't normally reach the brain. CureStuff must have developed some new technology to fix this because their website says they can be given in tablet form and are being used to treat depression. That's actually pretty cool." Jason realized he had been mumbling and looked around to make sure nobody heard him.

Jason sat for a few moments, staring off into space, trying to remember something he had seen recently. Then he started talking to himself again. "I remember seeing something on the news a couple of nights ago about a strange incident at a company in Research Triangle Park. Something happened to one of their senior vice presidents during a meeting of the higher-ups and she ended up in the ER; the report was kind of vague on the details. I wonder if it was CureStuff Pharmaceuticals. That's probably why the name sounds so familiar. I need to check it out."

• • •

That night, Chelsea brought Chinese takeout home for dinner and made chicken strips for the kids, their favorite. When Jason got home, she barely acknowledged him; she appeared to be preoccupied until they sat down to dinner. The girls were all chattering as usual, and the oldest, Lizzy was tormenting her younger sister, Lilly; nothing new there. Chelsea gave them her death stare and told them to behave, and things quieted down.

"Okay, monkeys, time to go upstairs, wash up and brush your teeth. I'll be up in a few minutes." The girls raced each other up the stairs, and when they were gone Chelsea turned her attention to Jason.

"So, how did work go this afternoon? Any more attacks from buxom brunettes, or was this a one-time thing? Are you still planning on carpooling with that woman? I've been thinking about it all day, and I still can't, for the life of me, figure out what could have happened. I'm supposed to believe that she attacked you, a woman you just met, and you had to take her to the ER for . . . well, you know . . . spontaneous orgasms? That's the craziest damned thing I've ever heard."

Lizzy yelled from upstairs. "Mommy, Lilly's picking on Lucy again."

Lilly yelled, "Am not. Am not. Lizzy's a big fat liar."

Normally, all the kid chatter and fighting drove Jason nuts, but he was actually glad to hear the kids interrupt Chelsea. It provided a distraction from an even greater explosion that he was expecting. To his surprise, Chelsea apparently decided not to erupt any further, for now.

"I'm going to go upstairs, spend some time with the girls, and think about this carpool thing some more. It just doesn't add up. I've been a nurse for twenty years, and I've never heard of such a thing as spontaneous orgasms. If I could manage such a thing myself, you might become unnecessary, in which case . . . well, who knows? Now could you please take care of the dishes?" With that, she got up and headed upstairs, an evil grin on her face.

Jason cringed. *I know she loves me, but she has a temper, and I'm probably going to catch major hell later, when I least expect it. I'd better go into hypervigilance mode for the next couple of days, sleep with one eye open, and maybe buy some flowers.*

The next day at work, Jason sat in his office, going through his files for the past five years, and he found a report that he'd written about a drug application he'd reviewed for a product named *Pleasuria* from CureStuff Pharmaceuticals.

Now I remember. They submitted the application to the FDA three years ago for treatment of depression. I've reviewed so many of these things that I can't keep them straight anymore. According to my report, the product was a monoclonal antibody designed to affect the pleasure center of the brain, the idea being to stimulate the brain pleasure center in patients with depression in order to make them feel good.

According to his review, there weren't any side effects reported, which was a good thing, but the drug just didn't work. It was given as an oral tablet.

Jason had assumed that the technology didn't work and the antibody never reached the brain to do its thing, so he had recommended against its approval. Based on his follow-up notes, FDA approval was never granted for this one.

He remembered that the original product wasn't very effective at treating depression, although he didn't recall reading about side effects like those Joanne experienced. *I think I would have remembered that. Who, in God's name, would design a drug that causes spontaneous orgasms as a way to combat depression, assuming that was the intended effect? Maybe it was a side effect, and they chose not to report it. If that were the case, the warning label should read, "Do not drive while taking Pleasuria," or "if experiencing repeated orgasms for more than four hours, go see a doctor," or perhaps "sudden death may occur due to intense pleasure."*

If they had listed spontaneous orgasms as one of the side effects, they would have probably sold the hell out of that drug. Jason doubted the drug was originally designed to have this effect; *but what if they accidentally hit on something that stimulates the part of the brain that controls sexual arousal?* That might explain how the SVP at CureStuff ended up in the ER and also what happened to Dr. Shipley.

Jason realized that whatever was involved, it may have almost killed someone at CureStuff and could have killed Joanne if he hadn't gotten her to the ER. If she'd been the one driving, it could have killed both of them, although at least she would have had a smile on her face when they crashed. He mumbled, "I think this calls for an investigation." Then he looked around his office and thought, *I hope the NSA isn't bugging my office. It wouldn't be good for the authorities to hear some of the things that I mumble to myself, I might end up in jail.*

Jason took out his cell phone and dialed Joanne Shipley. When she saw the caller ID, she almost didn't answer out of embarrassment. When she did, she spoke timidly.

"Hello, Jason."

"Hi, Joanne. Are you okay?"

"I'm fine. They released me from the hospital yesterday afternoon, and Tom brought me home. I've been ordered by the doctor to take a few days off to rest. I think maybe we should wait a couple of weeks before going back to carpooling. That should give me enough time to get myself together again. I'm still mortified and baffled by what happened to me."

"Joanne. Don't worry about it. You were obviously under the influence of something, probably a drug. I'm guessing that someone slipped you something without your knowledge." He eased into what he had to say next. "When I talked to your husband at the hospital, he told me you used to work at CureStuff Pharmaceuticals. He also said that he thought there was something odd going on at the company before you left. Can you tell me about that?"

Joanne sounded agitated. "Tom shouldn't have said anything. Why do you want to know? What does that have to do with what happened to me?"

"No reason to worry. It's just that the name *CureStuff Pharmaceuticals* seemed familiar to me for some reason, so I did a little digging when I got back to the office. I discovered that I reviewed one of their drugs a couple of years ago, an antidepressant named Pleasuria, designed to affect the pleasure center of the brain. It never received FDA approval. I also found out that there was an incident at that same company more recently, where one of their female SVPs ended up in the ER from a mysterious illness similar to yours. And now, I find out that you used to work for CureStuff before you moved to Northern Virginia. I can't help but wonder if this is all connected somehow."

Jason heard silence from the other end of the phone for a long time before Joanne responded.

"Jason, we haven't known each other very long, and I'm extremely embarrassed by what happened, but you might have some good points. I did work for CureStuff, and I knew Dr. Wendy Thompkins, the woman who ended up in the ER. I was told that she almost died of a heart attack, but she was in good health and the official details the company released were vague and suggested there was more to it.

"I also knew about Pleasuria; although, until you mentioned it, I didn't make the connection to what happened to me yesterday. There's no way that I can look into this. I didn't leave the company on the best of terms, and I signed a confidentiality agreement saying that I wouldn't talk to anyone about the work that was going on at CureStuff. I'm also pretty sure that no one in the company will speak to me, and I certainly will never be allowed back into the building. I'm not sure what to do."

Jason smiled. "Joanne. You're in luck. My day job is as a drug reviewer for the FDA, but I recently got my private investigator's license, and I'm available for hire if you would like me to investigate your case. I assume that you'd like to know what happened to you, who's responsible, and whether or not they were trying to kill you."

Joanne thought that perhaps Dr. Jason Longfellow was nuts. She had heard from colleagues at the FDA that he was a very good drug reviewer, but now he was telling her that he was also a PI on nights and weekends. This was almost as crazy as what had happened to her on the way to work.

"No offense, Jason, but whatever possessed you to get a private investigator's license? Wasn't getting a PhD in pharmacology and working as a drug reviewer enough to keep you busy? Why would you want a second job, and as a private eye? Watch too much TV or read too many murder mysteries?"

"Actually, after twenty years of reviewing drug files, I got bored, and I decided that I needed a hobby. I do love murder mysteries, and I decided to study online to get my private investigator's license, just for the hell of it. If it makes you feel any better, my wife also thinks I'm crazy, but what's the harm? And you have to admit, what happened in the past day or two has dumped an interesting case into my lap. So what do you say? Do you want to hire me to investigate this thing for you? I charge thirty an hour plus expenses, and I can only work nights and weekends. I already have a leg up, because I know a lot about drugs and what happened to you, plus I'm familiar with CureStuff. What do you say?"

I'll probably get fired by the government for taking this case, nosing around a drug company as part of a potential attempted murder investigation when I reviewed one of their drug applications. But who cares? I want to be a full-time PI anyhow, and Joanne probably won't realize there's a problem, since she's only been with the FDA for a short time. He was obviously in denial where his wife was concerned; it was highly likely that Chelsea would care—a lot.

Joanne sighed before she said, "This is insane. But I have to admit, you do have a leg up on this mess, and you are the one who made the possible connection between what happened to me and my old job at CureStuff, although I'm not convinced they really had anything to do with it. So yeah, go ahead and investigate, see if you can figure out what happened to me and whether or not they had anything to do with it. Spend a couple of weeks on it, and then get back to Tom and me and let us know if you found anything."

Jason was elated—his first case. But his mood immediately changed when he realized that he had no idea how to proceed.

He mumbled, "Oh well, what the heck. I'll just ask myself WWJD. What would Jessica (Fletcher) do?" He thought some more, and then continued to mumble, a more serious tone to his mumbling. "On a less happy note, Chelsea is going to be pissed when she finds out that I'm really going through with this private eye thing. She's already mad at me for doing this as a hobby, and she's still furious at me for what happened yesterday with Joanne. And now I'm going to start working for this same woman on my first case as a private eye? Oh crap. What am I doing to myself? Next thing, the police are going to be investigating my murder. Oh well. They always suspect the spouse first, so they'll probably catch her when she kills me."

CHAPTER 6

Jason's commute had only gotten worse. His current drive involved taking the Dulles Toll Road to I-495 North, across the Cabin John Bridge to Maryland, and on to the FDA White Oak Campus in Silver Spring, Maryland.

"My commute is torture," he told his wife. "Every day I have another near-death experience, and my nerves are constantly frayed from driving the eight lanes of wall-to-wall, stop-and-go traffic of the Washington Beltway, where you can be going seventy, turn a corner and find traffic at a dead standstill. I really hate this."

Chelsea was afraid he was using this as another excuse for quitting the FDA to become a private eye. "Well, dear, I suppose we could always move to Maryland. Then I could do the same commute in reverse."

"Sounds like a fine idea. Maybe we could find something within walking distance of the FDA campus. That'd reduce my stress level considerably."

"That's what you think. First, the schools here are better. Second, I'd be pissed and stressed all the time, and you know what they say. 'Happy wife, happy life.'"

"And an angry wife—sleep with one eye open? I know. I'm only kidding. More like wishful thinking. But between raising three girls, the stress of the commute and the boredom of the job, I'm losing my mind. There's got to be a better way. That's one of the things I like about the private eye gig. I can work from home."

He wished he hadn't said that, especially this early in the morning before Chelsea had her second cup of coffee. With her, coffee had a calming effect. But he actually thought he saw smoke coming out of her ears.

"Jason, I swear to God. If I hear anything else about private eyes, I'm going to scream so loud it'll shatter the windows. I understand you're bored; I get that it's tough raising three girls, and I know your commute is a pain. But, let me repeat this again, we need your government salary. If you want to diddle around pretending to be a private eye on weekends, go for it. But don't even think about quitting your day job right now! Go to work. I've got to get the girls up and ready for the day."

On this particular Friday morning, he headed out at five thirty to avoid the heaviest of rush hour, but traffic was already heavier than normal. After going through the toll booth he took the exit toward the Beltway, where three lanes of traffic were forced to merge into a single lane that carried commuters from the toll road onto the monster eight-lane highway, the slow traffic from all three lanes aggressively jockeying for position. He called the office on his cell phone, speaking to the administrative assistant, Janice Henderson.

"Hey, Janice, traffic's worse than usual. Must be an accident on the north Beltway. I may be a few minutes late for my first meeting."

As his car approached the entrance onto the Beltway, he heard the roar of engines behind and beside him. To his right he saw a new BMW sedan whose driver thought it a good idea to pass him in the emergency lane with the intention of cutting him off. At the same time, a white Corvette pulled up on his left with a similar idea as the BMW. Earlier in his career, Jason would have shoved the accelerator to the floor and died rather than letting these two idiots get in front of him, but over the years his nerves had frayed to the point where he was more about surviving than racing.

"Janice, I'm about to die. A Corvette and a BMW are planning to defy physics, by occupying the same space in front of me at the same time. Tell everyone at the office I said goodbye." With that, he closed his eyes, slammed on his brakes and prayed. To his surprise, he didn't hear a crunch, and when he opened his eyes the BMW was directly in front of him with the Corvette in front of it.

He heard Janice say to someone, "It's Dr. Longfellow. He's on his way to work and being overly dramatic, as usual; something about an impending car crash."

Jason said into the phone, "Janice, I'm not being overly dramatic. I really thought that was the end. Instead, all involved magically ended up in line and exchanged the one-finger salute. I'll still be there late, but I'm not dead yet."

• • •

The workday was fairly standard, in that he started by reviewing about a billion pages of data, until his vision had blurred. Then, he attended three meetings with various drug companies, ate lunch in the cafeteria on campus, read another billion pages, and when he could no longer see, he got into his car to navigate through the nightmare of Friday afternoon rush hour traffic.

On his way home, he called Chelsea on his cell. "Hello, dear. I'm headed home at a fairly fast clip for Friday night. Thought I'd give you a call to see what's for dinner." He had a terrifying flashback to his last big Friday night dinner and almost drove off the road. The stress was really getting to him.

Chelsea was already home, having a twenty-minute commute from Fairfax Hospital. "Drive careful. You know traffic can stop abruptly at any time, and you aren't leaving me to raise these three girls all by myself."

"Thanks, dear. Your concern is underwhelming." He realized she was probably still angry from this morning, but neither of them ever stayed mad for very long. All of a sudden, he yelled, "Oh shit!" and slammed on his brakes. He said to Chelsea, "Damn, that was close. I'm almost to the Cabin John Bridge, and all of a sudden traffic is at a dead stop. I had to set the 4Runner on its nose to avoid hitting the guy in front of me. It's got to be an accident on my side, or rubberneckers. Would you take a quick look at the news for me, and see if they are reporting any accidents on the Beltway?"

"Not that thrilled about a Friday night traffic report, but I'll take a look. Hang on while I turn on the TV. It doesn't matter much anyway. You can nuke the pizza if it's cold, if you ever get home. Friday night's always a nightmare." Chelsea was quiet for a couple of minutes and then came back on the phone and said, "No accidents reported near the Cabin John. You'll have to figure it out for yourself."

Just as she said this, Jason saw the problem. At the entrance to the bridge, a young woman, probably late twenties, had pulled off the road with a flat tire. She was currently bent over changing said tire, her short skirt not appropriate attire for the task at hand. Jason cursed under his breath at the damned rubberneckers, as his frayed nerves tingled and his head began to throb with frustration at this latest near-death experience. He said to Chelsea with self-righteous indignation, "Some young girl had a flat, pulled off the road right before the bridge, and is bent over changing the tire, her ass bared to the world. These rubberneckers are idiots." He reached the spot where the girl was changing the tire, slowed to a stop, and took a good long look before continuing on across the bridge. He failed to mention that part to his wife.

"Jason, are you staring at her ass? How long did you stop to look?"

"I did no such thing. It's not worth dying for." He looked up to the sky, waiting for the lightning bolt to strike.

Once he had passed the young lady with the hazardous rear end, traffic picked up again. About a mile ahead, he saw a large plume of dark smoke rising mysteriously from the road, and he got a whiff of the distinct odor of burning rubber. As he approached the source of the smoke, his mind had difficulty processing what his eyes were seeing. He said to Chelsea, "Lord God Almighty! I'm in a freaking NASCAR race! Up ahead, in my lane of course, is a blue Ford Fusion, spinning round and round like a top, black smoke rising from the tires as they slide sideways across the asphalt surface. Someone must have given this guy a NASCAR bump in the rear at high speed, and sent his car into an uncontrollable spin. Help me!"

"Jason, are you screwing with me? I'm going to hang up and go eat pizza. The girls are home, and we're all hungry."

Jason had mere seconds to decide how to avoid disaster; in the wall-to-wall traffic he had nowhere to go, and he was moving too fast to stop in time. For a brief moment he detected a small break in the traffic to his left, so he closed his eyes, said a quick prayer and jerked the steering wheel in that direction, expecting to crash into one or more of his fellow commuters. He screamed into the phone, "Aaaahh! Shiiiiit! I'm gonna die!" To his surprise, when he opened his eyes he was moving safely around the spinning car, and all he suffered was yet another one-finger salute, this time from the Mercedes sedan that he had cut off while avoiding death. He was glad he had Bluetooth, because he couldn't have pulled off that maneuver if he'd had a cell phone in one hand. He said to Chelsea, "Dear, are you still there?"

After a brief pause, he heard "Still here. I just served up the pizza. The girls all say hi, and they love you. Are you okay? I thought I heard you yell. Did someone cut you off?"

"Oh, I'm fine. I just had yet another scrape with death, but I'm still not dead yet. I hope we have a full bottle of gin, because I'm going to have several martinis with my pizza. And I hope it's pepperoni, because gin-soaked olives go especially well with pepperoni pizza."

An hour later Jason pulled into the garage of his home in Northern Virginia. Traffic had been stop and go the rest of the way. He turned off his vehicle and sat there for several minutes, trying to force himself to take regular deep breaths as an effort to calm down before facing his darling wife and three beautiful daughters. It was not their fault that his commute was the equivalent of driving the Indy 500, and he didn't want to take out his stress and frustration on them.

Eventually, Jason got out of his car and opened the door that led through the mudroom into the kitchen. It was good to be home—good old safe, peaceful home. As he opened the door connecting the mudroom to the kitchen, he heard raised voices, perhaps an argument. When he walked into the kitchen, his eldest daughter, Lizzy, saw him first, turned from her mother and charged toward him. He held out his arms, foolishly expecting a hug from his darling thirteen-year-old. Instead, she looked up at him, placed one hand under each of her newly formed breasts, pushing them up to emphasize their presence, and said emphatically, "Daddy, can I have a push-up bra? Mom says I'm too young, but I want one. What do you think?"

Jason blinked a couple of times, looking around to make sure that he was in the right house, began to shake uncontrollably, dropped his briefcase on the floor, and fled back through the mudroom and into the garage. He climbed back into his 4Runner, backed out of the garage, barely remembering to reopen the garage door first, and aimed the vehicle at the nearest bar, where he calmed his nerves with a couple of nice, strong drinks.

About an hour later, he drove home again, parked in the garage, and this time he went to the front door and rang the doorbell. He thought that maybe by doing so his family would not realize that it was Dad and he would have the element of surprise. Chelsea answered the door alone, and when she opened it and saw him, she looked daggers through him.

"What the hell! Where did you run off to? I had a bad day at the office, and I desperately needed some help corralling those three little hellions to get them ready for bed. Instead, you ran away, you big coward, and left me here to fend for myself. I can smell from your breath that you already drank your dinner, and the pizza's all gone anyway. There's some bologna in the fridge and bread in the pantry. You can make yourself one of your disgusting fried bologna sandwiches. I'll send the girls to the kitchen to say goodnight."

• • •

Jason was in bed reviewing his day, and for the first time, he started to think seriously about leaving the government and working full-time as a private eye. *I could work from home, and the commute from hell would end. I already have my PI license and my first case. Why not give it a try? Now, how can I do this without Chelsea finding out? How, indeed?*

CHAPTER 7

"What would Jessica do? What would Jessica do?" Jason was a mumbling mess.

It never dawned on him that people might think he was nuts if they heard him, especially if they knew his mentor was an old lady from a TV show.

He finally decided that he'd visit CureStuff Pharmaceuticals. He mumbled, "That's what Mrs. Fletcher would do. She'd go to CureStuff, ask a lot of questions, irritate the hell out of everyone, and see what happens. Means, motive, opportunity, and alibis."

Jason had no idea what he was doing. He wasn't even sure that this was attempted murder. If a drug caused Joanne's strange attack, the dose would be important to consider; a higher dose would have probably killed her. If the intent was not to kill but to induce intense sexual pleasure, she could have taken the drug herself, in which case there wasn't even a crime. *But where's the fun in that?* With that in mind, he called out of work for the day and prepared for a trip to North Carolina.

He suspected that Chelsea might not be too happy about his plans, and she did not disappoint. He sheepishly told her that he was taking a day of leave to visit CureStuff and interrogate some of the senior management.

"You really are crazy. You're abandoning me here with our three little monkeys, and by skipping out on your government job you are probably putting that in jeopardy. I love you, and part of me wants to support you on this little adventure of yours, but the other part of me thinks you're out of your mind and wants to kick you in the nuts." His only response was to cringe, grimace with imagined pain, and pack for his trip. A hug was probably out of the question.

When Jason was speaking with Dr. Richard Littlething, president and CEO, he would be careful not to say anything about working for the FDA. He dialed and an administrative assistant answered the phone.

"Hello. I'm Jason Longfellow, a private investigator hired by one of your former employees. I need to make an appointment with Dr. Littlething to question him about matters concerning Dr. Shipley. I'd also like to interview a number of the other senior management while I'm there. I'd prefer to come for a visit day after tomorrow. Would that work for Dr. Littlething?"

"I'm sorry. I'm not sure that Dr. Littlething is available for an interview with a private detective. I need to check with him. Please hold." Before Jason could say anything else, he heard the phone click, and elevator music began to play an orchestral version of Beatles songs. Finally, she came back on the line and said, surprise in her voice, "I must admit, I didn't think that Dr. Littlething would be interested in your interview. Sounds so, well, silly. I thought private detectives spent their time taking pictures of husbands and wives involved in extramarital affairs. Oh my God. Is someone here having an affair?" She paused. "Anyhow, much to my surprise, Dr. Littlething agreed to a meeting with you. It seems day after tomorrow will be fine."

Jason thought, *She makes my new job sound like I'm making a porn film.* Trying to sound confident, he said, "Thank you. I'm pleased that Dr. Littlething agreed to meet with me. I knew contacting him directly was the right thing to do. It's what Mrs. Fletcher would have done."

There was silence from the other end of the line, followed by a click as the administrative assistant shook her head. *I'm not sure who the hell this Mrs. Fletcher is,* she thought, *but I think I just made an appointment for my boss to meet with a lunatic.*

• • •

On the day of his appointment, Jason drove the four and a half hours to Research Triangle Park, parked in CureStuff's outdoor visitor's lot, and went through security at the entrance to the building without issue. From the looks of the place, the company had lots of money. The entryway and atrium leading to the elevators were gigantic, at least two stories, and filled with marble, stone pillars, and inlayed tile with beautiful and brightly colored designs. There was so much rock that it smelled a little like the inside of a cave, albeit a very expensive one. A large mural covered the ceiling, with four corners made up of a gigantic caduceus, a sphygmomanometer, a scene from a research laboratory—complete with beakers, test tubes, a microscope, and a picture of a hospital emergency room entrance featuring an ambulance with a large red cross on the side. These four items created a square, surrounding the branded emblem of CureStuff Pharmaceuticals: a picture of a globe with a 50s-cartoon-style face, a big, happy smile on it, and the words *CureStuff, for a Happy, Healthy World.*

One of the security guards waited with Jason until Ms. Harden, the perky assistant in her late twenties, came to get him. She was slender, with long sleek legs. She had short, bright-red hair, a cute nose, dimpled chin, luscious lips that looked highly kissable and rosy cheeks. There was something in her clear blue eyes and friendly smile that gave the impression of an intelligent young woman with more than her fair share of ambition. She was dressed business casual with a white blouse and light-blue skirt, though the skirt cut off high enough above her knees to get Jason's attention. Ms. Harden extended her hand.

"Dr. Longfellow? I'm Carol Harden, Dr. Littlething's administrative assistant. Pleased to meet you. Come with me, and I'll show you to his office." She thought, *He doesn't appear to be a lunatic. Looks fairly normal, although a bit on the tall side. He'd be a handful if he decided to run amuck.*

Jason shook her hand briefly while gazing straight into her piercing blue eyes. He believed that eyes were a mirror to a person's soul. He saw in her a youthful, energetic, playful spirit that for a moment brought back memories of a time when he was young and free. As she moved closer, he caught the light smell of lilacs, his favorite scent. *Ms. Harden, where were you when I was in my twenties?* Then reality hit him, and his smile wavered a bit. *Damned midlife crisis. My twenties are long gone, and I need to focus on the task at hand.*

"It's a pleasure to meet you, Carol. I appreciate you making this appointment for me, and I look forward to meeting Dr. Littlething. Also, you addressed me as doctor. I made my appointment as PI Jason Longfellow. How did you know I'm a doctor?"

She smiled and said, "I'll leave it to Dr. Littlething to explain," as she turned to lead him to his meeting.

They took a nearby elevator to the top floor, the home of upper management. "So, Carol, how long have you worked for CureStuff?"

"I've been Dr. Littlething's administrative assistant for three years now. I began working for him right out of college. Dr. Lance Harden is my father, and he introduced me to Dr. Littlething." she said, a twinkle in her eyes. "I majored in pharmacy at UNC and took the job as a way into the company, but I have plans to move on from here in the near future."

"Where do you eventually want to land in the company? With a pharmacy degree you obviously have potential."

"I have my eye on a position in the marketing department. Everyone knows that the marketing teams end up running most drug companies. It's unusual for someone new to start as the president and CEO's administrative assistant and move from there to a department like marketing, but I saw an opportunity and thought I'd give it a try. Plus, my father likes it that I'm in Dr. Littlething's office. I can keep an eye on things from here."

Jason was taken aback by her honesty. *Aha. It would seem that Dr. Harden has his daughter planted in Dr. Littlething's office to keep an eye on him. This makes sense.* It was Jason's understanding that Harden developed the company's new potential blockbuster antidepressant drug, so he had a large stake in the company and whatever the president and CEO was up to. "I wonder if there's a clue to what happened to Joanne in there somewhere. This Carol Harden could be useful," Jason mumbled.

"What was that you said? I couldn't hear you."

"Sorry, I was just saying how impressed I am with this elevator, the whole building really. I see the elevator has been inspected recently," he said, trying to recover from this latest bout of mumbling.

The elevator reached the top floor. "Yes sir, we have our elevators routinely inspected—not our primary goal as a company, but we do follow safety regulations. Is that what you came to talk to Dr. Littlething about, our elevator safety program?"

She led Jason up the hall on the right, where a set of large, ornate oak double doors sported a gold-inlaid sign announcing, *Dr. Richard Littlething, President and CEO, CureStuff Pharmaceuticals.*

"Wow, based on these doors and that over-the-top sign, this Dr. Littlething must be quite a character."

"Yeah, he's a real peach. Five feet four inches of pure bullshit. But I'll deny it if you tell anyone I said that." She thought, *The two of you should get along together famously. You're both nuts.*

She opened the door and they entered the office. She led Jason to a couch in a small waiting area near her desk. "Have a seat, Dr. Longfellow. Would you like some coffee?"

"Yes please," he said. "That would be great."

She left the room and returned a couple of minutes later with the coffee. "There's cream and sugar on the tray if you'd like. Help yourself. Meanwhile, I'll buzz Dr. Littlething and let him know that you're here. Enjoy your meeting with him, lucky you." She smiled and returned to her desk.

A few minutes later, a short man in a very expensive Armani business suit walked up the hall, approached Jason and offered his hand. Jason placed his coffee cup on the table in front of the couch, stood up, and reached down to shake hands with the president and CEO of CureStuff Pharmaceuticals.

"It's a pleasure to meet you, Dr. Littlething. Thank you for taking the time to see me."

Dr. Littlething looked to be in his late fifties. Dark, beady eyes peered through large dark-rimmed glasses resting on his bulbous nose, practically enveloped by his face, which was so large and round that his chin was nowhere to be seen, although it must have been somewhere south of the forced smile formed by his thin lips and small mouth. His only redeeming feature was a well-groomed beard and mustache, though even this could not distract from the 200 pounds that had been compressed into a five-foot-four frame. It was impossible for Jason to miss the fact that Littlething was balding, with a small crown of gray-brown hair surrounding the top of his head; more than a foot taller than Littlething, Jason had a clear view of the top of the man's head. When Jason took hold of Littlething's outstretched hand, the CEO tried his best to squeeze hard to demonstrate his power and masculinity, but his hand was so small that only the tips of his fingers made it around Jason's palm.

Dr. Littlething replied, in the surprisingly high-pitched squeal that was apparently his voice, "It's a pleasure to meet you, Dr. Longfellow. How are things at the FDA?" The man obviously took some gratification from the surprised look on Jason's face as he continued. "Yes, I googled you when Carol first told me that you wanted to meet with me. You introduced yourself as a private detective, but I found you online, and it seems that you're a drug reviewer for the FDA. Frankly, that's why I agreed to meet with you, although I'm quite curious as to why you're really here. Is there a problem with one of our drug applications?"

"I apologize for not being forthright about my job with the FDA, but I'm actually here on behalf of a client in my other role, as a private detective. I can assure you that I'm a legitimate PI. I have a license, business cards, a CCW permit, the works." He showed Littlething his bona fides.

Jason couldn't shoot worth a damn, but he was really proud of that permit. He didn't have to demonstrate good marksmanship to get it, just that he knew how to handle a gun safely. He had purchased a 9 mm Glock pistol, but he didn't actually carry it; he was afraid he might accidentally shoot himself.

"I would like to ask you some questions about what happened recently to one of your SVPs. I'd also like to discuss your previous relationship with Dr. Joanne Shipley. It's my understanding that she used to work for CureStuff?"

Dr. Littlething interrupted. "Dr. Longfellow, please. Isn't it a little odd that an FDA drug reviewer is also a private detective? Tell me why you're really here, or I'll contact our lawyers and security and have you removed from the building. I ask again, is there some problem with one of our drug applications?"

"Dr. Littlething. I assure you that I'm not here as an employee of the federal government. I'm on annual leave from my job with the FDA, and CureStuff's drug development programs have nothing to do with my visit. I'm here as a private detective investigating an alleged attempt at poisoning Dr. Shipley, and along those same lines, I'm also curious as to what happened to one of your female senior vice presidents recently. Now, could you please tell me about your relationship with Dr. Shipley when she was an employee at CureStuff?"

Dr. Littlething calmed down at this assurance. "All right. I'll take you at your word. Come along and we can go sit in my office to talk. Carol, please come along with us. I want you there as a witness when I speak with Dr. Longfellow, in case he tries to question me about any of our drugs or biologics."

He led the way down the hall to his office, where he sat down behind a very large and expensive oak desk, with an inlaid, dark-blue marble work surface and a thick, ornate border around the top consisting of two rows of detailed roses carved into the richly polished, light-brown wood. Jason and Ms. Harden were forced to sit in front of the desk in guest chairs that were built so low to the ground that when everyone was seated Dr. Littlething actually appeared to be the tallest person in the room.

Now eye to eye with his tall nemesis, Dick Littlething said, "To answer your questions, with respect to Dr. Shipley, she worked here in the Research and Development Department on one of our products, a monoclonal antibody. The project wasn't going anywhere, so the board of directors decided to stop funding. Dr. Shipley's services were no longer required at CureStuff. I don't know what she has told you about me, but you have to understand that I'm wealthy, good looking, and quite popular with the ladies. I'm also divorced, and free as a bird; quite a catch."

Ms. Harden leaned toward Jason and said softly, "That would be a cuckoo." She was seated so low that Littlething couldn't see her, so she wasn't concerned about detection.

Littlething continued. "Dr. Shipley was quite interested in me before she was dismissed from the company, and I even felt sorry for her and took her out for drinks one night, which eventually led us to my plush townhouse where we ended up in bed together. I fulfilled her every fantasy that night, and of course she wanted more, but I moved on to my next conquest and she has hated me ever since. Did I mention that I also drive a shiny new BMW and have a forty-foot cabin cruiser docked at the marina on Lake Norman? I'm quite a catch."

Jason glanced at Ms. Harden, and she just shrugged at him, a grimace on her face as she mouthed the words, "So full of shit." Jason was underwhelmed by Littlething's conceit. "Isn't Dr. Shipley married?"

"Not my problem," Littlething said smugly. "If her husband kept her satisfied, she wouldn't need to look for a stud like me to take care of her needs, now would she? I don't know if her husband ever found out or not, but I didn't hear anything from him. She got what she needed from me, and I moved on."

"So, assuming that any of this is true, Dr. Shipley is not one of your greatest fans. What about the SVP that, according to the news, recently had an outbreak of a mysterious illness here at your company?"

"You must be talking about Dr. Wendy Thompkins. As to her mysterious illness, she had some sort of fit or series of seizures during one of our senior management meetings, and ended up in the ER. It's my understanding that they never figured out what was wrong with her. Wendy was another one of the women in the company with the hots for me. A while back, she asked me out for drinks, and I agreed. She also ended up in my expensive boudoir, where I rocked her world, and after that night I again moved on. She started dating Dr. Harden shortly after, and that was that. I never heard from her again except as pertained to work."

Jason glanced at Ms. Harden, who was looking in his direction, her finger stuck down her throat with a mock vomiting motion. Jason realized that he wasn't going to get anything of value out of Dick Littlething. This man was so full of himself—and shit—that it was impossible to carry on a rational conversation with him. Jason said, "Dr. Littlething, thanks again for taking the time to speak with me. It sounds like you are not on the best of terms with either Dr. Shipley or Dr. Thompkins. I can't think of any more questions for you at the moment. Would it be possible for me to meet some of your other senior managers?"

Littlething walked around his desk so that he could see Ms. Harden. "Carol, I guess it would be okay for Dr. Longfellow to talk to a couple of our SVPs or VPs. Why don't you introduce him to Dr. Grayson and Dr. Chang?"

Jason rose. "Thank you, Dr. Littlething. I appreciate your time."

"You're welcome, Dr. Longfellow. And if you ever review one of our drug applications, be kind. We can use all the help we can get."

Jason reached down to pull Ms. Harden up out of her chair, and she led him out of the office and down the hall. As they walked, she said, "Let's try to find doctors Tanya Grayson and Lucy Chang. Tanya is our VP of Toxicology and Lucy is VP of Regulatory. They're good friends, and if we're lucky we might catch them together. It's about break time, and they're probably in the coffee room."

• • •

As Jason followed Ms. Harden to find Chang and Grayson, he couldn't help but compare the brightly lit, clean, shiny building, smelling of new carpet and oak furniture, with the dingy, old, dusty, musty government buildings that he had worked in for most of his career. They took several turns down multiple corridors that all looked alike, and he was immediately lost.

"I hope you help me find my way out of here. This place goes on forever."

Carol laughed. "No worries. If I left you to roam free in the building, Littlething would have my head. Here's the coffee room, and look at that. There are Tanya and Lucy, just as I'd hoped."

The two women were sitting at a small table together, drinking coffee, eating yogurt, and chatting. One of the women was obviously of Asian descent, in her mid-forties. Her hair was black, her face round and pudgy with prominent wrinkle lines below dark eyes. A small mouth with a friendly smile hovered above a double chin, and she had a large mole on one cheek that should probably be checked out by a doctor. She wore an oversized, casual jacket over a loose white blouse and dark-blue cotton pants with elastic waistband, presumably to cover the fact that she enjoyed the standard American fast food diet. The pink Nike walking shoes fit in nicely with the laidback look of the overfed.

The other woman, about the same age, walked to the coffee machine for a refill just as they entered the room. As she passed in front of Jason, her long, wavy blonde hair flowing over her shapely shoulders, he caught a whiff of Chanel. His midlife-crisis radar zoomed in on her outrageously alluring body, and when she turned in his direction, he felt a stirring in his manhood brought on by the sight of her tight blue blouse, unbuttoned at the top to show a more-than-ample bosom, and the matching short, blue, cotton skirt that revealed long, shapely legs and a perfect round buttocks that spoke of many hours at the gym. He also noticed her sparkling blue eyes and spectacularly beautiful face, which appeared mysterious and enticing. At first glance she looked like an angel, but there was something about her inviting smile and the twinkle in her eyes—a warning that any angelic tendencies might be a disguise. She held her smile and nodded in his direction, and his knees wobbled a little. He thought they might be having a moment—at least, he was having a moment.

Jason mumbled, "I'm liking this PI thing more and more. I'm gonna question the hell out of the blonde."

As they approached the women, Carol smirked and said to Jason, "Yeah, Tanya has that effect on most men."

"Hey, Tanya. Hey, Lucy. How are things? This is Dr. Jason Longfellow, a private detective from Northern Virginia. He's here to investigate issues concerning Dr. Joanne Shipley. He also wants to speak with you about what happened to Dr. Thompkins recently. He seems to believe there might be a connection?" She glanced at Jason for confirmation before continuing, "And by the way, keep in mind that Dr. Longfellow also works as a drug reviewer for the FDA. Littlething wasn't too happy about that, and I must confess, I'm not quite sure that I understand it either. Littlething said it's okay for you to talk to him, but only about doctors Shipley and Thompkins."

Jason approached the table where the two women, one tall and slender and the other not so much, were now standing, trying his best not to stare down at the blonde's breasts. He said to her chest, "Hello. It's a pleasure to meet you. I'm looking into the attempt on Dr. Joanne Shipley's life. It's complicated. I recently got my PI's license, and I do investigative work on weekends mostly. As Ms. Harden said, I also work for the FDA, although I'm on annual leave from the government today. When I'm working for the FDA, Joanne and I carpool to work together. It's possible there was an attempt on her life, so she and her husband may have hired me to look into the situation; I can't say for sure because a PI's not supposed to reveal the identity of his client. So here I am. As I told Dr. Littlething, I'm not interested in your drug development program, only in this attempt on Joanne's life, and also what happened to Dr. Thompkins here recently. I'm wondering if there is any connection between the two events." He thought, *This private eye thing was a great idea. I'm already meeting new and exciting people. Just hope Chelsea doesn't find out how exciting.*

Dr. Chang spoke first, waving her right hand in the air. "Hello, Mr. Private Detective. I'm over here, not that you seem to have noticed. I'm Lucy Chang, VP of Regulatory. What do you want to know?"

Jason blushed. "Sorry, Dr. Chang. I'm looking for a motive for someone to try to kill Dr. Joanne Shipley, and the same for Dr. Wendy Thompkins. Dr. Littlething told me that he had dated both Drs. Shipley and Thompkins, bedded them, and then dumped them the next day. I gotta be honest, after meeting Littlething, I'm not sure I believe his story."

The blonde, Dr. Tanya Grayson, spoke up, a wry smile on her face, "I'm Tanya Grayson, VP, Toxicology, and I must say, you are very perceptive, although your eyes seem to have a mind of their own. Anyhow, Littlething is full of it. He has hit on every woman in the building, and to my knowledge no one will go near him. We're all taller than him, and no woman wants to date a man when she has to gaze down at the top of his bald head all the time. And for some unknown reason he's delusional and thinks he's God's gift to women, which makes him even more repulsive and ridiculous. No amount of money in the world would convince me to go out with that man."

She paused, considering how much information she should share. "It's my understanding that he did hit on Wendy Thompkins several times, but she kept rejecting him. Joanne Shipley and I were good friends before she left the company, and I know for a fact that Littlething tried to hit on her. She wasn't as nice as Wendy since she's married. She told him to fuck off. That may be another reason why she got canned. Joanne and I used to make jokes about Littlething all the time. You know, tiny hands, tiny feet, tiny . . . well, you get my drift. Wendy Thompkins is dating Dr. Lance Harden now, Joanne has moved on, and I guarantee that Littlething never got his little thing anywhere near either one of them."

Dr. Chang spoke up. "Wow, Tanya. Don't sugarcoat it, girl. Just tell it like it is." She chuckled. "Well, Jason, as you can see this place is about as screwed up as it gets. I can confirm everything that Tanya says." In a lighter tone—"Tanya, darlin', weren't you interested in Lance Harden at one point? Or did I just hallucinate that one? It's so hard to keep up in this place. Between Littlething's imaginary flings and the actual affairs that are going on at CureStuff, someone should write a book."

Tanya Grayson said, "As for Wendy Thompkins, I don't think anyone's really sure what happened to her. She had some type of attack. I didn't see the whole thing, but rumor was it looked like she was having sex with herself, getting off again and again during a senior management meeting of all things. Pretty screwy, huh? They took her to the ER, gave her a strong sedative, and she survived. She hasn't been back to the office since, but I think that it's more out of embarrassment than anything. I don't think anyone ever figured out what actually happened to her, or who, if anyone, did anything to her. Is that about right, Lucy?"

Lucy Change responded, "That's what I heard. Everyone made a big fuss at the time, but it's all died down and most everyone's forgotten about it. I guess that's partly because Dr. Thompkins hasn't been to the office since the incident. You know, out of sight, out of mind."

Jason thought, *Very interesting. Having sex with herself. Multiple climaxes. That sounds strangely familiar.* "That's useful information. Thanks. Is there anyone else that you can think of that might have a motive for harming Wendy or Joanne? I need to figure out who had a motive for harming these two women, so I can solve this case." *I need to show Chelsea that I can do this. It's way more fun than working for the government.*

Lucy answered, "Well, let's see. There's Ted Conway, our VP of Marketing. After Wendy's episode at our quarterly senior management meeting, Dick Littlething called a follow-up meeting to figure out how to proceed with the clinical trial for our new antidepressant drug, Happiness, while she's out of commission for a couple of months. At that meeting, Ted mentioned he had an argument with Wendy about the future of the drug if it gets FDA approval. He wants to use his salespeople to try to convince doctors to prescribe the drug off-label for everything from excessive gas to the common cold, and Wendy disagreed with this approach. At that meeting, Ted tried to convince Dick to replace Wendy with someone more open to his marketing ideas. He seemed very angry with her."

Tanya spoke up. "Yeah, and Wendy told me that old Ted cornered her in her office one evening a couple months ago, when they were both working late, and tried to kiss her. Apparently he'd left the office, gone out for a few drinks, came back to finish some work, and found her here. She kneed him in the balls, and he backed off. She never told anyone else because she didn't want to get him fired, and I guess she'd made her point with him. According to her, he never bothered her again, but I guess that might be a motive for him to try to poison her."

Wow, the office gossip's flying now. This is good information. I'm really good at this. "That's great. So this Ted Conway sounds like he has a motive. How did he act during the meeting where Wendy had her attack? Did he appear guilty, look nervous?"

Lucy said, "Come to think of it, Ted wasn't at the meeting where Wendy went to the ER. I believe he was on vacation that week. Isn't that right, Tanya?"

Tanya thought for a moment. "I believe you're right. Ted wasn't here when Wendy got sick; he just got back for the follow-up meeting."

Jason said, "Crap. It sounds like this Conway has an alibi for Wendy's poisoning. Well, that's not much help." *I'm getting the hang of this, using words like "motive" and "alibi," and collecting all this useful information, and some not so useful. Chelsea'll be impressed when I tell her, and she'll have to agree that I should quit the government and be a full-time PI.*

Tanya said, "There is someone else that might have a motive. Joe Bly, our SVP of Manufacturing. He's always sucking up to Dick Littlething, cutting manufacturing costs to the bone and skimping on product testing to increase profits. At our follow-up meeting, Joe was complaining about Wendy because she kept raising hell with him for the quality of the drug that his group was providing for the clinical trial. He was also angry with Wendy and agreed with Ted that she should be replaced."

"Was Joe at both meetings?"

Lucy responded first. "Yes, I distinctly remember Joe being at both meetings."

Tanya said, "Yep, he was there for both."

"Good. That means he had both motive and opportunity. Anyone else?"

Lucy spoke up. "Only other person I can think of would be Donna Smart, our VP of Human Resources. Donna and Wendy have been going at it since Donna interviewed her for head of Clinical Trials several years ago. Donna's kind of a petty person, and she'd just had her office redecorated the week before she interviewed Wendy. The story goes that during the interview Wendy made some comment about the color of the carpet, called it 'blood red,' or some such thing. It was a small thing, but Donna had picked the color, and like I said, she can be really petty. I'm guessing that it was more than that—some sort of conflicting personality thing. Anyhow, Donna was the only one that recommended against hiring Wendy, and she was pissed when Wendy was hired anyway. Later, Wendy found out, and there has never been any love lost between those two."

"Wow. Trying to poison someone over the color of a carpet is kind of extreme, but it doesn't sound like they got along. I haven't been at this very long, so I can't say I've ever seen anyone murdered for dissing the color of someone's office carpet. . . . This is all good stuff. Thanks."

Carol Harden said, "Well, Jason. What do you think? Any more questions? Your ears must be on fire, what with all that gossip."

"Nope. I'm good. Just one more thing. Do you think that I could speak to your father, Dr. Harden?"

"I don't know why not. I know that he's here today. I'll take you to his office." Carol said to the two women, "Thanks for your time, ladies.

I'm sure you gave Detective Longfellow plenty of food for thought. The way it goes around this place, everyone probably has a motive for trying to kill everyone else. I've heard that the main motives for murder are money and sex, and there's plenty of both at CureStuff."

Carol led Jason up another hall and down several more corridors before arriving at her father's office door. She knocked and then entered. Jason followed her into a large interior office. No window view here, even though Dr. Lance Harden was allegedly the discoverer of the company's latest potential blockbuster drug. As Jason entered, Carol said, "Hello, Dad. I've brought you a visitor."

CHAPTER 8

arden was in his early fifties, six-foot, with a medium build at about 180 pounds. If Jason had met the man on the street, he would have thought him a drug dealer, or old hippie, or maybe even homeless person. Dr. Harden had a pleasant enough face, with hazy brown eyes and a sort of goofy smile, but his full head of long brown hair was unkempt, not particularly clean, and had grown well over the ears; the man was in desperate need of a shave. He wore small, round, gold earrings in both ears and a smaller one in his left nostril.

Dr. Harden walked from behind a cheap-looking metal desk and shook Jason's hand. He was wearing well-worn blue jeans, a wrinkled black T-shirt with large white peace sign on the front, and sneakers. Jason was surprised at the man's appearance since pharmaceutical company employees generally dressed more conservatively. Dr. Lance Harden was definitely not your everyday pharmaceutical executive, emphasized by the pleasant smile that seemed to be unusually mellow for someone facing the high pressures of the industry. Then, Jason caught the faint, sweet odor of what was unmistakably weed.

This man has been smoking marijuana in his office, and not too long ago. Why would two professional women be interested in this scruffy-looking character? Does he share his supply of weed with them? Is he a dealer? Maybe he has an endless supply of little blue pills. The pharmaceutical world is a wonderful place.

Carol continued, "Dad, this is Dr. Jason Longfellow, or I should say Detective Longfellow. He's a private eye here to look into a recent attempt on Joanne Shipley's life up there in Northern Virginia. Strangely enough, Jason is also a drug reviewer for the FDA, works with Joanne, and carpools with her to work. He would like to ask you some questions about Joanne, and he's also interested in what happened to Wendy Thompkins a few weeks ago. He seems to feel that the two things are connected."

The two men exchanged pleasantries, and then Harden said, "Have a seat." He gestured to a small couch positioned against one of the walls. Jason and Carol sat on the couch, and Harden sat on the corner of his desk.

"So, you work for the FDA, and you're a private detective? How does that work? Can you really come to CureStuff, a drug and biotech company, and investigate an alleged attempted murder without it being a conflict of interest with your job as a drug reviewer? Seems a little odd. That must have driven Littlething nuts." He flashed a devilish smile.

"As I told Dick Littlething, I'm on annual leave from the government and am here solely for the purpose of finding out what happened to my fellow carpooler, Joanne Shipley. It was the strangest thing I've ever seen. I was driving us to work and all of a sudden she started getting what appeared to be sexually aroused. She was having orgasms all by herself in the passenger seat of my SUV, and she couldn't seem to stop, so I had to take her to the ER. She had no idea what happened, and the ER couldn't find anything specific, so they gave her a strong sedative, which stopped her strange reaction and probably saved her life. Can you tell me anything about Joanne Shipley? I know she worked here. Actually, Dick Littlething told me that he dated her, bedded her, and then dumped her. He told me a similar story about Wendy Thompkins. But doctors Chang and Grayson explained to me that this was all, how did they put it . . . 'bullshit.' They don't seem to have a very high opinion of their boss. What can you tell me?"

"Orgasms all by herself, in your SUV? That's quite a story. In the interest of full disclosure, I actually dated Joanne Shipley when she first joined the company, before she married. She was a young scientist that was hired to work in my lab, although when we broke it off she moved to a different lab and was later dismissed from the company. As you probably know by now, I'm currently dating Wendy Thompkins and have been for a couple of months, or at least I was. I haven't seen her since her bizarre reaction during the senior managers' meeting a while back. It's interesting. Her reaction was somewhat similar to what you described with Joanne, some sort of hypersexual response, and it happened in front of most of the CureStuff senior management. I think the poor thing's too embarrassed to see me or to come back to work. No one knows what happened to her, and the ER docs apparently couldn't figure it out. It's very frustrating; she won't answer my calls."

He paused, stared off into space for a few moments. "So, I have had relationships with both of these women, although I can assure you that I had nothing to do with whatever happened to either of them. It's a shame, because Wendy and I were getting along so well before that incident."

"Just one more question. It's my understanding that there's a new potential blockbuster antidepressant drug, or biologic, that has been developed here at CureStuff and is currently in clinical trials, and that it was developed in your lab. Is that true?"

"Yes, that's a fact. It's in clinical trials, and we are hearing good things. Actually, Wendy planned those clinical trials, and she's still monitoring the latest study, working from home. We're very hopeful that the study will prove the drug is effective. The earlier clinical studies showed that it's safe, and the behavioral animal study results suggested that it should work for treating depression."

"So, Dr. Thompkins planned the clinical studies for this new blockbuster drug? What about Pleasuria? I understand that earlier in your career you developed a drug called Pleasuria, also for the treatment of depression, and it failed in clinical trials. Did Wendy Thompkins put together the clinical studies for that drug too?"

"So you know about Pleasuria. I see you did your homework, although aren't we supposed to be talking about an attempt on Joanne Shipley's life and not CureStuff's drug development program?"

"I'm just looking for a motive for someone to try to harm Joanne or Wendy. So, what about Pleasuria? Why did that one fail?"

"All right. I get your point. In my opinion, those clinical trials failed because Wendy didn't include a high enough dose in the studies. We argued about it at the time, and I tried to get her to include a higher dose, but she insisted that the risks were too great. The drug did show some promise with depression, but the data were not convincing enough for the FDA. If she had done what I asked, I believe it would have worked. The FDA turned down the application on the first try, the project ran way over budget and CureStuff's board shut it down. I realize this doesn't sound good for me. I admit that I was upset with Wendy for refusing to follow my recommendation, but we discussed it, got through it, and we were fine. I would never hurt her. As I said, Wendy also planned the clinical studies for the current drug for depression, and things are looking much better this time."

Jason noticed that a young blonde woman in her late twenties had taken a seat in the waiting area outside of Lance Harden's office. She wore a white lab coat, and Jason figured she must be one of Harden's lab techs, or perhaps a young scientist. She appeared to be paying attention to their conversation, and he realized that she probably heard much of what they had said since Harden's office door was open. When she noticed that Jason was looking in her direction, she became obviously nervous, and after a couple of minutes stood up and bolted. Harden didn't appear to have noticed her.

Jason turned his attention back to Harden. "I'm glad to hear that your new drug is showing promise. I wish you the best. I don't have any more questions, so perhaps I should leave you to your work. Thank you for taking the time to speak with me."

Jason stood up and shook Harden's hand again. Carol also stood and said, "Thanks for taking the time to meet with us, Dad. I appreciate it. I'll show Detective Longfellow out of the building. This way, Detective."

She led Jason out of the office and started down the hallway. After a few steps, Jason said, "Carol, could you please direct me to a men's room? It seems that all the coffee has gone through my system, and I need some relief before heading out."

She said, "Sure, no problem. The men's room is just down this hallway. Turn right and it should be just on the left. I'll wait here for you."

Jason thanked her and headed toward the men's room at a quick pace. All the coffee he drank while speaking with Littlething had indeed gone through him. When he exited the men's room, he was all turned around.

He walked for a couple of minutes and then thought, *Crap. I must have taken a wrong turn out of the bathroom, and this place is an impossible maze of hallways. I'm hopelessly lost, and I don't have any way of contacting Ms. Harden since I don't have her cell phone number. Maybe if I just keep walking, I'll find an exit eventually. Better than stopping to ask for directions and looking like an idiot.*

He turned yet another corner and ran directly into the young blonde woman that he'd seen outside of Dr. Harden's office. At first, he thought that it was a chance collision—a not totally unexpected event in a crazy building with so many intersecting hallways. She took him by the arm, led him into a nearby empty conference room and said quietly, "I'm Shelly Carson, a lab tech in Dr. Lance Harden's lab. I know you saw me outside Lance's office, and I overheard most of your conversation. So, are you really a private detective or are you with the FDA? I'm confused on that point. I have wanted to speak with someone from the FDA for quite some time, but I'm not sure if you are the right person to hear what I have to say."

Jason repeated his situation. Shelly said, "Detective Longfellow, you sound like a man with an identity crisis, but if you really work for the FDA, you may be my only chance, so I'm going to tell you what I know. I worked on the original animal studies during the development of Lance's first drug, Pleasuria. There were some animal study results that CureStuff, and mainly Lance, chose to withhold from the FDA. In the rat studies to test for the safety of the drug, there were some strange side effects. When I gave the animals the high dose of the drug and put them back in their cages, they started humping each other frantically. Gender didn't matter—males humping females, males humping males, females humping males and females. And when I reached into one of the cages to remove an animal for further analysis, some of the rats tried to hump my finger, and one of them jumped on my arm and started humping my wrist. It was very disturbing.

"This strange behavior continued for several hours. The animals were obviously distraught, suffering, and worn out from all the humping, which they apparently could not stop. A couple of them actually died, from exhaustion or cardiac arrest. Eventually, I was forced to euthanize the entire lot, all of the high-dose animals. I included this reaction in my lab notes, and I even took video of some of the humping on my cell phone. Lance had company security confiscate both my lab books and my cell phone, and I was told that if I ever said anything to anyone about this, I would be fired and would never find another job in the pharmaceutical industry. Lance was so mad, I wasn't just scared for my job, I was afraid for my life."

"So what the hell does this drug do? How is it supposed to treat depression? And why does it make rats hump each other? Do we really need a drug that makes rats do that? Aren't there already enough rats running around?"

"The original drug, Pleasuria, was not actually a drug. It was a biologic, a monoclonal antibody, similar to the proteins made by the human immune system. Monoclonal antibodies are targeted therapies, like antibodies made by the immune system that are designed for specific binding to chosen cells in the body. Most people are familiar with monoclonal antibodies designed to kill cancer cells, like trastuzumab for breast cancer, which specifically attacks certain cancer cells."

"I get the concept of biologics and a monoclonal antibody, but for the sake of this conversation, let's just call Pleasuria a drug. Right now I have on my detective's hat and don't want to get too lost in the technical stuff."

"Okay. In the case of 'the drug' Pleasuria, it was designed to specifically stimulate a part of the brain called the amygdala, part of the limbic system that regulates emotions and includes the human pleasure center. The idea was for the antibody to bind to the pleasure center of the brain, causing good feelings in the patient and counteracting the depression. Monoclonal antibodies normally don't get into the brain; they're also destroyed in the digestive juices in saliva and the gut, so they can't be given as a pill. They are typically given intravenously, but Lance developed a special formulation for Pleasuria, a pill that allowed the antibody to be taken orally, cross the blood-brain barrier, and get to the brain without being destroyed in the gut. So Pleasuria was a miracle drug, but in doing this, the antibody's properties must have been changed to cause this bizarre humping thing. This part of the brain also includes sexual arousal, and Pleasuria not only makes a person feel better, but it has the side effect of somehow inducing hypersexual arousal, like humping-yourself-to-death-type sexual arousal. You know, like 'the head bone's connected to the neck bone, and the brain's connected to the boner bone'; you get the idea."

"Very interesting. That would explain why Wendy Thompkins didn't want to give a higher dose to the patients in the clinical studies, even though your boss tried to convince her to do so. Is it possible that someone is now using this failed drug, Pleasuria, to attempt to murder people, including Wendy and Joanne? It'd have to be someone who knew about the animal data and these bizarre humping side effects at the high dose. It's likely that Lance, and perhaps Dick Littlething, would have known, and they both have motives for harming these two women."

"That's not all. What most people don't know is that the new investigational drug, designated PQRST123, also called 'Happiness,' the latest potential blockbuster for treatment of depression, is really just a new formulation of the failed drug Pleasuria. Lance believed that if Wendy Thompkins had given the patients a higher dose of that drug, those clinical studies would have been a success. So, he did a minimal amount of work to make a new formulation from the old drug and told everyone that it is a completely new drug. In fact, if she had given the patients a higher dose of Pleasuria, they might have humped themselves to death, or who knows, they might have died from terminal orgasms, way too much of a good thing. It's my theory that's what happened to Wendy. Someone slipped her some of the drug."

Jason was getting excited. Here he was, a real private detective, finding clues, uncovering information, solving an attempted murder—or two. "Wow! Now we're getting somewhere. If Lance Harden knew about those animal data, he certainly had a motive for killing Wendy Thompkins. She must have known about the humping side effects, which is why she wouldn't give the high dose to the patients. He would have wanted to keep her quiet, to keep the side effects a secret. Especially since his new blockbuster drug is pretty much the same as the old one, with the hump, hump, hump. If Littlething knew about those side effects, he would have wanted to keep Wendy quiet too. He also has another motive; both women rejected him when he tried to hit on them. This whole thing's about humping—humping rats, Littlething trying to hump his employees, Harden humping everyone. Sounds like a motive for murder to me."

Shelly interrupted. "If that little perv knew about the humping side effects, he would've probably given both women the drug in the hope it would help him get into their pants."

"And both Harden and Littlething would have access to a supply of the original Pleasuria and to the new drug as well. But didn't those same side effects appear in the animal studies for PQRST123? Did CureStuff withhold data from the drug application to the FDA for this drug too?"

"Worse than that, they only gave lower doses of PQRST123 to the rats in that study, so they would be sure not to see any of those side effects. I don't know why the FDA didn't ask for a study with the higher dose, but I know for a fact that the rat study for PQRST123 only included a non-humping dose."

"Well, I'm Detective Longfellow right now, not Dr. Drug Reviewer Longfellow, so I'm not going to think about that. Besides, I don't know who at the FDA is reviewing the submissions for PQRST123, but it's not me. I now have two good suspects with motive and opportunity, and they could both have gotten their hands on the drug. Now, I just have to figure out how Joanne and Wendy were given the drug without their knowing it. Thank you for sharing this information with me, Shelly. I promise that I won't reveal my source to anyone. We should probably split up now. We don't want to be seen together. Please tell me how to find my way out of this crazy building. I feel like a depressed rat in a maze, and I sure as hell don't want any of CureStuff's antidepressants, thank you very much."

• • •

Jason drove home, and the next day he visited Joanne Shipley in her office at work. She wasn't ready to carpool with him yet, so the only way he could speak to her in person was at the office. He knocked on her door and she invited him in, although he noticed that she blushed when she saw him, and their being together felt uncomfortable.

"Joanne, I visited your ex-colleagues at CureStuff yesterday. I spoke with doctors Littlething, Harden, Grayson, and Chang. From what I could determine, Littlething and Harden both have motives for trying to harm you. Depending on who you talk to, Littlething hit on you and you either rebuked him or had sex with him. He told me that he bedded Wendy Thompkins too, and she is the senior manager at CureStuff that recently had an attack of hypersexual arousal. I also found out that Lance Harden dated you for a while when you worked in his lab, and then you broke up. Can you give me any insight as to which of these two men is the more likely candidate for trying to poison you?"

"You certainly found out a lot in one day. You must be pretty good at this detective thing. Maybe you should quit the government and do it full-time."

He smiled because that was his thought too. *Maybe she should talk to my wife.*

"First of all, it might be best if you don't share any of this information with my husband. He doesn't need to know about Littlething or Lance Harden. To answer your question, Dick Littlething is all bluster. He's a tiny little man who feels the need to act tough, but he's really scared of his own shadow. If you said boo to him he'd hide under his desk. He acted all tough when he hit on me, and I told him to take a hike, but I don't think he has the balls to actually hurt anyone. On the other hand, Lance Harden is a serious type of guy. I know that he looks like an old hippie from the 60s and he seems laid-back, but he's extremely passionate about his drug development, and he was really angry when Pleasuria failed the clinical trials. I thought he was going to strangle Wendy Thompkins when she refused to give a higher dose to the patients, and he liked her. I admit to dating him when I first joined the company, and I was the one who broke it off because he was too intense, no fun, and didn't have a sense of humor. Of the two, I think Lance is the more likely candidate. But I don't want to believe that either one of them would want to hurt me, or Wendy."

"One last question. When I talked to Tanya Grayson, she said that the two of you were good friends and you both used to poke fun at Dick Littlething—you know, small hands, small feet, small . . . well, you know. If that's true, I'm surprised the president of a company would put up with that kind of thing. Is it true? Did you do this in front of other people?"

"Again, I must confess, after he hit on me I was really pissed. He lied and started a rumor that he had slept with me, and that's when Tanya and I went after him. We got him pretty good at a couple of the senior management meetings. He had this tiny gold-plated laser pointer that he used with the slides during his quarterly budget presentations. It was a gift from some trade association, and he was proud of it. We used to ask him if he handled his tiny self as gently as he did that tiny laser pointer, and I might have said this in front of a few of the other senior managers. He pretended to ignore it, but his face got so red it would have lit up the room in the dark. I guess that was mean, but he was a bastard and we thought he deserved it."

CHAPTER 9

Sunday morning, a week after his visit to North Carolina, the kids were playing in the basement and Jason and Chelsea were having coffee in the kitchen.

"Chelse, my commute is killing me, and Northern Virginia's getting more and more crowded every day. My job is still boring as hell, and being cooped up at home with the kids is driving me crazy. We need to get out of here for a while. How about we take a vacation? I was thinking we should try a camping trip."

"I hear you, but how do we take three daughters camping? It's hard enough to keep them corralled and safe in the house. And we don't know anything about camping. Where would we even go?"

"Give me a chance. I'll look into places to go camping within a reasonable distance of home. Meanwhile, I have a buddy at work that bought a long-wheelbase Ford panel van and had it converted into a camper for him and his wife. He found a place in Maryland that'll do the conversion for you for a reasonable price."

"You've lost another marble. But I guess I already knew that. You always go all in on everything. Now you want to go camping, but we can't just take tents somewhere—you have to buy a van and pay someone to convert it into a camper? How expensive is that? How can you fit all five of us into a single van? And how are you going to afford it if you give up your day job and do this PI thing full-time?"

Jason just smiled. "Chelse, trust me. I'm not going to quit my day job just yet. And we can set up a long-wheelbase van to hold you, me, and all three girls. I'll get on the van thing, and once we have that, we can go camping whenever we want."

Chelsea didn't believe he was serious or that he would go to all that trouble. He was just venting frustration, she figured. So, she humored him so he would drop it.

"Okay, Jason. I'll go camping with you if you manage to come up with a converted van and find a reasonable place to go camping. I guess the girls would probably enjoy it. So, let's go camping." She smiled, shrugged, and figured that was the end of that.

A month later, Jason drove home in a brand-new long-wheelbase Ford van, converted into a camper. He called Chelsea and the girls out to give them the tour and invited Chelsea inside. She took a seat on the strange-looking couch thing that appeared to serve as a rear seat.

"The van has been modified for camping, with carpet and a back seat that automatically re-adjusts itself into a comfortable bed at the push of a button." He pushed a red button on the side of the couch thing, and it began to automatically unfold itself into a bed, carrying Chelsea along with it.

Chelsea screeched. "Jason, what the hell? Are you trying to kill me?"

"Stay cool, woman. Just go with the flow. I want you to see how comfortable the bed is."

The three girls all laughed, watching their mom slowly recline as the couch automatically flattened into a bed.

"Mommy has to put a quarter in the cuss jar," Lucy giggled.

Jason continued to show them the finer points of the conversion van. "See here? They also included space for a modified crib for Lucy next to the bed, and floor space for sleeping bags for Lizzy and Lilly.

I had them modify a crib for Lucy because at her age she's so active I figured we needed bars to contain her."

Lizzy interrupted, "Lucy's gonna sleep in a baby crib? What do you think about that, little one? You're still a baby."

"Am not a baby," Lucy cried. "Tell her, Daddy."

Jason ignored his daughters and continued. "The windows have been fitted with screens and a small fan for proper ventilation. We'll all be very comfortable in here, nice and cozy together." He could hardly wait to take the new van on their first camping trip.

Chelsea said, exasperated, "I don't know how you expect both of us to sleep on this bed. You're six foot seven, and there won't be enough room for me. And we can't all live in this thing for an entire weekend. We'll all go crazy. More important, how much did this monstrosity cost? When we talked about this, I agreed with you because I didn't think you'd actually go through with it. I just agreed to shut you up. I should've known better. Now we're actually going to go camping, in the woods, with the bugs, and snakes, and bears."

"Bugs and snakes and bears? We're gonna die!" Lizzy groaned.

"Mommy, I don't wanna die!" Lucy pleaded.

"No worries, my children. Daddy will protect you. After all, I am an official private detective, and I am much-man. I even have a gun. I'll wrestle that bear to the ground and bite off his ear, and if that doesn't work I'll shoot him."

Chelsea rolled her eyes. "Oh boy, I feel better already. Can we leave the gun at home, though? I'd rather be eaten by a bear than accidentally shot in the ass. And if much-man is going to wrestle a bear, maybe I should increase his life insurance."

"Mommy has to put a quarter in the cuss jar," Lucy said.

"Chelse, don't worry about fitting in the van. We're just going to sleep in it. We'll bring along a couple of large screened tents too, one for a kitchen and the other as a family room in case it rains. So we'll have two tents and the entire outdoors as a playroom. It'll be great."

"Judging by the size of the bed, much-man may find himself sleeping in one of the tents, or better yet, in the playroom," she fired back.

A couple of weeks later, on a weekend in May, they decided to do a trial run. Jason had them all corralled in the kitchen.

"I made reservations for a campsite at a small place just outside Front Royal called Land of Lakes State Park. It's only about an hour away, and if things don't go well, we can easily flee back to the comforts of home. But what could possibly go wrong on a simple camping trip?"

Chelsea just rolled her eyes. "Yeah. What could possibly go wrong?"

Jason loaded up two large tents, packed enough food and clothing for a two-night trip, and they headed out Friday after work. They arrived at the park around seven that evening, just an hour before dusk. It had started raining lightly about a half an hour into the trip, and Jason and Chelsea were already getting a bad feeling. Jason spoke up first, false hope in his voice.

"No worries, it's just a light rain. It'll cool things down, keep the bugs away, and tomorrow will be a beautiful day."

Chelsea looked at the girls in the back seat. "No worries. We're gonna have a great time. We'll toast marshmallows, and your father will protect us from the bears and stuff."

The girls' eyes got really big. Lilly said, "Bears? Are there really bears?"

"Mom, there are no bears around here. Are there?" Lizzy asked.

Lucy cried, "There are too bears. And Daddy said he will protect us. He will wrestle the bear to the ground and bite off his ear."

"Don't worry. Your father will protect us. Won't you, dear?"

"Who's gonna protect me?" Jason smirked.

"As you are so proud of pointing out, you got a CCW permit with your PI license, Detective Longfellow. Didn't you bring your little pistol with you?"

"I have a 9 mm pistol, and I can't hit the side of a barn with it. Worse, even if I was able to hit a bear, it would just make him mad. And besides, you told me not to bring it."

"My much-man. My protector. Maybe you should have brought your gun. If you threw the thing at the bear and hit him in the head, it might scare him away. And by the way, I did increase much-man's life insurance to a cool million, so go ahead and wrestle all the bears you want."

Jason sighed and kept driving.

As they drove through the park towards their assigned campsite, Chelsea said, "Oh look, dear, Land of Lakes State Park does, indeed, have three man-made lakes. Or, more accurately, there's a very small man-made lake, and two man-made mud puddles. Only one of the lakes has actually been filled with water. But the good news is, if it keeps raining, maybe the other two will fill up, too."

Jason flinched at her barb as he backed the large van onto their campsite, consisting of a raised gravel platform with retaining wall on the lake side. At least their campsite was located on the lake that actually contained water.

"Chelse, could you please get out and guide me so I don't back over the retaining wall, through that small patch of trees and into the lake."

She got out and walked around to the back of the van, stationing herself so that he could see her in his side mirror. "Straight back now, slowly, slowly. Just a little more. Stop! You don't want to put this thing in the lake. I'm betting your fine conversion van won't float, and our daughters are still inside."

"I'm inside too. What about me? Don't you care if I sink to the bottom of the lake?"

Chelsea laughed. "Sink to the bottom? Jason, you could stand up in the middle of this so-called lake, and your head would be entirely out of the water."

Once he had set the emergency brake, the girls got out and Jason and Chelsea began to unload the tents and set up camp in the light rain. It took well over an hour for them to finish, and by then it was almost dark and they were both soaking wet. Jason said, shaking his head to fling the rain out of his drenched hair, "See, that wasn't so bad. And now we're all ready for a good night's sleep."

Chelsea responded, "But dear, we haven't had dinner yet. I'll fire up the gas stove and boil us up some hot dogs. Meanwhile, why don't you corral the girls and do campsite things with them?"

The rain had subsided for the moment, and Lizzy, Lilly and Lucy had wandered off. Jason said to Chelsea, "I don't see the girls. Where the hell are they? I hope they didn't go down by the lake. They don't have on life jackets, and Lucy can't swim yet. I better look for them." He yelled. "Hey, monkeys, where are you? Are you okay?" He said to Chelsea, "I'm going to go find the girls. I'll be right . . . Aaahh! Shiiiit! Umph!"

As he jumped off the end of the retaining wall and his feet hit the ground, he slipped in the mud and fell hard on his rear end. The result was a sore rear end and muddy hands. In spite of the pain, he was very worried about the girls, so he bounced right back up and continued on through the trees toward the water's edge. He yelled to Chelsea, "I'm okay. I'm not dead yet. Stupid rain!"

When he broke through the trees, he didn't know how to respond to what he saw. Lizzy and Lilly were standing several feet from the water's edge, laughing hysterically, and there was poor little Lucy, sitting on a fallen tree trunk, completely naked, her body the bright-blue color of a Smurf. In fact, she looked a lot like Smurfette. The girls had gotten bored with Mom and Dad setting up the tents, and the two older children had taken some chalk from their drawing kit, mixed up a bright-blue concoction with muddy lake water, and used it to paint their little sister head to toe. Lucy was crying, and Jason couldn't tell if it was from chalk in her eyes, the fact that she was cold, or the fact that her sisters were laughing at her.

"What did you do?" he bellowed at his two older daughters. "Are you crazy?" To Lucy he said, "Are you okay, little one? Your sisters have lost their minds, and there will be consequences. Let's get that stuff off of you and get you into some warm clothes." To the other two, he said, anger in his voice, "You little monsters go to your rooms . . . I mean, go to the van. You're both banished to the van until I figure out your punishment."

It took a while, but Jason finally got Lucy washed clean of the liquid chalk and dressed in warm, dry clothes. Meanwhile, Chelsea had finished fixing hot dogs and beans, and she yelled, "Soup's on. Come and get it. Come on, girls, the hot dogs are getting cold."

But Jason intervened. "Those two need to stay in the van and go without dinner. What they did to their little sister was unacceptable." He was struggling, because it had been mean, but Lucy had also looked pretty funny and kind of cute all painted blue. Those girls needed to be taught a lesson.

He walked to the van and opened the side door. "Girls, you need to be nicer to your little sister. What you did to her was terrible, and dangerous. She can't swim, and you had no business taking her down by the lake without Mom or me. And painting her all blue was just mean." He realized that he was being ignored. They were watching one of their favorite movies on Lizzy's laptop, both wearing earbuds. He climbed into the van, closed the laptop, and pulled out their earbuds. "You two are making me crazy. I'm trying to have a family outing. Camping can be lots of fun. But instead you paint your sister blue, and then you plug yourselves into your laptop. What am I going to do with you?"

Lizzy said, "Well, Daddy, you sent us to our room and we were bored, so we decided to watch a movie. What's wrong with that?"

"I sent you to the van as punishment for painting your sister. It's no punishment if you just watch a movie. You need to sit there and think about what you did wrong."

Lilly said, "What's wrong with what we did? Lucy liked it. She laughed and laughed, until she got cold and started crying. She's such a big baby."

Jason's eyes started to bulge; his blood pressure soared again, and he yelled, "Chelsea. Help me! Your children are impossible!" He just couldn't seem to keep up with three daughters. He started mumbling.

"Three daughters. Help me. One's a handful, two are barely manageable, and three, well, three are freakin' impossible. Lucy's still little, but somewhere between eleven and thirteen they magically change, and at that point I'm completely lost. By that age, they constantly argue and talk back; all of the sudden I've turned into the enemy, and somehow, according to them, I'm dumber than a bag of rocks. Sometimes I think, who are you, and what have you done with my sweet little daughters? I have no idea how to talk to them, discipline them, nothing. It's like being on an alien planet, and the aliens are mysterious, yet somehow familiar, and always hostile."

Chelsea walked over to the van, looked in at the girls. "Now, girls. Look what you've done. Your father is babbling uncontrollably, poor man. What you did to Lucy was wrong. It was mean and dangerous. I want you to apologize to her, and I never want you to do that again."

Lizzy and Lilly looked at Chelsea with their sweetest faces and said in unison, "Yes, Mom. We're sorry. We'll apologize to our sister, and we'll never do that again."

"All right then. Now, let's have some dinner. Hot dogs and beans it is—real camping food."

The two girls crawled out of the van and headed for the cooking tent. Chelsea said to Jason, "See, dear. You just have to stay calm, talk to them like adults, and they will respond. Now, let's eat."

Jason screamed inside his head. The girls had gone virtually unpunished, his ass hurt, and he had no idea what had just happened. He mumbled, "When I talk to them, they do nothing but give me lip. When Chelsea talks to them, they do what she says. What am I doing wrong?"

By the time they finished dinner, it was nine o'clock and it had started raining again. The girls were all wound up, and the tent simply wasn't big enough for the five of them. Lucy was especially energized, excited by her new surroundings. Jason and Chelsea were sitting in the kitchen tent, drinking coffee, and the two older girls were as far to the other end of the tent as possible, plugged into their laptops. Jason looked up and yelled, to be heard over the earbuds, "Oh crap, where's Lucy? Girls, do you know where Lucy went?"

"I think she just sneaked out of the tent."

Then they heard a crash, followed by crying. "Aaaahh! Bleeding. I hurt myself!"

Jason, the protector, jumped up and fearlessly ran out into the rain to rescue his youngest daughter. He yelled to Chelsea, "She's okay. She fell off of the retaining wall and landed on her hands and knees. Her pants are torn, her knee and one hand are scratched up, and she's muddy from head to toe, but she's okay."

Jason carried Lucy into the tent, and Chelsea cleaned her up and bandaged her knee. At that point Jason was exhausted. He said, "Okay, monkeys. Let's all go to bed. Mom will take you to the restroom, where you can shower and brush your teeth, and then it's off to bed for the night. We'll get a good night's sleep, and start fresh in the morning. I'm sure the rain will let up by then."

After the usual arguing and grumbling, Chelsea managed to herd the three girls off to the campsite facilities. When they returned, Chelsea said, "The bathrooms are disgusting. Next time, pick a better place to camp."

Jason had the van set up for the night. "Okay, girls. Lizzy and Lilly, snuggle down into your nice warm, comfy sleeping bags. I'll put Lucy into her crib thing, and we can all go to sleep." He picked Lucy up and placed her in the converted crib. She was very active, and they thought that by converting a crib into a bed for their five-year-old, they would provide sidewalls that would keep her in place for the night. "Good night, Lucy. We love you."

Jason and Chelsea got comfortable on the fold-down bed. The older girls were surprisingly quiet, tired from the hard work of painting their little sister blue. After some shuffling around in the converted crib, Lucy seemed to quiet down, too. Jason, lying on his back as usual, had just nodded off into a pleasant and sorely needed sleep when he felt a sharp pain in his groin, followed by pressure on his upper torso as Lucy crawled up his body, placed her face just above his, looked him in the eyes and said, "Hi, Daddy."

Jason and Chelsea both laughed when they realized what had happened. He took her in his arms, placed her back in her crib. "Come on now, Lucy. It's bedtime. Time to go to sleep. You need to stay in your cage . . . I mean bed."

But Lucy wasn't having any of that. She was wide awake, and time after time, all through the night, she kept escaping the crib, climbing up Jason's body, never once missing the chance to plant a foot or knee in his groin, and then looking him square in the face and saying, "Hi, Daddy." This went on until six in the morning, and Jason and Chelsea got no sleep at all.

Jason was exhausted. "Chelse, I wish we'd have thought to bring something to put over the top of that crib thing. Four walls just aren't enough. We need a full-blown cage."

With no sleep at all, Jason and Chelsea decided to get up and fix breakfast. When Jason looked out the window of the van, it was starting to get light outside, and he saw that heavy cloud-cover still hung over the campgrounds. Just as he started to open the side door of the van on his way to the bathroom, the sky opened up and it felt like someone was dumping bathtubs full of water on him. He was drenched the second he stepped foot out of the vehicle. To no one in particular he bellowed, "Damned camping! Damned rain! Whose stupid idea was this, anyhow? You gotta have a screw loose to leave the warm, dry comfort of your home for this!"

He heard Lilly say, "Daddy has to put a quarter in the cuss jar."

The bathroom was damp and filthy; at least one toilet was clogged and the odor of human waste hung in the air. Jason looked around, and said to no one in particular, "This is nice. The showers look like they've never been cleaned, the green mold covering the shower curtains is most attractive, and the musty smell is almost as bad as the toilets." Jason relieved himself, noticed there was no soap or paper towels and was afraid to wash his hands in the grimy sink. He gave up and fled back to the van.

When he got back from the bathroom, Chelsea was sitting on the bed with her hands over her ears. All three girls were yelling at once. Lucy was crying, wailing above the noise of the storm. Lizzy and Lilly were screaming that they were cold and hungry and wanted to go home. Chelsea looked like she was going to strangle him, then jump out of the van and run away. Jason, standing there, looking at his distraught family through the side door of the van, made a command decision. "Family. We're getting the hell out of here. Chelsea, let's pack up and head home." He looked at Lucy. "I know, another quarter for the damned cuss jar."

In the pouring and blowing rain, he walked to the back of the van, frantically yanked down the two large, soaking-wet tents, wadded them up and threw tents, stakes, clean and dirty kitchen equipment, the whole lot, into the back.

"Chelse, push the button to convert the bed back into a bench seat, buckle everyone in, and let's get the hell out of Dodge." For once, no one argued with him.

They made good time getting home, and the girls slept the entire trip, but it took those tents over a week to dry out hanging in the garage. That was that for family camping. The camper van appeared for sale on eBay the very next week.

CHAPTER 10

Captain Harold Jennings was a well-respected pilot for United Airlines, based out of Charlotte Douglas International Airport in Charlotte, North Carolina. He was in his early fifties, tall, slender and still in prime physical shape. Women considered him attractive, with his dark hair, graying at the temples, dark-brown eyes, dimpled chin and friendly smile. While he made a striking figure in his captain's uniform, he was considered a little eccentric, as he had been seen dancing up the gangway toward the plane with a red rose in his teeth on at least two occasions. Some worried that drugs or alcohol might be involved, but he had always passed the requisite testing, and to date his safety record was impeccable. He was seldom home, volunteering for extra flight time with United and moonlighting as a cargo pilot.

His lonely wife had hooked up with a neighbor and got the house in Charlotte in the divorce. Jennings purchased a townhouse in Greensboro, not far from Raleigh-Durham International Airport, where he kept his private plane, a Cessna TTx.

On a beautiful sunny Saturday in June, Captain Jennings, exhausted from long hours at both jobs, decided to fly his Cessna to Tampa for a couple of days at the beach. He filed his flight plan and taxied his plane onto the runway. The air traffic controller said from the tower, "You're cleared for takeoff, Captain Jennings. Have a good flight." The controller was an old friend of the pilot and was aware of his destination and plans for the weekend.

Captain Jennings piloted a smooth takeoff, and responded to his friend, who heard, "Hello there. Who are you, and what are you doing in my cockpit? Damn, you're a looker." Then Jennings said, "Oh baby. We're gonna have a blast at the beach. God, you are hot. You have the body of a goddess."

"Captain Jennings . . . Harold?" the controller radioed. "What did you say? Please repeat. Is everything okay?"

Jennings said, "That's it. Take off your blouse. Hell, let's get naked right here, right now. We'll do the mile-high thing, but instead of the bathroom we'll do it right here in the cockpit. Bring that bodacious body over here!"

The controller was even more confused and more than a little alarmed when he saw the Cessna unexpectedly change course, heading due west instead of southwest. "Harold, what the hell are you doing? You are off course. You need to get that Cessna back on your scheduled flight plan or you are going to cause a major disaster!"

Jennings didn't respond and instead said, "Oh baby, do that some more. Don't stop! Yes, I want you bad, real bad. Damn, we need a bigger cockpit! Careful, don't pull that, it controls the flaps. Oh yeah, do pull on that. That's real nice."

The Cessna continued to fly off course, and the controller became frantic, as he could see on his screen that a large passenger jet was headed for a collision with Jennings's plane. "Harold, please respond! You are off course. Repeat, you are off course. Please return to your assigned flight plan, or you're going to collide with a passenger jet. Repeat, return to your assigned course, immediately!"

The controller heard, "John, leave me the fuck alone. I'm setting a record for the mile-high cockpit club. Gina here is one hot babe, and we're about to set this plane on fire. Oh baby!"

The controller checked the flight plan for the Cessna again, but as he already knew, Captain Harold Jennings was the only one scheduled to be on board the flight. He said, "Harold, who the hell are you talking to? There's no one scheduled for your flight but you. Did you sneak a woman on board? What the fuck are you doing? This is highly irregular."

Again, no response from Jennings, but he heard, "Oh God! Oh God! Gina, ooooh! Please don't stop! I'm just about there! Oh yes, yes! Do that!"

Finally, after several more tense moments the controller heard, "Aaaah. Oh my God, so good, I'm gonna explode!" And then, "Oh *shit!*"

The FAA discovered the remains of the plane in a field just southeast of Greensboro, North Carolina. Only one body was found in the debris, a male, presumably Captain Harold Jennings. When the FAA investigators interrogated the air traffic controller, he seemed completely befuddled. "Just after takeoff, I heard Harold . . . Captain Jennings talking to someone in the cockpit, although there was no one else scheduled to be on the flight. Captain Jennings described the other person as a hot blonde, and said they were going to set the record for the mile-high cockpit club. I'm not sure that's even a thing. Anyhow, the rest of what he said sounded like the dialogue of a porno movie. It sounded like this other person, Jennings called her Gina, was doing things to him to bring him to . . . well . . . a happy ending. He seemed to get there right about the same time the Cessna hit the ground. Talk about your big time climaxes. This one ended in an actual explosion. I was kind of jealous of Harold, right up until the time his Cessna ate dirt."

CHAPTER 11

Jason's life was more hectic than ever, what with his job at the FDA and his first case as a private detective. When they met at home on Friday night, about a month after their ill-fated camping trip, Chelsea informed him, "Jason, you need to spend more time with the girls, especially our little one, Lucy. You've been working on that stupid case for the past couple of weekends, and the girls have missed you. Tomorrow I'm taking the older girls shopping for some new clothes. Lucy's a handful, and if we take her with us to the mall, we'll spend the whole time chasing her and won't get anything done. She likes to ride the escalators. Remember the leash?"

Jason groaned. "How could I ever forget that? We tried the leash after she decided to get on the crowded mall elevator by herself and ride to the third floor. I had to sprint up two down escalators to get to her before she got off and lost in the crowd. That was scary as hell."

"I still can't believe you actually found a leash designed for a small child. I'll never forget that large woman screaming at you for treating your daughter like a dog, and then beating you about the head and shoulders with her folded umbrella, until a mall cop finally pulled her off of you."

Jason sighed. "Yeah. That was painful. We threw the leash away and gave up. If we ever take Lucy to the mall again, one of us has to hang onto her at all times while the others shop. You'll definitely get more done if I stay home with her. We can play in the basement. You know me, I like to spend time with the girls. I'm just a big kid myself."

Chelsea rolled her eyes. "No argument from me. Like the time you bought Lizzy a radio-controlled car when she was six? I'm still convinced you bought that thing for a much larger kid. And then you took her into the garage to play with it, yelled at her when she kept crashing it into the walls, and took the controller away from her so you could *demonstrate* how to use it. If memory serves, you never gave her back the controller."

"Yeah. I remember. And you had no right to take the car away from me . . . us. You did that eye-roll thing that you always do, and confiscated the car. That was mean, and not fair to Lizzy, or me."

"And I still stand by my statement that it's a pain raising four children," Chelsea said.

Jason knew he didn't have a chance with this argument, so he gave up.

The next morning Chelsea, Lizzy and Lilly headed off to the mall, and Jason stayed home with little Lucy. He told Lucy, "So, how about a healthy breakfast of chocolate-covered cake donuts?" Both he and Lucy were quite fond of this wholesome choice. Jason thought it must be a genetic thing. He continued, "Mommy forbade me to give you girls donuts for breakfast. But Mommy's at the mall, now isn't she?"

After breakfast, Jason asked Lucy what she would like to do. "Daddy, I want to go down to the basement and play dress up." These were not words that Jason ever liked to hear from any of his daughters. He'd been there before with the other two, and he knew how this story ended. Lucy saw Jason's reluctance, immediately gave him *the face*, and said, "Come on, Daddy, please, oh please."

Jason saw the sad puppy face and said, "Lucy, not the face. I'm onto you. Your sisters used that on me, and I've learned my lesson."

Lucy's lower lip quivered, and her puppy face got even cuter and sadder. "Pretty please, Daddy, just for a little while."

Jason's really hated playing dress up, and his resolve was strong as she took him by the hand and led him to the basement, where the makeup kit was already set up. "Take it easy on me, Lucy. Last time it took me three days to wash off all the makeup."

Chelsea had made the mistake of allowing Jason to furnish the large finished basement of their home. Instead of regular furniture, he had chosen to construct a large plastic castle-type jungle gym, complete with slide, in the middle of the room. In one corner he placed a couch facing a TV cabinet with a flat-screen TV and not one but three different video-game consoles and a DVD player. There was even a small, electric-powered car for Lucy to drive around the large room, and there were nerf swords, a gun that launched nerf balls, and a small trampoline. When Lucy was still a baby, Jason and the two older girls had spent many hours on weekends staging nerf wars as the troll, a.k.a. Jason, attacked the jungle gym castle with the damsels inside, while baby Lucy crawled around on the carpeted floor.

Lucy was determined to play dress up, Jason's least favorite thing in the world—with the possible exception of reading Dr. Seuss's *Hop-on-Pop* for the eight millionth time. Jason tried to distract her, "Hey, Lucy. How about a game of troll? Or a ride in your car? You can chase me around the basement in your car. Wouldn't that be fun?"

But she wouldn't be deterred. She led him over to the makeup table against the back wall of the room and said, "Daddy, sit. I'll make me pretty first, and then it's your turn."

Jason groaned as he struggled to sit on the floor, leaning against the wall. His large behind just wouldn't fit in the child-sized beauty parlor chair. "Go easy, Lucy. Mommy will be mad at me if we make a big mess, or if it takes hours to clean you up."

At age five, Lucy had become quite sophisticated at the art of applying makeup. First, she got all dolled up in one of her sequined pink party dresses, complete with feathered hat. Jason said, "Well, don't you look beautiful."

"Thanks, Daddy. Now, one for you." Then she got out a larger pink hat, also sporting several large feathers and covered in multicolored sequins, and put it on Jason's head.

From there, she got out the makeup, applying eyeliner and rouge first to her face, and then to Jason's face. "Go easy. I have to go to work Monday morning, and if I can't wash this off I'll get all kinds of funny looks."

Then, it was time for the lipstick. Lucy looked around for it and said, "Daddy, I can't find my red lipstick. Do you see it?"

Jason looked around the room and shook his head; toy debris was everywhere. "Lucy, I'm afraid you're going to have to pick another color. I doubt we could find anything that small in this mess."

Lucy said, "I'll bet it went under the couch to hide." Jason wondered how Lucy was going to search under the sofa, since it had short legs and was not very far off the floor. He was impressed when she used one of her makeup mirrors to search under it for the lipstick. She held the mirror near the bottom of the couch at an angle so she could see underneath in the reflection. She squealed with joy, and said, "There it is, Daddy. There's my red lipstick." She reached her small hand under the couch and pulled out the lipstick tube. He was impressed with her ingenuity but also sad that she found it because he knew what came next; he was in store for a set of bright-red lips.

Lucy took the lipstick, opened it, and said, "Okay, Daddy. Pucker up so I can put on your lipstick. You'll be so pretty with bright red lips."

When Chelsea, Lizzy, and Lilly returned from the mall, they searched the house for Dad and Lucy. Lizzy found them in the basement, snuggled up on the sofa with the final credits for *101 Dalmatians* rolling on the TV screen. There was Dad in a pink feathered hat, pink shawl, and full makeup, sitting on the couch asleep with his head slumped forward, and Lucy, also asleep with her head resting on his arm. Lizzy, a firm believer in social media, called softly to Dad, and when he opened his eyes and looked up she snapped several photos with her iPhone, which she immediately posted to Facebook, Twitter, and Instagram. As Jason slowly woke up, he realized what had happened and he began to panic.

"Lizzy, what did you do?" he said loudly. "You can't post those photos on social media. I'll be a laughingstock. What about my job . . . my jobs! The government will think that I'm dressing in drag! And no self-respecting hard-boiled private eye would be caught dead like this. Where did you post those pictures? Give me your damned phone! Take down those posts. Recall those pictures! Someone help me!"

Chelsea heard all the commotion and went downstairs to see what was going on. When she saw Jason sitting there in his pink garb, she laughed hysterically. The other two daughters had tried a similar treatment on him when they were younger, but neither of them had gotten him this good.

"You look like something between a drag queen and a hooker from hell. How on earth did Lucy get away with dressing you up like this? She must have given you an extra special puppy face."

Then she noticed the iPhone in Lizzy's hand, and she said to her daughter, "No you didn't! Your poor father is going to lose his job . . . both jobs, although I wouldn't mind if he lost the PI thing. I want you to take down whatever posts you put on social media and call back whatever photos you sent to whomever. It's not that your father didn't deserve this, after what he let Lucy do to him. But we can't really afford for him to lose one or both of his jobs. God forbid the government fires him because then all we would have is good old PI Longfellow, and I'm not sure I could live with that."

Jason, who had been planning to tell her about his decision to quit the government, died a little inside. He wasn't even thinking about the fact that the photos of him were already out there in the internet-o-sphere and would always remain there throughout eternity. He was more concerned about how he was going to tell his wife that PI Longfellow was who he wanted to be.

CHAPTER 12

Jim and Mary Hutchinson were seventy-five-year-old retirees living in Raleigh. They looked like an average elderly couple, white hair, wrinkles, and ravaged by age, gravity and overeating. He stood only five-six due to poor posture and a bad back, and she was an inch shorter, and her once-pretty face and shapely body now looked like an overstuffed version of her younger self. Jim had retired as a professor in the English Department at North Carolina State University, and Mary was a high school history teacher at the Raleigh Charter School. They were longtime North Carolina residents and were very happy with their lives. Despite being in their mid-seventies, they were both still relatively healthy and self-sufficient. Jim spent his time hanging out with friends at the club or watching TV, while Mary played bridge, attended her book club where they drank copious amounts of wine, and enjoyed gardening in the backyard of their suburban home.

One evening in July, they went to bed after the late evening news, as usual. After forty-eight years of marriage, they still slept together in a king-size bed, although in the past couple of years Mary had taken to placing a long pillow in between them to mark her territory. As they settled in for the night, Jim said, "Dear, I don't think you'll need your pillow wall tonight. I'm exhausted. I doubt I'll move once I'm asleep. We stuffed way too much into a single day. I didn't mind the marathon grocery shopping; we bought enough food for a month, you and those damned coupons. But when we got home from the store and put away the food, did we really have to weed your garden? We were already tired, and the heat and humidity were too much. We're not spring chickens anymore."

"Yes, dear, but I'm not taking any chances. You thrash around in your sleep like a fish out of water, and you've already pushed me out of bed three times in the past year, always in the middle of the night. That last time I just gave up and slept on the floor. It's either the pillow barrier, or we're gonna have to go to separate beds."

Jim frowned. "I remember a time when you used to like to go to bed; you were a passionate woman. Now, there's a pillow wall, and you're talking about separate beds. Are we really that old? How'd that happen?" They were both asleep by the time he finished his last sentence.

Around two thirty, Jim was awakened by the sound of his wife's voice. He heard her say, "Oh my! That feels good. I haven't felt anything like that for a long time. What are you doing, you naughty boy?"

Jim, groggy from being woken in the middle of the night, said, "Mary, who the hell are you talking to? What are you doing? It's the middle of the goddamned night."

She didn't respond. Instead, he heard her say, "Oh yes. That's so good. Right there. Don't stop. It's been so long; I forgot what it's like. Oh God! Oh God!"

At this point, Jim was baffled. It sounded like his wife was having sex with someone, and it was apparently not him. They hadn't had any intimate contact for years. He reached out to the nightstand, turned on the dim lamp, looked in her direction, and saw his wife in her pajamas, covered from the waist down by the sheet, massaging her breasts through her pajama top and moaning with pleasure.

"Honey, what are you doing? There better not be anyone over there with you. Damn it! I can't see a thing without my glasses. You can't do that without me. It's not fair."

He fetched his glasses off of the nightstand but still didn't see anyone else, and from what he could remember of sex, his wife was approaching an orgasm. She moaned, "Oh God, yes. Let it come. It's been so long. Just let it come. Oh yes, yeeesss!" With that, her entire body shuddered, she arched her back and screamed with ecstasy.

Jim was dumbfounded. He didn't know what to do, and he was kind of jealous. He said, "Mary, what the hell's going on? You haven't let me touch you in years. I'm right here, and would be happy to help."

Jim had seen a movie recently where the ghost of a woman's dead husband had returned and made love to her, and he wondered if maybe this wasn't something like that.

"Mary, are you having sex with a ghost? Who is it? I'll kill him."

She was somewhere else, somewhere that he wouldn't mind visiting. He wanted to move to her side of the bed and participate, be a part of this thing, whatever it was. But the other side of the pillow wall was taboo, and she had such a large smile on her face and such a look of contentment that he didn't have the heart to interrupt. He was actually beginning to feel happy for her.

Mary climaxed and when she calmed down Jim said, "Darling, I know it's been a while since we had sex, but I seem to remember that you need to touch certain parts for a woman to climax. I'm watching, and I don't see any touching. Is this something that you learned about on *Oprah*? If so, I want to see that episode."

He was beginning to relax, comforted by the thought that maybe she was in a deep sleep and had just had one hell of an erotic dream. Then, she started up again. She said, much louder this time, "Oh God. That's unbelievable. Yes, do that. Right there. Don't stop doing that. Ooooh! I'm going to come again. Yes, oh yes, oh yes!" Her entire body shuddered again, her back arched and she appeared to experience another, even stronger orgasm. She screamed, much louder this time, and her eyes appeared to roll back in her head.

Again, Jim looked around the room, trying to figure out who or what was doing this to her. Her hands were nowhere near her orgasmic region; this time they weren't even on her breasts. Her hands were just waving randomly over her head, almost like she was dancing, kind of like jazz hands. Deciding this must be some type of erotic dream, Jim said, "Mary, wake up! This is your husband, and I want in on this action. What are you dreaming? It sounds like wild sex, but your hands look you are dancing. You can't do this without me. You're in your mid-seventies, you're getting too agitated, and I don't think this is good for your heart. Mary, snap out of it! I'm afraid you're going to stroke out."

He really got concerned when, for the third time in the span of no more than five minutes, he heard her say, "Oh God. Yes. Again. And again. And again. Do it to me. Right there. Yes, touch me right there. Yes, harder, faster, deeper. Please, don't stop. Please, take me there, again, and again, and again. It's been so long, and it feels so good!" And for the third time, she screamed, her body shuddered, her back arched and she had what looked like the grandmother of all orgasms. Her face was contorted with pleasure.

"Goddammit, woman, I don't know what's going on, but you need to share. You can't keep doing this without me. It's just not fair." He was becoming downright indignant until he noticed that she had stopped moving

"Oh shit," he said. "Mary, are you okay? Talk to me!" She was suddenly quiet and still. He courageously crossed the pillow wall and tried shaking her, but still no response. He felt for a pulse, but it was very faint and her breathing was very shallow. "Thank God, still alive."

Jim dialed 911 and heard, "What's your emergency?" Jim realized that he hadn't thought this through. What to say? How to explain what had just happened?

After a lengthy pause, he said, "This is Jim Hutchinson. My wife Mary is here in bed beside me, she's barely breathing and her pulse is very weak." He paused again for a few seconds before continuing, "She just had some kind of fit, a seizure, or something."

The 911 operator asked, "How old is she and what was she doing before this seizure?"

Jim's mind was frantically trying to sort it all out and do his best to explain the situation. "My wife is seventy-five, and I woke up to find her sexually aroused. She was moaning, talking out loud, in her sleep I think. Then she, well, she seems to have had three consecutive orgasms, apparently really good ones . . . without me."

"You mean at seventy-five, you and your wife were having sex, and she had three orgasms? What did you do, call 911 to brag? I don't know whether to be outraged or really impressed. This service is reserved for emergencies, sir, not fairy tales."

He could tell that she was about to hang up on him, so he blurted out, "No. We weren't having sex. We haven't had sex in years. I don't know what the hell was going on. She appeared to be talking to someone else, but there was no one but me in the room. She kept making noises like she used to make when we were in our twenties, and we would . . . well . . . you know. I think the kids today call it hooking up. But I was on my side of the bed, busy not touching her, and she was having climax after climax, without me, I counted three in all. I was really getting pissed that I wasn't included, but then her breathing got really shallow and her eyes went up into her head."

"I still don't understand. Do you mean that your wife was masturbating and got carried away? Did she hurt herself? A girl's got to be careful with some of those battery-operated things. Do you need an ambulance?"

"No, she wasn't touching herself. She was waving her hands around in the air. It was like she was dancing, on her back. Anyhow, no one touched her, including her; there was no masturbating, and I'm sorry to say that I was also left out of the equation. I am trying to tell you that I don't know what happened, but we need an ambulance. She's unconscious, barely breathing, and her pulse is almost nonexistent. Please send help. Hurry!"

The operator heard the desperation in Jim's voice. "Don't worry, sir, I'll dispatch an ambulance immediately. If you like, I can stay on the line with you until they arrive."

Jim said, "Thank you. There's not much you can do. I'll make a cold compress from a wash rag and put it on her forehead. For all I know, she could just be overheated."

CHAPTER 13

The following Monday, Jason saw a notice on a bulletin board at work announcing the upcoming appearance of Dr. Lance Harden, SVP, CureStuff Pharmaceuticals, at an FDA conference to speak about CureStuff's research program related to antidepressant drugs. Jason called him and invited him to dinner while he was in town, and Harden accepted. To Jason's surprise, Dr. Harden was dressed in suit and tie like everyone else. His presentation appeared to be purposefully vague with respect to his research program. The symposium ended at six and Jason drove Harden to a nearby Wendy's. Jason intended to question Harden further about his research, but he had to be careful not to let on to Harden that one of his own lab techs had ratted him out on the "humping" side effects of Pleasuria. Jason didn't want to get her fired; it could prove handy to have someone on the inside.

When Jason pulled into the Wendy's drive-through, Harden looked confused. He said, "Dr. Longfellow, when you asked me out to dinner, I assumed we would be eating somewhere with plates."

"I'm a little low on cash right now. I work for the government, I'm trying to start my own PI business on the side, and I only have one client at the moment. No one's going to reimburse me for this meal, and it's not ethical for you to pay since I also work for the FDA. So, Wendy's it is, unless you'd prefer McDonald's, just up the road. Besides, I thought we would have more privacy if we ate in the car. If you insist on a plate and silverware, we could go inside, if a paper plate and a spork would do."

Harden responded indignantly. "Oh, for Heaven's sake. This is fine. Let's just get this over with."

Once they received their orders, Jason parked the 4Runner and handed Harden his bag of food. Jason asked, "So, Dr. Harden, when I visited CureStuff, I heard from a number of people that it was your research that led to the discovery of the company's new potential blockbuster drug to treat depression. You must be very proud of your staff. I hear that the drug's supposed to be worth hundreds of millions. Is that true?"

"Well, it depends on the how the clinical studies go in the next few months. I must confess, I am hopeful. As you know, the data can't be unblinded until the study is finished, but I've been hearing some good things from the clinical researchers."

In order to make Harden as uncomfortable as possible, Jason left the windows up in the car. Temperatures were in the 80s. Then, as a further distraction, Jason cleverly dropped a greasy french fry on Harden's pant leg. "Shit, that'll make a mark." He said, "Let me get that for you," as he smeared french-fry grease into Harden's pants, trying to wipe it off with a paper napkin.

Harden slapped Jason's hand away, took the napkin from him, and started wiping himself. "Please, let's finish eating and you can take me back to my hotel where there's a wonderful air conditioner and no you."

Jason didn't take offense. He saw that his plan was working; Harden was starting to sweat through his business suit. While he had Harden distracted and miserable, he changed the subject abruptly. He didn't expect Harden to confess that the new drug was just a quick makeover of Pleasuria or that ubiquitous humping had been seen in the earlier animal studies. Jason was more interested in finding out who might have a motive for harming Joanne Shipley. He was new to the PI game, and he needed to be subtle enough to keep Harden from becoming suspicious.

"I hope you're enjoying your meal. By the way, I met Dr. Dick Littlething during my visit to CureStuff. I heard from some of the employees that he was quite the ladies' man. Is it true that he tried to date Wendy Thompkins at one point and she shut him down? Same for Joanne Shipley? And what about Tanya Grayson? Did he try to hit on her too? Do you think Littlething is capable of trying to kill these women because they rejected him? Do you think he's a murderer? Do you know who tried to murder them? What about you? Did you try to kill Joanne Shipley and Wendy Thompkins?"

Jason thought, *I need to work on my interrogation technique. Subtlety is not one of my strengths.*

Harden looked surprised. He had expected questions about his research, and he was prepared to be vague about that. But he hadn't expected questions about a murder or accusations that he was a killer. He also had french-fry grease on his dress pants and was about to pass out from the heat.

"Excuse me, Dr. Longfellow. It seems that you've switched from your role as FDA reviewer and put on your Sherlock Holmes hat. I wasn't expecting you to grill me about the alleged attempt on Wendy Thompkins life, or that of Joanne Shipley. Do you really think I had anything to do with those attempted murders, if that's what they were? Also, as a government employee, I don't think you're allowed to torture someone you're interrogating. And if you are, can we please go back to the hotel, and you can waterboard me? I'm pretty sure I'd prefer that to Wendy's food, french-fry grease and being cooked alive in your car."

"Sorry. I'm just curious about Dr. Littlething. When I spoke with him at CureStuff, he seemed to be a legend in his own mind when it came to the ladies. He told me that he had had sex with all of them, Thompkins, Shipley, and Grayson, and they were happy to oblige. But when I spoke to those women, they all laughed at my questions about their relationships with Littlething, and to a one, each of them made fun of him as a balding, pathetic little man. One comment was something like 'little man, little hands, little thing.' You can see how this might provide Littlething with a motive for harming these women. As for you, sorry about that. I got kind of carried away. I'm new to this PI thing. I don't think you are the killer, but just in case I thought I'd try to catch you off guard."

Harden, eyes crossed and gasping for breath, said, "No worries. Happy to answer your questions. Could you please open the windows a crack? I can assure you I had nothing to do with whatever happened to Joanne and Wendy. As for Dick Littlething, I'm not one to take much stock in gossip. But, to your point, I have heard rumors that Dick tried to hit on Joanne and Wendy, and I also heard that they both refused his advances. As for Tanya Grayson, my experience is that she continually makes fun of Dick, both behind his back and to his face, but I don't believe that he has ever tried to approach her. I don't think he likes her very much. In fact, I think he's afraid of her. Tanya can be nice, but she can also be, well, a bitch. Dick is arrogant and self-absorbed, but I still felt sorry for him the couple of times I saw her put him in his place. Now, for God's sake, please open a window!"

"Thank you for the insight into Littlething's possible motive. I'll be happy to open the windows and drive you back to your hotel now."

• • •

After dinner, Jason dropped Harden off and then went back to the hotel near the FDA offices, where he was staying during the conference to avoid his normal commute. He watched the late-evening news before going to bed and caught a story about a suspicious small private-plane crash in North Carolina. The news report got Jason's attention when he heard an air traffic controller say, "I knew the pilot, Captain Harold Jennings, and was in constant contact with him during takeoff. When he leveled off, he left his headset on, and I heard him talking to someone in the cockpit. He described her as a gorgeous blonde, and

I heard him say she was undressing, then moaning sounds like they were going at it in the cockpit. He said they were trying to set some sort of mile-high record. I thought he was just pulling my leg because Harold was always a joker and the flight manifest listed the pilot as the only passenger. But it became clear he was no longer focused on me, or even aware I was listening. I was afraid he'd lost his mind and taken an escort on the plane with him. Odd thing is, I never heard anyone else's voice but his. I really started to worry when the plane veered off course, and then started to plummet straight for the ground. After the crash, I heard that the FAA only found one body in the wreckage—Harold's. I don't know what really happened, but it's a shame. Harold was a good guy, and to tell the truth, I was kind of jealous at what I was hearing through my headset, right up until Harold kissed the ground."

Jason chuckled. *An old pilot flying along in his private plane while an escort serviced him—that would certainly explain the crash. Talk about your friendly skies.*

Then he saw a second story, in which an elderly woman was rushed to the hospital with some mysterious ailment. The reporter interviewed the seventy-five-year-old husband, a Jim Hutchinson, who said, "My poor wife, Mary, woke up in the middle of the night, having some sort of fit, or sexual dream, in which she was having way too much fun without me. We haven't been intimate for years, and she was really going at it. At first, I thought there was someone else in the bed with her; my damned eyesight's bad and I couldn't see a thing. When I turned on the lights and put on my glasses, she was there, by herself, climaxing all over the place. Did I mention that she was doing this without me? I still can't figure out what the hell happened, because her hands were waving over her head like she was dancing on her back. Anyhow, whatever was going on, she was enjoying it so much that I was afraid her heart would give out. Her last climax was so strong she seemed to levitate above the bed. I got scared and called 911 when she appeared to stop breathing. It isn't fair that she had so much sex that it almost killed her, and I haven't had any for years." The old man didn't seem all that concerned about his wife; he just kept repeating how unfair it was that he'd been left out.

The news reporter joked, "Apparently the wife survived, and is in the hospital in stable condition. I must say, I'm a little jealous myself. It sounds like this elderly couple is seeing a lot more action that I am."

Jason mumbled, "I think I'm getting the hang of this PI thing."

Both news stories took place within driving distance of CureStuff Pharmaceuticals, where they developed antidepressant drugs, at least one of which caused unreported side effects of rats humping themselves to death. Both stories included victims suffering from some type of hypersexual response.

"Coincidence? Probably not. There has to be some connection here, but what? And what do an airline pilot and an old woman have to do with the attempted murders of Wendy Thompkins and Joanne Shipley?"

CHAPTER 14

It was Lucy's sixth birthday. Chelsea invited several of Lucy's friends for a party, complete with games, cake and ice cream. One of the games was "pin the tail on the daddy," Chelsea's idea. She thought the kids would get a laugh out of this, so she made up some paper donkey tails and talked Jason into letting the kids chase him around the house, trying to pin them on his posterior. This started out as fun, with several squealing little girls chasing the daddy donkey. As he fled from the swarm of five and six-year-olds, Jason said, "Thanks, Chelse. I always dreamed of being chased by hordes of children. And the mask and ears make it even better."

Chelsea yelled over the squeals of the delighted children, "Run, donkey, run! They're gonna get you." She couldn't help but laugh.

Jason was overwhelmed by a swarm of small children, three of whom planted their tails squarely on his rear end. Jason yelped, "Ouch. What in the heck! That hurts. Woman, what did you do?"

Chelsea said, an evil grin, "Why, whatever do you mean, dear?"

Jason turned to look at his backside. Removing one of the tails, he said, "What? Wife, I assumed you'd use Scotch tape. These tails have actual pins in them, and three of them penetrated my blue jeans and stabbed me. Why would you do that? That wasn't nice at all."

"Well, you normally use pins when you play pin the tail on the donkey. Did it hurt much? Maybe, if you were a stricter disciplinarian with our thirteen-year-old or weren't hell-bent on this PI thing, this game might have involved Scotch tape. I guess I was just distracted trying to keep the girls in line. Plus, I didn't really think the pins would penetrate your jeans," she said, feigned innocence in her voice.

The game abruptly ended after Jason removed the three pins from his rear end. He looked at Chelsea, and said, "I won't be able to sit for a week."

She gave him one of her mischievous grins. "Oh, don't be such a big baby. You'll be fine. I'll make it up to you later." She didn't have a puppy face, but she had her own way of making Jason do her bidding

After games, it was time for cake and ice cream. Everyone gathered around the kitchen table, Chelsea delivered the cake with six candles to Lucy, everyone sang "Happy Birthday," the birthday girl blew out the candles, and Chelsea cut the cake. Chelsea said, "Jason, please serve the young ladies their drinks."

Jason asked the girls, "So, ladies, what's your pleasure? We have iced tea or soda, Pepsi, root beer and Fanta orange."

Jason delivered a cold drink to each guest. The birthday girl was last. "Here, Lucy, a nice big glass of Pepsi on ice. That should go good with cake and ice cream."

Jason made the mistake of sitting the glass too close to the edge of the table. He turned his back for a second, to go to the refrigerator for his own drink, when he heard a crash followed by, "Daddy! I'm all wet! My pretty dress!" Then he heard his daughter crying. He turned and saw the empty glass on the floor and a very wet birthday girl covered with sticky soda and ice.

One of the guests said, "Lucy's all wet. Lucy's all wet. Look what her daddy did." The children all laughed. Lucy cried even harder.

Another guest chided, "Poor Lucy. Are you okay? I'll bet the ice is cold. I'm sorry your daddy spilled soda on your new dress. Bad daddy."

Lucy stopped crying. "Daddy, what did you do? You've ruined my bestest new dress. How could you! You are so mean." Then she began to cry all over again.

Chelsea gave Jason one of her death stares. "Way to go, Dad. The poor thing's drenched. Come on, Lucy. Let's go up to your room, clean you up, and get you into some dry clothes." Again, to Jason, "Good luck entertaining a room full of five and six-year-old girls. Maybe you could play another round of pin the tail on the donkey."

As Chelsea and Lucy started to leave the kitchen and head upstairs, Lucy's oldest sister, Lizzy, spoke up in a consoling voice. "Don't worry, Lucy. You shouldn't feel too bad. Daddy spilled iced tea on me at my seventh birthday party."

Lilly said, "Yeah, Lucy. And he took me to the movies for my eighth birthday and spilled a large soda all over me and my popcorn. I was all wet and had to eat soggy popcorn during the movie. Sometimes Daddy's just mean."

Jason was mortified and said, "So each of my daughters has a list of the mean things that I've done to you over the years? What else is on these lists? Am I really such a bad dad?"

He was immediately sorry he'd asked as his daughters started rattling off all his fatherly mistakes. Lizzy, never bashful when it came to speaking her mind, said, "Well, let's see. You promised you'd be there for my gum surgery, but you had to go to work that day instead. You hugged me in front of my friends. And one day you dropped me off at McDonald's to have lunch with some friends, and you refused to let me out of the car around the corner so no one would see that my dad drove me. You also talked to my boyfriend. You really can be mean."

Lilly chimed in, "Yeah, and he spilled soda on me on my birthday, embarrassed me by asking me if I did my homework in front of my friends, and refused to take me for a ride on the riding lawn mower or let me drive it. Lizzy's right. He can be a meany."

He asked, "So each of you has a list. Out of curiosity, do you all have a similar list for your mother? What horrible things has she done to you?"

The girls said, in unison, "There's no list for Mommy. She never does anything mean. She's a good mommy."

Chelsea smiled. "Come on, Lucy. Let's get you cleaned up."

Jason was devastated. He tried so hard to be a good dad and a loving father. He had no idea why each of his daughters had such a nasty mental list. He mumbled, "This seems really unfair, but there doesn't seem to be anything I can do about it." He looked around the room at all of the five and six-year-old girls, bundles of energy that were literally bouncing in their seats or frantically running round and round the kitchen table, and he simply shrugged, gave up, and said, "Okay, so, how about another game of pin the tail on the daddy?"

CHAPTER 15

Todd DeMarco was a construction worker building a skyscraper in downtown Charlotte, North Carolina. He was an ironworker known for his fearlessness when it came to walking the high steel. He was fifty years old and tall. His most prominent feature was a massive beer belly, suggesting that he drank a couple of six-packs a night, although his disheveled brown hair with gray sideburns and round, wrinkled face were also quite noticeable. A large mouth with thin lips, a weak chin, large teeth and a chicken neck accompanied his small, brown, bloodshot eyes and bulbous, reddish nose, which served as further evidence of his voracious thirst for cheap beer. In spite of his passion for drink, he had amazingly good balance on the high beams. However, since he had no waist, his belt had difficulty holding up his pants, which were at risk of falling down around his knees and tripping him, launching him off the building.

On Thursday morning he showed up for work with a mild hangover and coffee from a nearby food cart and took the construction elevator up to the fourteenth floor, where he was welding steel girders into place. Two other men, an electrician and a carpenter, were in the elevator with him. The three of them grunted at each other, and DeMarco said, "Another day, another dollar. Too damn bad we're on the high steel. Can't see the babes walkin' by."

The electrician said, "Better not be lookin' for babes up there. That's a long way to fall for a look at a nice ass."

The carpenter said, "Yeah, but if he lands on his head, he'll be fine." Both men laughed, and they all exited the elevator and took their places on the high steel.

DeMarco sat on a steel beam for a few minutes, drinking his coffee and looking at the stream of tiny people down below headed to work. He finished his coffee and suddenly began to feel strange. He couldn't stop thinking about sex, which wasn't all that unusual, but this was different. Something seemed to shift inside his head, and he heard a noise behind him. He turned around and saw a woman standing on the high beam a couple of feet from him. She was a tall blonde whose ample bosom poured out from a see-through nighty, barely long enough to drape across her smooth behind, leaving what felt like six feet of strong, tan legs fully exposed. Her dark eyes had a mischievous glint to them, matched by her pouty grin.

The other two men working nearby heard DeMarco say, "Well, hello there, darlin'. Ain't you a hot little number! What the hell are you doin' all the way up here? Don't get me wrong, I ain't complainin', but ain't you kinda cold with the wind and that flimsy nighty? How about you come over here and I'll warm you up."

The other two men were only a couple of steel beams away from DeMarco, close enough to see and hear what was going on. One of them, the electrician, a stocky Mexican gentleman named Jorge with prison tattoos covering his arms and neck, looked in DeMarco's direction and said to Tony, the large Italian carpenter, "What the hell's DeMarco doin'? Who the fuck's he talkin' to?"

Both men watched as DeMarco walked across the steel beam, reaching out with both hands to . . . something? Someone? But there was no one else on the beam anywhere near him. He kept saying,

"You're one hot broad. Come to papa." He kept walking forward until he reached one of the upright steel girders. He reached out, placed both arms around the girder and began to hump it like a crazed dog.

Jorge said, "Jesus Christ. He's gone loco. He's trying to bang that steel girder. Somebody musta put somethin' in his coffee. I never seen nothin' like this before."

Tony responded, "Me either. I've heard of lovin' your work, but this is fuckin' nuts. Man, look at him go. He reminds me of my dog, Buck, when he was a puppy and he first met my mother-in-law. He went after her leg like there was no tomorrow. I didn't make him stop right away, and man, was she pissed. My wife chewed my ass out, but I loved it." He laughed as they both watched DeMarco continue to go after the steel girder.

Finally, Jorge said, "Hey, Tony. Shouldn't we do somethin'? He's gonna hurt hisself, or else he's gonna lose his balance and fall. He's a crazy bastard, but he's one of us. Don't want to see him die."

Tony said, "No, let's just let him be. He's not gonna fall. He's got a death grip on that girder. If he keeps it up, worst thing'll happen he'll mess his pants. I don't want nuthin' to do with that."

Just as Tony finished, DeMarco let go of the girder, turned and started walking in the other direction on the bare steel beam. He reached out his arms again, and they heard him say, "Oh boy, a redhead. I just love redheads. So fuckin' much passion. Come here, darlin'. Don't be shy. C'mere and I'll keep ya warm. Maybe you can join me and the blonde over there for some real fun."

He reached out again and began to walk faster, like he was chasing someone, but Tony and Jorge still didn't see anyone else on the steel beam. Jorge yelled, "Hey, DeMarco, what the hell you doin'? You better slow down. You're gonna fall."

DeMarco seemed to hear Jorge, was startled, turned to look in his direction, missed a step and fell fourteen stories to the ground. As he fell, they heard him yell, "Sonofabitch. I was about to get me a two-fer, the blonde and a redhead. *Sheeit!*" Then they saw him hit the pavement in a spatter of red that continued to spread across the sidewalk.

Jorge said, "I don't see no blonde or redhead, but I hope he at least got his rocks off before he hit the ground. What a bummer."

Tony said, "I've been at this a long time, and I ain't never seen nothin' like that. DeMarco went batshit crazy. He went after that steel girder like a wild man, and now he's a skid mark on the sidewalk. He musta took some kinda drug or somethin'. I'd know if there was a hot blonde or redhead up here. All I see is you, and you ain't no hot babe, that's for damn sure. I better call 911, though I don't think it'll do much good at this point."

CHAPTER 16

Jason had hit a wall with his investigation. He had interviewed Dick Littlething, Lance Harden, Tanya Grayson and his carpooler, Joanne Shipley, and hadn't been able to remove anyone from his list of suspects. Seated at his desk in his home office, he was drawing a diagram of the case on a whiteboard—a group of suspects on the left represented by stick figures in a dress or pants, along with their names, motives, and a line pointing from each suspect to a specific victim, similarly depicted in a separate group on the right.

"Let's see." Jason mumbled, "Littlething was rejected by Wendy Thompkins and Joanne Shipley, and apparently held a grudge against them." He drew lines from a very short stick figure in pants with Littlething's name to both of the victims, lady stick figures in dresses. "Harden had dated Shipley earlier, she broke it off with him, and he's now dating Wendy Thompkins. Even though they're dating, he blamed Thompkins for the failure of his first antidepressant drug, Pleasuria, because she refused to give a high enough dose in the clinical trials, so he had motives for harming both women." Jason drew lines from Lance Harden's name and much taller stick person in pants to both victims.

More mumbling. "So, Littlething and Harden are my prime suspects, although I have no idea how either of them managed to administer a drug or poison to Joanne Shipley when they were in North Carolina and she was in Northern Virginia."

Jason sat and stared at the whiteboard for a few minutes. "Oh crap. Joanne Shipley might also have had a motive for harming Wendy Thompkins. Joanne dated Lance Harden, who broke up with her and went on to date Wendy. Maybe Joanne, an alleged victim, actually faked her own poisoning in order to draw attention away from herself, and she was the one who really tried to kill Wendy." He drew a line from a stick person in a dress with Joanne Shipley's name under it to Wendy Thompkins's stick figure, and another line in a circle from Joanne Shipley to herself.

"This detective stuff is hard," he mumbled. "I'm literally going around in circles. I have no idea what I'm doing, what the hell's going on, or how to figure it out. But I can't let Chelsea know. She's already pissed at me for thinking about quitting the government. I also need to do a better job of interrogating this Lucy Chang. I only spoke with her briefly, and I have no idea if she has a motive for harming these two women. This stuff is exhausting. I actually have to talk to people. I hate talking to people. They're so annoying."

He had another thought. The only person he could reasonably cross off his list of suspects was Tanya Grayson. Tanya was way too good looking and hot to be involved in murder. *Why would such a drop dead gorgeous woman need to kill anyone? She can get whatever she wants from any man just by asking. What kind of horrible world would it be if such a good-looker murdered people? No one would have a chance.* It just couldn't be her. In fact, there were men that would probably kill just to get next to her. Maybe that's what happened.

He wrote Tanya Grayson on the whiteboard, drew a stick figure in a dress, and then gave this stick figure an ample bosom as an afterthought. He placed this stick person off to the side with no interconnecting lines.

Jason was confused by his own logic and frustrated by his inability to identify the killer. Lucy Chang had mentioned that Tanya was interested in Lance Harden at one point and that Lance had been dating Wendy Thompkins at the time, but that was probably nothing. Maybe it was just Jason's testosterone talking, but he couldn't believe that a woman who looked like that, dressed like that, and smelled like that could be jealous of anyone, and certainly not enough to kill because of it. It just was not possible.

Then, Jason asked himself, *What would Jessica do?* and he decided that at this point Mrs. Fletcher would try to annoy people to death by asking a lot of meaningless questions. So he phoned Dick Littlething to make an appointment for another visit to CureStuff.

When he finally got Littlething on the phone, he said, cleverly lying to convince the president and CEO to meet with him again, "Hello, Dr. Littlething, I'm making considerable progress on this case and need to meet with you again. During my visit to CureStuff, I would also like to interview Lucy Chang. And, while I'm there, I might as well interview Tanya Grayson again, just to be thorough." He thought, *Yes, I'll have to give her a thorough going-over, just to make sure she really is in the clear.* He tried to picture what she might be wearing when he saw her this time. And he tried not to think about his wife, Chelsea, killing him.

There was a long pause as Jason pictured Grayson in her short skirt and tight top, and Littlething said, "Dr. Longfellow? Are you still there? I seem to have lost our connection."

Jason's fantasy of Tanya Grayson had deteriorated to a nightmarish vision of Chelsea smothering him with his own pillow while he was sleeping, and he abruptly came back to reality.

"I'm still here, Dr. Littlething. Sorry, I went away there for a moment, but I'm back."

Littlething said, "Detective Longfellow, I would be happy to meet with you again to discuss your case. I hope you still don't consider me a suspect in whatever happened to Wendy and Joanne. And you're welcome to speak with Lucy and Tanya while you're here. I'll leave that to you to figure out." Littlething was thinking that if he met with this nut job again, he might somehow gain an advantage when it came time for the FDA to review their application for a license for Happiness. Maybe he could even bribe the loon, or convince Tanya to manipulate him; she could be quite persuasive.

"Excellent. I'll be down tomorrow, and perhaps we can meet in your office, say two in the afternoon? I'll probably need a couple of hours for a thorough interrogation . . . I mean interview. Does that work for you?"

Littlething agreed, and they hung up.

• • •

The next day, in Littlething's office, Jason tried to throw the doctor a curve. He said, "I'm looking for motive and opportunity for someone to have committed these alleged crimes. Can you think of any reason why Joanne might have wanted to harm Wendy Thompkins? If so, when would she have had the opportunity to give her something to try to kill her?"

Littlething looked puzzled. "How would Joanne have given poison to Wendy Thompkins here in North Carolina when she lives up your way? And wasn't she a victim of attempted poisoning herself?"

Jason said, "I thought about that. It's possible that Joanne took a small dose of the drug, or poison or whatever, giving her some of the symptoms without killing her, to cast suspicion away from herself. Or she might have faked the symptoms, although I gotta say, I was there and it didn't seem like an act to me. If it was an act, she should be doing porn. But no one would suspect her if it appeared she was one of the victims. I'm more concerned about how she could have administered a drug or poison to Wendy Thompkins."

Littlething thought for a moment and then said, "Well, Joanne worked for CureStuff until recently, when she took a job with the FDA in Maryland. She and Wendy were friends, and I suppose it's possible that she could have given Wendy something that looked innocent but was really intended to kill her. Say, for example, she gave Wendy some aspirin but replaced some of the tablets with something that looked similar. Wendy's demise would depend on when she got a headache or some other ailment that required her to take aspirin. I doubt this happened, but I suppose it is possible."

"Interesting. But what about Lance Harden? Is there any reason why he'd want to harm Joanne and Wendy?"

"Well, Lance insists he should get full credit for development of the new drug, Happiness, even though Wendy Thompkins also worked on the project with him; she planned the clinical trials. Come to think of it, Joanne Shipley also worked on that project while she was at CureStuff."

"Interesting. Joanne didn't say anything to me about working on Harden's Happiness project. It's my understanding that Lance developed another drug, named Pleasuria, also for treatment of depression, and that drug failed in clinical trials. Did Joanne work on that project too?"

"Well, yes, I believe she did. She may have actually been dating Lance at the time."

Jason mumbled softly, "Now I'm getting somewhere. She didn't tell me that she worked on both of those projects. I wonder why she left that information out of our conversation. I'll just have to ask her, now won't I?"

"What? What did you say?"

Oh crap, did I say that out loud? "Nothing. I was just about to ask you about Tanya Grayson. Did she work on any of Lance Harden's projects?"

"Why yes, I believe she worked on both of them, Pleasuria and Happiness. There's a toxicology component to all drug development programs, you know, potential safety issues. But Tanya is all about the work. She doesn't date colleagues at the office. In fact, she seemed totally uninterested in me, which made me think she must be, well, you know, a lesbian. Although, I do remember that she stayed late with Lance on several occasions, and they went out for coffee together a couple of times. I'm sure it was just business for Lance because he was dating either Joanne or Wendy at that time, I don't remember which. But, come to think of it, I'm not so sure it was all about business for Tanya. She usually dresses nice, but if I remember correctly, back then she was wearing some pretty provocative clothing, you know, low-cut front, short skirts, that sort of thing. But I'm pretty sure Lance Harden didn't go for it."

"Interesting. You're just full of little tidbits of useless information. Tanya's a lesbian because she didn't go for you. But she might have been interested in Lance. Surely you can do better than that. On another subject, are you aware of the recent incidents reported in the news in your area? The first one involved a pilot, a Captain Harold Jennings, who died when his private plane crashed. The second was an elderly woman, a Mary Hutchinson. She's still alive, but in the hospital in critical condition. Both incidents were reported to involve hallucinations of a sexual nature, or hypersexual responses of orgasmic proportions, similar to what happened to both Joanne and Wendy. There may be no connection, but it's likely not a coincidence that four people currently or recently living in the same area of North Carolina experienced unusual spontaneous sexual reactions leading to their injury or death. Don't you think?"

Littlething looked puzzled and said, "No, I hadn't heard anything about those two incidents, but I don't watch the news very often. Too damned depressing. Nothing but politics, politics, politics. Come to think of it, Washington is one place where sexual hallucinations and weird sexual behavior are probably the norm.

"Dr. Longfellow, or should I say Detective Longfellow? Am I correct in assuming from your line of questioning that one or more of our doctors or scientists are suspects in the attempted murders of Wendy and Joanne? I am shocked that you could suspect such highly educated individuals of violence. Studies have shown that most killers are of low to average intelligence. I'm afraid that you are barking up the wrong tree."

"Interesting. Where were you when the attempt was made on Wendy Thompkins's life? It's my understanding that you attended that same business meeting. Actually, you ran the meeting, and I'm guessing that you had easy access to any beverages that were served to the attendees. Furthermore, your colleagues have told me that you hit on both Wendy and Joanne, and they shut you down and made fun of you. So, you have both motive and opportunity with Thompkins and motive with Shipley. I don't know how you would have given Shipley the poison or drug, but your theory about the aspirin is interesting. Maybe that's how you did it, by giving Joanne Shipley a bottle of aspirin laced with something else, something to improve her sexual satisfaction, to death."

Littlething recoiled. "How dare you come into my office and accuse me of trying to kill these women. I'm friends with both of them, and they both worked for me. I would never harm anyone. I don't think I want to talk to you anymore."

Jason realized that he probably tripped over some invisible line and he wouldn't get any more information from Littlething. So he said, "Well, thank you, Dr. Littlething, for your time. Now, if you could please show me to Tanya Grayson's office, I have an appointment to speak with her while I'm here. It's probably a waste of time because I doubt that any woman that looks as good as she does would need to harm anyone to get what she wants. With most men all she would have to do is ask, and they'd probably give her anything—the keys to their car, their house, whatever." As he said this, visions of a skimpily clad Tanya Grayson danced in his head, immediately followed by visions of Chelsea dancing on his head with spiked heels. This midlife crisis was going to get him killed.

Littlething, now calmer, said, "You got that right. That woman is good looking, hot as hell, and dresses to show it off. I can't imagine her hurting anyone. Well, I can imagine it, but only in a good way." Then he seemed to change his mind mid-thought. "But, as I said before, she didn't want anything to do with this." He gestured with his hand to call attention to his rotund body and finished with, "So, I'm guessing she's probably gay. Good luck with that."

• • •

Littlething pointed Jason in the direction of Tanya Grayson's office, and off he went. When Jason knocked on her door, he heard an alluring voice say, "Hello. Come on in. Detective Longfellow, I presume."

Jason entered the room, a large corner office with full windows on two sides, and Tanya stood up behind her desk to shake his hand. She was just as he remembered—an exceptional female with long, wavy blonde hair, possessing the stunning face of a model and voluptuous body of a Playboy centerfold; she was dressed in a tight black dress with a hemline so high that it stopped just below the buttocks and a low-cut front showing substantial cleavage, right there for the viewing. Jason detected the scent of a very nice perfume wafting across her desk, a light fragrance that was both clean and erotic at the same time. He took her hand, with its long, sensual fingers and silky smooth skin, and he felt a little dizzy for a moment, his knees buckling slightly. She smiled.

"Are you all right, Detective Longfellow? You look a little woozy."

"I'm fine, thank you. And I must say, you are looking great this afternoon. I approve of your business attire. Very professional, a real attention-getter, highly motivating, stimulating . . ." He tried his best to focus his eyes on her face, but it was like they had a mind of their own.

"Why, thank you, Detective. You seem to be tongue-tied this afternoon. Perhaps you would like some coffee."

He took a seat opposite her desk "No thank you, Dr. Grayson. Please sit. I have a few questions that I need to ask you."

"Please, call me Tanya. Yes, you said on the phone that you had some questions. And, by the way, my face is up here. You seem to be speaking to my chest, which is fine with me, but it's my mouth that will be answering your questions."

Jason blushed. "Sorry, I woke up with a stiff . . . neck this morning, and I'm having trouble holding my head up. I'll try to do better. Is there any reason why you might want to harm Wendy Thompkins or Joanne Shipley? Some of your colleagues have told me that you were interested in Lance Harden at one point but that he was already involved with these two women."

"Lance and I are just friends. As you probably already know, I worked with him on both the Pleasuria and the Happiness projects. Toxicology studies are required for all drug development programs.

I don't know what anyone else has told you, but there is not, nor has there ever been, anything between Lance and me." As she said this, she bent forward and propped her elbows on her desk.

Jason's eyes followed her ample cleavage, his head shifting forward so quickly he pulled a muscle in his neck, causing him to grab his neck and wince in pain. "Are you okay, Detective Longfellow? Be careful. We wouldn't want you to hurt yourself."

He tried desperately to compose himself and focus on his next question. He suspected that she was purposefully trying to distract and fluster him, and it was working extremely well. Finally, massaging his neck, he said, "I'm okay. Must have slept in a funny position last night. My neck muscles are really tight. So, Dr. Grayson . . . Tanya, have you heard about the recent incidents, one fatal, here in North Carolina involving a pilot and an elderly woman? Both cases involved some type of hypersexual response, sexual hallucinations and repeated . . . let's say, happy endings. Have you heard about these incidents on the news, and do you think that they have anything to do with what happened to Wendy Thompkins or Joanne Shipley?"

She smiled, purposefully licking her bright-red lips, flirting with her eyes. "No, I haven't heard anything about any such incidents. But I must admit, the repeated orgasms do sound intriguing. Where does one go to sign up for that?" She sat back in her chair, straightened her shoulders and crossed her long, sleek legs, giving Jason a clear view all the way up to her lacy black panties. At this point Jason involuntarily leaned forward and almost toppled out of his chair.

"Detective, are you sure you're okay? You look woozy again. I thought for a moment there you were going to fall on your head." She laughed.

Jason struggled to compose himself. "I'm fine. My stiff neck muscles just contracted and I experienced a momentary spasm. I'll be okay."

"Detective, do I understand correctly that I'm a suspect in the alleged attempted murders of Wendy and Joanne? These women are friends and colleagues of mine, and I would never consider harming either of them. Why, how could you even think such a thing?" She pushed her shoulders forward just a little to give Jason a clearer look at all that cleavage again, and his eyes glossed over for a second.

"I don't really consider you a suspect. A fine-looking woman like yourself would have no reason to be jealous of anyone, and you certainly wouldn't need to harm anyone to get a man. I just have to ask these questions. It's part of my job." His mind told him that she was a possible suspect because she had reason to be jealous of both of the victims, but his testosterone was arguing furiously that this woman could not possibly kill anyone.

"Thank you. I assure you I had nothing to do with harming Joanne or Wendy. But I do think that I know who the murderer is. I don't know anything about a pilot or old woman, but I believe that Dr. Littlething is the one who tried to kill Wendy and Joanne. He was angry with them because he tried to hit on both of them and they shut him down. Also, Joanne and I were good friends and we may have made fun of Dick in front of the other senior managers on one or more occasions, based on his diminutive size. So, he has a motive for harming both Wendy and Joanne, and frankly I'm afraid that he might come after me. I just don't feel safe here anymore."

Jason wanted to walk around the desk, take her into his arms and comfort her, but he heard the voice of Chelsea in his head, telling him that if he did so he had better sleep with one eye open from now on. So, he refrained.

"I hear what you're saying. I agree that Dick Littlething is my number one suspect at this point. If you are concerned for your safety, maybe you should talk to the local police. They might be able to put a guard on your body . . . I mean, assign you a bodyguard, to protect you until these attempted murders are solved and the perp is in jail. Just a thought."

"Thank you for your concern, Detective. I appreciate it. I don't actually think that I need a bodyguard, but I will be careful."

Jason's eyes glossed over yet again as he imagined guarding that body, but he heard Chelsea's voice in his head say, *Dead. You are so dead,* so he came back to reality.

Tanya stood, signaling the end of their meeting. Jason just sat there for a moment, staring at that little black dress, but finally he stood too, shook hands with this gorgeous, clearly innocent woman, and walked out the door, thinking, *I'm really likin' this PI gig.*

• • •

While driving home to Virginia, Jason could not stop thinking about Dr. Grayson and that little black dress. He said to the empty car, "No woman should look that good. If I wasn't married, I'll bet I could charm her right out of that dress. But I am married, to a nurse, with access to scalpels, and needles, and drugs, and who probably knows lots of ways to inflict pain, and death. Let's see, little black dress versus pain and death?" He thought about this for a minute and then said, "Oh crap! Damned black dress. Damned midlife crisis. I'm almost home, and I got so distracted by Dr. Grayson's hotness that I forgot to interview Lucy Chang. Oh, what the hell. She's probably innocent anyhow."

CHAPTER 17

T he following Saturday morning, Chelsea had an appointment for a haircut and style, leaving Jason home alone with the three girls. Lizzy was upstairs, keeping an eye on her two younger sisters. Jason was in the small workshop in the basement, located near the bottom of the heavily carpeted stairs. He was painting a small birdhouse that he had built when he heard Lilly say, "Okay, Lucy, climb aboard the train. It's time for a train wreck, and you're the only passenger."

These were not words that a parent wanted to hear his eleven-year-old daughter say to her five-year-old sister, and the voice was coming from the top of the stairs. Jason continued painting, assuming that Lizzy would intervene in whatever Lilly was up to. After all, he was paying her to watch them. But Lizzy never appeared on the scene. Jason heard Lilly say, "Okay, Sis. Off you go!"

Jason dropped the paintbrush and ran for the basement door. He yanked it open and looked up to see Lucy sitting at the top on a small toy train engine designed for little kids to ride while pushing with their feet. Lilly was standing just behind the vehicle, ready to give it a hard shove and launch her little sister into the air and down the stairs. All

Jason could do was scream, "Noooo!" as he started to run up the stairs.

Lucy screamed, "Whee, this is fun!"

Jason had on a pair of slippery slippers resembling cat's paws that Chelsea had given him for Christmas, having not yet learned his lesson after slipping and falling on the carpeted stairs while showing them off to the girls. He yelled again, "Lilly, No! *Do not push!*" As he said this, his foot slipped on the bottom step, and he fell forward, smashing his face and stomach into the stairs. "Umph," he groaned as the wind was knocked out of him.

Lucy squealed, "Whee! Here I come, Daddy!" as the toy locomotive launched into flight, Lucy at the wheel. Then Lucy yelled, "Aaaah. Help me!" as the locomotive went one way and she went the other.

Jason almost blacked out as the heavy plastic locomotive hit him in the head then continued to roll down his backside on its way to the basement floor. "Oh, my head! . . . Lucy, where's Lucy!"

He got his answer when Lucy landed hard on her hands and knees in the middle of his back where she grabbed hold for dear life and was able to stop her rapid fall. Jason said, "Umph! Ouch! Sonova . . ." He felt several vertebrae move in odd directions. He lay there for a few seconds, trying to catch the breath that Lucy had knocked out of him and said, "Lucy, are you okay?"

Lucy, now crawling up Jason's back, sharp knees poking him in the kidneys, giggled, "I'm fine, Daddy. Let's do it again. It was fun! And you need to put a dollar in the cuss jar."

When Jason was able to push his body off the stairs and stand, he noticed that Lilly had disappeared and Lizzy was also nowhere in sight. He yelled, "Girls, where are you? Lizzy, you're supposed to be watching your sisters. And, Lilly, you are not supposed to throw your little sister down the stairs. Where are the two of you?"

A moment later, Lizzy appeared at the top of the stairs. "What the heck happened? Are you all right?"

"I'm fine, but Lilly threw your little sister down the stairs. You're supposed to be watching them. Where were you?"

Lizzy said, "I watched them for a while, but I got bored, so I went to my room to play video games on my laptop. Sorry!"

"Where's Lilly?"

Lizzy responded. "I saw her run down the hall to her room. I think she's hiding in there, probably in the closet. That's her favorite place."

The front door opened and Chelsea came in, headed for the kitchen with an armload of groceries. She saw Lizzy and Lucy standing there, looking up at Jason. Chelsea looked at him too, top to bottom.

"Jason, really? Still wearing those slippers? I thought you threw them away."

CHAPTER 18

The plane crash that happened several weeks back in North Carolina had been tormenting Jason. There had to be a connection.

"I need to go to North Carolina to investigate an airline pilot that was reported to have died in a crash under strange circumstances. I need to search the guy's place for clues to try to figure out a motive for his murder and see if it's tied to what happened to Joanne Shipley and Wendy Thompkins."

Chelsea said, "So, you're going to take leave from your government job again? You're going to get fired screwing around like this. I don't know what you hope to prove. And how the hell do you plan on getting into this guy's house? For that matter, how are you going to get to North Carolina? Are we going to have to spring for gas and a motel room again for this folly?"

"Well, dear, for your information, I just bought a set of illegal lock picks from a guy who knew a guy who sold stuff out of the back of a pawn shop in Vienna. I'm anxious to give them a try."

"So, now you're going to North Carolina to get arrested on a B and E charge. Don't count on me to come bail you out. I think you've lost your mind".

He ignored her snide comment. "As to how I'm getting to North Carolina this time, I'm going to take the red rocket. I'm looking forward to the drive, top down, wind in my hair."

Jason was aware that his venture into the private eye business was probably motivated by his current midlife crisis, and it was a really big crisis. So, in addition to deciding to quit the government and become a full-time private detective, he had also bought a shiny new red sports car. A couple of weeks previously, he had told Chelsea, "Honey, I need a new car. I'm tired of my 4Runner. It gets sucky gas mileage, and it's no fun to drive. I want a fun little sports car. How about we go to the dealership this weekend?"

"Are you out of your mind? You're thinking about quitting your job with the government, you don't know anything about being a private detective, and now you want to buy a new car? Where's the money coming from? Do you have a screw loose?"

But Jason had been determined, and his OCD kicked in. "Come on, Chelse. Go to the dealership with me. I'll take you to your favorite restaurant if you'll come with. Please, oh please!"

She finally said, "Oh, all right. I give up. You won't shut up until I go with you and you have a new car. This midlife crisis is going to be the death of both of us; you for sure."

They left the girls with a neighbor and headed to the Mazda dealership to trade in his Toyota 4Runner for something sporty. On the drive, Jason said, "I've been reading about the new Mazda Miata. It's an awesome little car with six-speed manual, convertible, rear-wheel drive, good gas mileage, and fun to drive. I can just see myself tooling down the road in one."

Chelsea just rolled her eyes. "Yeah, sure. But isn't a Miata a two-seater? Where are you going to put the girls? And just how much do these things cost?"

"Sometimes a guy just wants to hit the road so he can clear his head and find some peace. And sometimes you and me could take a ride by ourselves, leave the girls with the neighbors or a babysitter. Just think about it, Chelse, top down, warm sunshine on your face, hair blowing in the wind. Besides, when we need to take the girls, we can drive your SUV. It's plenty big to haul everyone."

"When the hell do you think we're going to find time to take these rides, with our two jobs—or three, if you count 'Detective Doofus'—and three daughters. We barely have time to sleep now."

"Don't be such a downer, honey. I'm just trying to have some fun, for both of us."

Chelsea rolled her eyes again, a clear message—she thought he was being ridiculous. Before she had a chance to respond, they arrived at the dealership. Jason pulled up in front of the showroom, and they went inside. A slick-looking young man in Dockers with a button-down shirt and tie greeted them at the door and introduced himself.

"The names Pete, Pete Carlson. What can I do for you?"

"Hi! I'm Jason, Jason Longfellow, and this is my wife, Chelsea. I'm here to look at sporty cars. I'm interested in a new Miata."

Chelsea thought, *This salesman must be pissing his pants. Jason is way too eager. No way he's going to get any kind of deal acting like a kid in a candy store.*

Pete Carlson said, "Step right this way. I have several new Miatas in stock, including a bright-red one parked out front." He led them through the front door. Pete continued, "The new Miatas are really nice. This one has a cloth top that raises and lowers with the push of a button. We also have one with the mechanical convertible hard top. It's entertaining just watching that sucker in action, like watching a robot flip its lid. Would you like to take a test drive?"

"Oh, hell yes!" Chelsea rolled her eyes, and elbowed him in the ribs.

When Pete Carlson left to get the keys, Chelsea sighed and said, "Jason, calm down. This guy saw you coming a mile away. You're acting like you'd give anything to get hold of one of these cars. That's no way to negotiate a deal. You need to act casual and be willing to walk away if he doesn't give you the deal you want." She really did want him to walk away, but she knew Jason, and this was already a lost cause.

Pete returned with the key, put a license plate on the back of the car, got in and put down the top. Then he got out, held the door open and said to Jason, "Go ahead, get in. Since there's only two seats, you and Chelsea can take her for a spin around the block. I'll wait here and do a few numbers while you're gone."

Jason walked around the car, opened the door for Chelsea. "After you, madam. Your chariot awaits." She shook her head in frustration and got in the passenger's seat.

Jason walked around the car and struggled his way into the driver's seat. His head extended above the top of the windshield, and he could barely get his legs into the car. He looked at Chelsea. "Wow, this is comfortable. I'll bet it's a blast to drive. And just smell that new car aroma. How sweet is that?"

Chelsea tried to roll her eyes, but this time she was so frustrated and stressed that they crossed instead.

"Babe, are you all right? What's wrong with your eyes? Is something wrong?"

"Uh, Jason, I can't help but notice that your head is higher than the windshield. Is that a good thing? How are you going to put the top up if it rains?"

"No worries. It's fine. I'll show you." He turned the key to the accessory slot and pushed the button to raise the top. As the canvas top swung up behind them, completed its apex over their heads and began to descend to the point where it would attach to the windshield, Jason realized that his head did, in fact, extend above the windshield. As the top came down towards its connection point to the windshield, Jason was forced to lower his head until his chin was touching his chest to allow it to finish its descent. He said into his chest, "Might be a little snug, but it's fine."

"You look comfortable. And you can smell the new car smell a lot better with your nose pointing down like that. So, how are you going to drive while looking at your crotch?"

"Ha, ha. Funny woman. This is no problem." He managed to find the button on the dashboard and push it again to lower the top. As the top traveled back into its resting place in the trunk he said, "Damned car manufacturers. They all discriminate against tall people. But no worries, I'll just drive the car with the top down, when it's not raining, kind of like I would a motorcycle. That's it—I'll consider this my little red motorcycle."

Chelsea rolled her eyes yet again. "Idiot. What're you going to do about the bugs that you get in your teeth because most of your head is above the windshield?"

But Jason was having none of it. He was determined to drive this little red sports car home. He started the Miata. "Okay, Chelse. Get ready for the ride of your life." To the salesman he said, "We'll be back in a while. I'm going to take my new baby, here, for a spin." He put it in first gear and rolled out of the parking lot for a test drive.

As he struggled to drive the car, Chelsea said, "Jason, be careful. I don't know how you are working the brake and clutch pedals, since your big feet barely fit in the footwell. And is your left knee supposed to hit the steering wheel every time you depress the clutch? Honestly, you look like you've been stuffed into a sardine can. Please, just get us back to the dealership alive, and let's go home and forget this insanity."

"Chelse, it's fine. This thing is a blast to drive, and eventually I'll limber up some and be able to shift without banging my knee on the steering wheel."

"Limber's got nothing to do with it. You would need to shrink by half in order to fit in this damned car."

Pete met them at the front door, and Jason handed him the keys. "So, how'd it go? Ain't that a sweet ride?"

"Yes, it's great. I had a blast. How much?"

Chelsea's jaw dropped as he said it; this was not going to go well. "Jason, I would like to speak to you alone for a moment."

She took him by the arm and forcefully pulled him several feet away from Pete. "Are you out of your freaking mind? You don't fit in that thing. You looked like a very large child sitting in a toy car. That car's not safe for you to drive, and again, no room for the girls. Let's just get out of here."

But cars were Jason's weakness, at least one of them. He also liked tight black dresses, but that was an issue for another day. "Chelse, honey, what's your problem? I can drive the car just fine. It's a little tight, and I admit I can't get the top up. But I told you, I'll only drive it when the weather's nice, just like I would a motorcycle. It'll be my little red sports motorcycle. I'll call it the red rocket. It'll be fine. Now, let me make a deal, so I can drive the thing home and have some fun."

As Chelsea had predicted, it did not go well. Jason ended up paying the full MSRP, and the cute and curvaceous young saleswoman that sold the add-ons talked him into buying the seven-year, 100,000-mile extended warranty, the undercoating, and the paint sealant. And Jason had forgotten to look up the current value of his 4Runner, so the salesman really lowballed him on the trade-in value. Chelsea was very close to a stroke, or to killing her husband, by the time they headed for home.

After they got home, Jason asked, "So what do you think, Chelse? Ain't it a beauty? I mean, we are gonna have some fun with this baby."

"Yes, it's a beauty, all right. And you only paid the full price, bought all the useless add-ons and paid over two thousand for an extended warranty when you're going to be crippled and have to sell the car within a month. I love you, dear, but frankly, right now I'd like to run over you with your little red sports motorcycle; problem is, it's so small it probably wouldn't kill you, just maim you a little."

• • •

So, Jason drove the red rocket to North Carolina. When he got there, he stealthily drove past the address for the dead pilot to make sure that no one was home. He parked a block away to avoid detection and walked to the house. He approached from the rear, sneaking in through the backyard, intending to enter through the back door. "Now for the new lock picks," he mumbled softly so no one would hear. "I can do this. Piece of cake."

Forty-five minutes later he mumbled, "Ah, screw it!" as he jammed his elbow through the small glass windowpane at the top of the door, reached in and unlocked the deadbolt.

Once inside, Jason mumbled, "So, what am I looking for? I need to find out why someone would want to kill this guy. I guess I'll just search the place and see what turns up. That's what Jessica would do."

He started in the kitchen and found a lot of old, spoiled food, some dirty dishes and a can of coffee on the counter. He opened the refrigerator, gagged, and mumbled, "Jesus, that's bad. I guess no one's come in to clean up since the guy's death. You'd think he would have a relative that would take care of the place now that he's gone." He swallowed several times and said to no one, "This really stinks. I'm afraid I'm going to barf."

He fled the kitchen and searched the bathroom. He looked in the medicine cabinet and found the usual—Zocor for cholesterol, Nexium for gastric reflux, Xanax for anxiety. He pocketed the Xanax; Chelsea was still causing him a great deal of anxiety over his new red rocket. He mumbled, "I don't see any prescriptions from CureStuff Pharmaceuticals. Damn! I thought sure this guy would have a prescription for one of their antidepressant drugs." He also found a hand mirror, which was strange for a man to have.

"Well, this sucks," he mumbled. "Nothing useful here. Why would he have a hand mirror? Maybe he used it to look at a bald spot on the back of his head? Maybe he had a girlfriend. Who knows?"

He didn't find anything in the bedrooms either, except a bunch of dirty clothes in a hamper and several pilot uniforms hanging in the closet. Then on to the living room, where he searched bookshelves, the guy's CD collection, under the couch cushions, and found nothing. He whispered, "I have an idea. Lucy used a hand mirror to search under the couch and found her lipstick. I'll try her trick. Maybe there's something useful under there."

He retrieved the hand mirror from the bathroom, used it to check if he had a bald spot on the top of his head, and then he got down on his hands and knees and used it to look under the couch. To his surprise, he saw what looked like a pill bottle, located as far back as he could reach. "Well, I'll be damned, somebody must have dropped this and it rolled under the couch," he grumbled. "This idea from my five-year-old turned out pretty well. I'll have to look to my daughters for ways to solve all my crimes. Unfortunately, this means that I'm no smarter than a five-year-old, but I won't tell anybody, especially Chelsea."

With some effort, he was able to retrieve the pill bottle. The label on the bottle was not from any pharmacy. It read, *Investigational Drug, Happiness, Dose: 200 mg; Take as Directed*. The label also listed CureStuff Pharmaceuticals as the manufacturer.

"Well, this is interesting," Jason mumbled. "It looks like this pilot may have had a connection to CureStuff Pharmaceuticals after all. I wonder if he was a patient in the clinical trial for their new antidepressant drug."

He heard noises outside, looked out the front window, and saw the garbage truck, men collecting trash from cans placed in front of all the houses on the street except that of the pilot. "I better get out of here."

While sitting in his car, Jason thought he might give Jim and Mary Hutchinson a call to see if they were home before paying them a visit. Mary was one of the other people in North Carolina that had been in the news recently with a strange affliction that seemed to fit the pattern of the other victims in his case. He had gotten their address and phone number from the internet—at least, he hoped he had the right Hutchinson. He dialed, the phone rang several times, and then he heard a recording of an old man's voice.

"Hello, this is the Hutchinson residence. Mary is out of the hospital, and after her health crisis, we have gone to Hawaii to rekindle our relationship. We still don't know what happened to her, but the emergency room doctors gave her a strong sedative that seemed to do the trick. They ran some tests, found nothing unusual, and one of the docs suggested that someone may have slipped her something in her food or drink that caused her strange reaction. If you are the one who did it, I'd like to thank you, because whatever you did has awakened something in Mary, something very good. I'm not sure when we'll be back, but my vote is that the something stays awake for a long time, in which case don't look for us anytime soon. Please leave a message after the beep."

Jason just laughed and hung up. He mumbled, "Well, I don't know if this was an attempt on Mary Hutchinson's life or not, but in this case it seems to have had a silver lining, at least for her husband. It would be helpful to know if this woman was taking a certain antidepressant drug, but I think I'll just leave these two elderly love birds alone. Besides, if I interrupt them, Jim might hurt me."

CHAPTER 19

While in North Carolina, Jason decided to stay a couple of extra days and drive his red rocket to Charlotte where the dead murdered construction worker had lived. He phoned the FDA to tell them he was still sick, as he was using his sick leave for this trip, and then he phoned Chelsea to let her know his plans. He wasn't thrilled with the thought of speaking to her.

When she answered her cell, he said, "Hello, dear. I found something interesting at the dead pilot's house. Since I'm on a roll, I decided to stay in North Carolina for a couple more days to visit the home of a recently deceased steel worker in Charlotte, whose death was also reported to include strange circumstances. I hope that's okay with you. I'm still on the case."

Chelsea sighed. "Jason, I don't know what to do with you. This midlife crisis of yours is killing me. First, the private eye's license, and you pick Jessica Fletcher as a role model? You realize that was just a TV show, right? Then, you want to quit your steady government job, and you bought the red rocket. Now you're running around North Carolina breaking into peoples' houses. If I hadn't known you for so long, I'd think you have lost your mind. Please, be careful. What are you planning to do if someone catches you at your B and E? I have the girls and my job here, and I can't just pack up and come bail you out of jail. You're on your own. Good luck. Hopefully I'll see you in a couple of days." She sounded exasperated.

When the call ended Jason thought, *Gee, she sounds upset. I'm just trying to have some fun at my new career.* His thoughts strayed to Tanya Grayson and that little black dress, but the fantasy that started with his talking to Tanya abruptly ended with visions of Chelsea and a meat cleaver. He mumbled, "Probably not a good idea to share my entire adventure with the wife."

It started to rain during his drive to Charlotte, so he had pulled his plastic rain cape and hat out of the trunk and put them on. As he drove in the rain, top down, he thought, *This isn't so bad. I'm staying fairly dry, although I'm going to need to take a hair dryer to the rocket's upholstery when I get to the hotel to avoid mold. Hopefully, the rain won't get any harder and short out the car's electronics.* The rain had stopped by the time he pulled the red rocket into a parking garage three blocks from the steel worker's place.

The address turned out to be one half of a duplex, one of many that covered two square blocks of the city. Jason surveyed the area. The front stoop was located very close to the sidewalk, so it would be too conspicuous for Jason to stand at the front door trying lock picks for forty-five minutes. Instead, he would walk around to the back of the building and try to enter there.

In the back, he found a small patio that led to a set of sliding glass doors. He quickly climbed over a white rail fence, apparently more for show than protection, and approached the sliding glass door. Being a clever detective, he tried the door first, and to his surprise it easily slid open. *Wow, this is too good to be true. I'm getting the hang of this. On TV they usually use lock picks, or break down the door.*

He walked across the threshold into a nice, large living room, complete with oak-paneled walls and ceiling, tile floor, comfortable furniture and a large flat-screen TV. Jason mumbled, "This guy lived well for a construction worker. I should live so well." As he gently shut the slider behind him, he heard a low growl. He immediately smelled the odor of dog, turned, and saw a large Doberman, teeth bared, sitting in the archway to the kitchen only a few feet away.

Jason turned slowly toward the dog, hands out in front of him, and said quietly, "Easy there, fella. Good dog. I don't mean you any harm. I'm just here to take a look around, and then I'll get out of your way. Please don't eat me."

The dog approached, growling. Jason backed slowly away toward the sliding glass door, placing his hand on the door handle as he did so. He stood in front of the door and taunted the dog.

"Come get me, you big dumb brute." He actually barked back at the dog, hoping that in dog-speak he was challenging the Doberman to attack. "Woof, woof," he said loudly. "Grrrrr. Come and get me, you big bastard."

The dog lunged and Jason jumped out of the way, yanking open the sliding glass door as he did so. As soon as the dog was through the opening, Jason violently pulled the door closed.

"Yes! Take that, you beast. Wow! I'm smarter than a five-year-old and a dog." The dog stood on the patio barking fiercely for a few seconds, until it realized that it was outside, and free. Once that realization set in, it got briefly distracted by a cat that had the misfortune of wandering in the yard before heading up the street. Jason breathed a sigh of relief, turned back to the living room, and, once the adrenaline rush subsided, began his search.

He searched the kitchen, living room and the master bedroom. The place was a mess. Piles of dirty clothes everywhere, a musty smell and the distinct odor of sweaty construction worker. This guy was definitely not married, or else his wife was a slob too. *This place reeks of chaos, and I hate chaos.*

Jason wandered into the master bathroom. It was a mess in there, too. He said to the room, "Someone forgot to flush the toilet, and it smells like a sewer. The shower curtain surrounding the tub is full of mold, and there's a pile of soggy towels in the middle of the floor, a delightful combination of sewage and musty smell." Jason went to the medicine cabinet, in a hurry to get out of there before he barfed.

He opened the medicine cabinet, and several items fell out into the empty sink.

"Let's see, lots of old pill bottles, Q-tips, toothpaste, dental floss, loose bandages, and a bunch of other bathroom-related crap." This guy never cleaned anything. There was mold growing on the shelves, and some more musty smell, not normal for a medicine cabinet. *Hope to hell I don't catch something contagious from this mess.* He sneezed as he started going through the pill bottles, those in the cabinet and the ones that fell into the sink. He said, to the sink again, "The usual meds again. Zocor, Nexium, Xanax, and this time a heart medicine. I'll just take this Xanax." *Now I've got two full bottles to combat whatever grief Chelsea has in store for me when I get home.*

As he was about to give up the search, he noticed a fat pill bottle on the far right of the top shelf. He took it down and read the label. It said, *Investigational Drug, Happiness, Dose: 200 mg, CureStuff Pharmaceuticals.* Jason was elated.

"Freakin' awesome," he mumbled, and patted himself on the back, hurting his shoulder in the process.

Jason smiled, pocketed the bottle of pills, and walked back to the living room with the intention of exiting through the sliding glass door. However, he heard something, a key in the door. Someone was entering through the kitchen. *Oh shit! Better get the hell out of here.* He moved quickly toward the sliding glass door. *Oh crap. The beast is back, and he doesn't look happy.* The Doberman stood on the patio, snarling. Jason quickly headed back up the stairs to the other bedroom. He saw a large closet door, opened it with the intention of hiding there, and, surprise— shoes, wigs, women's clothes, makeup, fake eyelashes, earrings, jewelry. And this guy really liked blue; dark, navy-blue pants suits, neon-blue dresses, light-blue blouses, every shade of blue imaginable.

"This would be disturbing if I weren't about to die or be arrested for a B and E." Then he thought, *Oh crap, did I say that out loud again? Think, don't talk, or you're gonna get caught.*

Then Jason remembered what his two older daughters had done to Lucy, painting her to look like a Smurf. Jason thought, forcing himself not to mumble out loud, *Jason, old man, it's Smurf time.* He grabbed two tubes of blue lipstick and some blue eyeliner off of one of the shelves and quickly painted his exposed skin, hands and face as blue as possible. He even painted his eyelids so they would be blue when he closed his eyes. Then he quietly closed the closet door and positioned himself just behind a rack of blue dresses and blouses, with his head sticking up above the clothing. His face was all blue, and he had taken a floppy blue hat from another area of the closet and placed it on his head to cover his graying hair.

Jason heard footsteps on the stairs, and someone entered the bedroom. The person opened and closed a couple of dresser drawers and made the sounds of someone undressing. *Who the hell is this? Must be the dead construction worker's roommate?*

Just then, the closet door opened and the light came on. Jason froze, his blue head protruding above the rack of blue clothing. He was amazed. A man in his fifties, medium height, large round head, rough-looking face, big shoulders, bigger beer belly, dropped the bath towel that had been wrapped around his body. The man stood there stark naked, reached into the closet, and removed a black wig with long, straight hair, several articles of makeup, high-heeled shoes, and a flowing blue gown.

The man was singing happily, and Jason heard him say, "Tonight's the night. I'm going to perform my new number, and I'll be the star of the show." Then he blurted out a few lines of some song that Jason didn't recognize. At one point, the man approached the rack of clothing directly in front of Jason, took a blue blouse off the rack very near Jason, looked up directly at where Jason was hiding and said, "I wonder if I should dress in my formal gown, or go more casual, like jeans and blue blouse. Nah. My song calls for a more formal look. I'll go with the blue gown."

Jason had closed his eyes, and was furiously thinking, *I'm invisible. I'm invisible. He can't see me. My eyes are closed.* The man looked right at him and didn't see him. Jason was amazed. The Smurf look was working. When the man continued the discussion with himself concerning whether he should dress in formal attire or go for a more casual look, Jason almost answered. It just seemed natural. *With a body like that, go casual dude. You just aren't built for a formal gown. And if you go with the gown route, you definitely need to shave those legs.*

Eventually the man finished dressing and applying makeup, and Jason heard his footsteps as he went back into the other upstairs bedroom, just up the hall. He didn't seem to notice that the dog was outside on the patio. *I guess he must really be looking forward to his performance tonight. I still have to get out of here without being caught.* Then he remembered the slippers that Chelsea had given him, and his plummet down the basement stairs. *If I can figure out a way to make the stairs slippery, I can run down the stairs and out the door, and this guy won't be able to follow me if he falls on his ass. They're carpeted, so he probably wouldn't break anything. Just slow him enough that he can't catch me.* Jason stepped from behind the rack of blue dresses and quietly searched the shelves for something slippery. He found a tube of Vaseline, probably used to remove makeup, or for other purposes he didn't want to think about, and his plan took shape.

He heard the man in the bedroom up the hall, practicing the song for his upcoming performance while presumably dressing for the evening. Jason quietly slipped out of the bedroom, went to the top of the stairs, applied a large glob of Vaseline to the top two carpeted steps, and then rapidly fled down the stairs toward the sliding glass door. He heard the man say, "What the fuck? Who's out there?"

Jason turned to look behind him as he ran toward the patio, and they saw each other. The large man in his black wig with red lipstick, large gold earrings, long dark eyelashes, and his prominent beer gut easily visible through the flowing blue gown yelled, "What the fuck are you doing in my house? And what the fuck are you?"

"No worries. I'm just a private eye on a case. And I'm normally not blue."

Jason kept running, and the large man sprinted down the upstairs hall toward the stairs. He hit the top step in his high heels, his foot slipped, and he plummeted butt-first and bounced down the stairs, starting on his ass and ending in an impressive barrel roll. As he fell, he cursed, "You motherfucker. If I catch you I'm gonna kick your ass." Then he hit his head at the bottom of the stairs and lay quiet.

"Jesus, you are one crazy violent man, and you move fast for a guy with a beer gut running in high heels. I'm glad I used the Vaseline." When Jason reached the sliding glass door, there sat the large Doberman, so he turned and bolted out the front door.

• • •

When he got home, he parked his soggy red rocket in the garage. It was partially dried out as the sun had come out halfway through the trip. He entered the kitchen through the mudroom. Chelsea was sitting at the kitchen table with Lucy, helping her with first-grade homework. Jason tried to sneak past them with a quick, "Hello, how are you? I love you guys." But Chelsea never missed anything, and she immediately noticed the blue tint of her husband's skin.

"Welcome home, dear. The girls missed their PI daddy. Did you catch the bad guy? Find any new clues? Paint yourself blue?"

Jason sighed, walked to her, kissed her on top of the head and said, "If you must know, I'm getting close to cracking the case. I found evidence that two of the recent victims of murder in North Carolina are probably linked to CureStuff and may be participants in one of their clinical trials. I still haven't put all the pieces together, but I'm getting close."

"Glad to hear it. You might want to take a look in the mirror. The visible skin on your face is bright red, I'm guessing from sunburn, what with driving for hours with the top down on the red rocket. And the rest of your face is bright blue. If you painted your eyelids white, you'd look very patriotic. I shudder to think why you painted yourself blue, but I don't have the courage or the stamina left to ask, so please keep whatever bizarre secret this is to yourself."

Lucy, sitting at the table next to Chelsea, said, "Mommy, does Daddy have to go to his room and stay grounded for a week? That's what he did to Lizzy and Lilly when they painted me blue. It's only fair."

"Yes, Lucy. I think that Daddy should go to his room and try to get whatever blue stuff that is off of his face and hands. But there'll be no grounding him. Daddy needs to go back to work tomorrow, or we're going to be living in a box under one of the Beltway bridges."

CHAPTER 20

Jason was watching the national news when he saw another report of a bizarre death in North Carolina. This time, it was a NASCAR driver. The onsite reporter said, "Jimmy Jeb Johansen, one of the newest drivers on the NASCAR circuit, was running in a Sprint Cup Series race at Charlotte Motor Speedway in Concord, Virginia when his car suddenly turned into the pit area doing 150 mph and crashed, killing Jimmy Jeb and several members of another pit crew. During a brief interview with Jimmy's pit crew, this reporter learned of a strange conversation with their driver just before the crash, but police told the crew that the specifics of the conversation were not to be released, pending further investigation. Studies have shown that there's a less than 1 percent chance that a race car driver will take a wrong turn during the race and head into the pit area at full racing speed. In fact, it's actually quite difficult to do, since the track is an oval, and all the driver has to do is go around the same road over and over."

Chelsea walked into the living room just as the news report began and heard the report.

"Oh no! Not another one. I guess you and the red rocket will be off to Charlotte again. Can you at least do it over a weekend so you don't miss any more work? They're going to fire you, and you aren't making enough as a private eye to feed yourself, let alone the rest of us. I wish you'd get a grip and let go of this ridiculous private eye thing."

All Jason heard her say was the part about doing it over the weekend.

"Yes, dear. I'll drive down to Charlotte next Friday after work. I'll get there late, but I can investigate on Saturday and Sunday if need be. I'm gonna crack this case or my name isn't Jessica Fletcher."

Chelsea just rolled her eyes and headed for the kitchen to fix the kids breakfast. All three girls came downstairs together, still in their pajamas. Lizzy said to Chelsea, "So how's Detective Daddy doing? Have you knocked him in the head yet, like you said you were going to?"

"No, sweetheart, not yet. But the day's still young."

That Friday afternoon, Jason loaded up the tiny trunk of his red rocket with a toothbrush and toothpaste and headed for the Charlotte Motor Speedway. He arrived at the Holiday Inn late at night, got a few hours of sleep, and then it was up and off to the races. He went to the track, conned his way into the garage by pretending to be a reporter, and found Jimmy Jeb Johansen's pit crew prepping their back-up car and driver for the next race. He approached the crew.

"Guys, truth be told I'm actually a private detective looking into the possible murder of Jimmy Jeb. I heard rumors that he was talking a little crazy from his car, just before the crash. Can anyone elaborate for me? What did he say?"

The pit boss, Todd Masters, answered. "Well, I didn't think you were a reporter. You look more like a giant nerd. So, you think Jimmy Jeb might've been murdered too? A police detective stopped by and asked a lot of questions yesterday. He told us not to say too much until he had a chance to investigate, but fuck him. Besides, you ain't no reporter, this ain't the first fatal NASCAR crash to ever happen, and the cops usually don't come snoopin' around. I don't know what happened to Jimmy Jeb. It don't make much sense, and I don't like to talk bad of the deceased, but I thought he was losin' his mind. During the race, I heard his voice on the radio, but he weren't talking to me. He seemed to be talking to someone else, like there was someone in the car with him, but I know for a fact there weren't. That's not possible. There's only one seat in them things, for the driver, and there's barely room for him in there."

"What was he saying?"

"Well, it sounded like he was talking to a woman, a good-looking one from what he said. He told her she was one hot babe, and he asked her if she'd like to go to dinner and then go back to his place. I know it sounds batshit crazy, but that's what I heard. From what he was sayin', she said yes, and then she put her hand on his leg and started rubbing his parts. I used to race one of them cars, and I can tell you that you gotta pay attention to what you're doing to keep from killin' your damn self. Jimmy Jeb sounded like he was real distracted. I heard him moan and say how good what she was doin' felt. Next thing I hear, it sounds like she's givin' him a blow job, and while he's drivin' a hundred ninety miles an hour. Then, he says they gotta find them a little privacy, and he yanks the wheel and turns into the pit area, doing at least one-fifty. You should have seen them pit crews scramble. It was a real slaughter; some were run over, but most died in the explosion. Strangest part is, when they searched through the wreckage, only bodies they found were Jimmy Jeb and crew members, all men. There weren't no sign of a woman anywhere."

"That's quite a story. You're sure there was no one in the car but the driver?"

Masters answered, "Just as sure as I can be. Jimmy died cause for some reason he had released his seat belt, and he was thrown from the car. If there had been a woman in the car, her body would have been burned bad, but it would have turned up, somewhere. They found nothin'. It's the strangest damned thing I ever heard of. No way would any driver in his right mind take a woman in his car during a race, good-lookin' or not. It takes all their focus and energy just to survive, let alone to win. And Jimmy Jeb was a real competitor. None of this makes any sense."

Jason was convinced that this was another murder and it had

something to do with the other ones he was investigating. *I'd bet the farm that when I look in this guy's medicine cabinet, I'll find a bottle of Happiness with his name on it.*

Jason got Jimmy Jeb's address from his interview with the surviving pit crew. When he went there later that afternoon, he saw a car parked in the driveway, a shiny new red Corvette. According to the pit crew, Jimmy Jeb wasn't married, but he was popular with the ladies and active on the current dating scene. Since there appeared to be someone home, instead of using his lock picks he rang the doorbell.

A tall young woman, slender and well proportioned, answered the door. She had medium-length, dark-brown hair with natural curls, a pretty face with blue eyes, a perfect nose and full lips, and was wearing a tight blouse and tighter blue jean shorts that revealed colorful dragon tattoos on both of her arms and a picture of a large black rose in the small of her back. With the tattoos, she presented an interesting combination of sensual female and tough biker broad. She had been crying.

"Hello, I'm Private Detective Jason Longfellow. I'm investigating the recent crash and death of Jimmy Jeb at the Charlotte Motor Speedway. Could I please come in for a few minutes?"

She opened the screen door. "I'm Brenda Jones, Jimmy's roommate. Todd Masters, Jimmy's pit boss, called me and said you might be coming by. Come on in. What can I do for you?"

Jason walked through the door, following the woman into the living room. As she walked in front of him, his eyes, still with a mind of their own, were acutely focused on her round, perfectly formed Jennifer Lopez-esque buttocks squeezed into those very tight shorts. This was one of Jason's favorite parts of the female anatomy, and the part that had originally drawn his attention to Chelsea in their youth.

Without realizing it, Jason mumbled, "What a spectacular rear end. Damn, I like this job more and more all the time."

"Excuse me. What's that you said?"

"Sorry, I was just saying that this was a tragic way for Jimmy Jeb's career to end. Poor Jimmy Jeb; that was a spectacular accident."

She started crying. "I can't believe it. We talked just before the race, and he told me he loved me and wanted us to get married. He said I brought him good luck. When Todd told me he thought he heard Jimmy talking to some blonde woman in his car just before the accident, I couldn't believe it. I know there wasn't really a woman in the car. There's barely room for Jimmy. But the fact that he might have even been thinking about some other bimbo after he told me he wanted to marry me, that really pisses me off. If the bastard wasn't already dead, I'd kill him myself."

She's not upset about this guy's crash; she's pissed about the rumors that he was thinking about someone else before he died. Sounds like I got myself another suspect. Maybe he was stepping out on her before the race, and she did him in.

"Ms. Jones. Did you and Jimmy have any problems recently? Was there another woman, or did you suspect anything? According to the pit crew, Jimmy sounded convinced that there actually was a woman in the car, doing . . . well . . . you know . . . things to him. I realize that's unlikely since, as you say, there's barely enough room for the driver in one of those cars and there was no woman's body found at the crash site. It's all very strange, don't you think?"

She placed her hands over her face to cover the tears. "I don't think there was another woman in the car. But I do know Jimmy liked to drink, and maybe he fucked up and took a few shots of Jack to build up his courage. He was fairly new to the NASCAR circuit, and he was having trouble sleeping nights—fear of what might happen on the track. If he was drunk, he might have been thinking about another woman, and that could have gotten him killed. I don't know. It's all so horrible."

"Well, studies have shown that race car drivers that drive drunk, especially during a race, often crash and burn." He then asked, "I know this is a tough time, but would you mind if I look around the place a little? Sometimes I can learn things by searching a man's house, especially his bedroom."

Brenda was still crying softly, her emotions a mixture of grief and rage that Jimmy might have been unfaithful. She pointed towards the stairs. "Go right ahead and search. If you find anything that suggests there was another woman, please let me know. I'll get me a lawyer and use the information to make sure I get my share of Jimmy's stuff, now he's dead."

Jason headed upstairs in the direction of the bedroom. He had lied; he wasn't interested in the bedroom. He really wanted to get a look at the guy's medicine cabinet. *I'd bet my left nut that I'll find a bottle of Happiness.* He entered the master bathroom, opened the medicine cabinet, and sitting on the top shelf he saw a large bottle with the label *Investigational Drug, Happiness, Dose: 200 mg, CureStuff Pharmaceuticals.*

"Damn, I'm good, and I get to keep my left nut. That's a relief," he said. "This bizarre death must be related to the others. Now I need to find the connection between these deaths and the attempted poisonings of Wendy Thompkins and Joanne Shipley. There's got to be one."

Jason pocketed the bottle of pills and headed back downstairs, where Brenda was sitting at the kitchen table softly crying while sipping on a cold bottle of Bud Light. "Well, did you find anything? Any evidence of another woman? I've never seen anything like that, and I've been staying here with Jimmy for a while. But you're a trained detective, so you must know how to do a proper search."

Jason smiled. *Lady, if you only knew how little I know about this private detective thing. But it's in my best interest for you to believe.* He said, "No, I didn't find anything to suggest another woman or to explain what happened to Jimmy in that car. You may be right. Maybe he drank some Jack Daniels to shore up his nerves, or maybe he got hold of some marijuana brownies for all we know. For some reason, it sounds like he hallucinated or was fantasizing about a blonde instead of paying attention to what he was doing, and that can be fatal at one hundred and ninety miles an hour. I'm very sorry for your loss. You're an attractive young woman, and I'm sure that you'll land on your feet. Thanks for talking to me."

It wasn't her feet that he was checking out as he passed her on his way out the door. *I love Chelsea, but this midlife crisis is driving me crazy. I can't stop thinking about "What if?" What if some gorgeous young thing was interested in me? What if she wanted to—*

This thought was abruptly cut off when he pictured what Chelsea might cut off if he ever followed through with one of these midlife crisis fantasies.

• • •

Jason stayed in the Holiday Inn overnight with plans to head home in the morning. He bought a local paper and was reading it over his final cup of coffee of the day when he saw a newspaper article:

Ted Jacobson, of Charlotte, came home from work last night, and, according to Mr. Jacobson, heard the sounds of his wife in the throes of passion with another man. Mr. Jacobson burst through the bedroom door with a 12-gauge shotgun and killed his wife. He is being held on a charge of premeditated murder. The police were vague when asked about the wife's lover.

Jason thought the news account strange because there was no mention of the man killing his wife's lover, yet they were holding him for premeditated murder. He wondered if maybe there was no lover. People were dropping like flies, and while Jason had some good leads, he still hadn't figured this out. *I need to solve this thing before more innocent people die.*

He needed to stay over on Monday to investigate this shooting in Charlotte, even though Chelsea was going to be really pissed. He had already missed work a couple of times because of his investigation, and she was right that he wasn't making enough to support them without his government job. He phoned her Sunday morning.

"Hello, Chelse. It's your lover, Jason. Guess what! There's been another bizarre murder down here. This time, a guy killed his wife, and maybe her lover, with a shotgun. There's something strange about it, because the guy's being held for premeditated murder even though he supposedly found them in bed together, which suggests a crime of passion. I need to hang around tomorrow and talk to the Charlotte police. This one might also be connected to my case. I know you are already not happy with me, but I need to follow through on this."

He was expecting a blast of expletives. To his surprise, he heard only a click as she hung up on him.

"Well," he grumbled to himself, "that's different. I'm sure it means she's over-the-top pissed, but at least that was easier on the old eardrums. I'm going to have to come up with something really special to get myself out of this one."

The next morning, Jason got the bright idea that while he was in North Carolina he might as well visit CureStuff Pharmaceuticals one more time and talk to Dr. Littlething. He still hadn't quite eliminated him as a suspect, so he thought, *Why not? I'll have another chat with him, and who knows, maybe I'll run into a certain little black dress while I'm there.*

Jason phoned Littlething's office, and when he asked if he would see him that afternoon, Littlething said, "I would be happy to meet with you again, Dr. Longfellow. I can't imagine what else there is for us to talk about, but the last thing I want to do is upset you, what with our company planning to submit a license application for Happiness to the FDA in the near future. Are you going to show up wearing your Sherlock Holmes hat or your FDA cap?"

Jason assured him that he was only interested in talking to him as a private detective about the attempted murders of Wendy Thompkins and Joanne Shipley. They set a meeting for three.

Jason drove the thirteen miles to Charlotte and visited the police station where Ted Jacobson was being held. He entered the building and presented himself.

"Hello. I'm PI Jason Longfellow." He presented his credentials. "Mr. Jacobson's parents hired me to investigate what happened last night, and I need to speak to him, try to find out where best to start."

The officer on duty replied, "I'll get the detective in charge of the case. His name's Detective Horton."

A couple of minutes later, a plainclothes detective, clearly defined by his cheap suit and patent leather shoes, of medium height, rough-looking, and sporting the beer gut of a forty-plus-year-old man approached Jason.

"Are you the gumshoe here to see Jacobson? Normally we wouldn't let a gumshoe anywhere near an active case, but this guy seems legit, genuinely distraught and confused about what happened. We're slammed with work, and maybe you could spend some time on the case. I'm thinking there's more to this mess than meets the eye. I'll let you talk to him, but in the interrogation room, and I'll be watching."

The two men sat across a wooden table from each other, with Jacobson's hands cuffed and a policeman standing just out of earshot.

"Hello, Ted. I'm Detective Jason Longfellow. I'm a private detective looking into your case. It seems to have some things in common with another murder I'm currently investigating. If you answer my questions, I may be able to help you. Please, help me out here."

"Everyone else thinks I'm crazy. I had to work late Thursday night, and I didn't get a chance to call Jenny to let her know I'd be late. Normally, when I came home late, she'd heat up dinner for me and we'd eat together. But there was no Jenny and no food in the kitchen. I walked down the hall and heard noises coming from our bedroom. I couldn't believe it. We were so in love, and she would never step out on me. But I stood outside the closed bedroom door, and I heard her moaning and she said, 'Yes, oh yes, that's really good. Don't stop. Yeah. Right there. Oh God, I'm going to come.'

"Then I heard her scream, just like she always does when we make love and she climaxes. That's when I lost it. I walked up the hall, took my 12-gauge off of the rack, loaded it and kicked in the bedroom door. It was dark when I entered the room, and I was in such a rage that I just started shooting. I must have fired off three or four blasts before my eyes adjusted to the light, and I realized that there was only one person in the bed, Jenny. At first, I thought that the guy must have heard me coming and somehow fled from the room, but there was no place for him to go. It's a small bedroom, the windows were all closed, and I was blocking the only exit. It was then that I realized I had killed my poor wife, and there was no one else in the fucking room." Ted started weeping.

"That's terrible. I'm so sorry for your loss. Do you have any idea what happened? Why was she acting that way? Was there a ghost involved?" He threw that last thing in because he couldn't think of anything else to say. He was still getting the hang of this interrogation thing.

"I don't know what happened. She had never done anything like that before. She's a good-looking woman for her age, and she works as a female barista at Starbucks, where she meets lots of men. But most of the men she meets are quite a bit younger than her. As far as I know, she has always been faithful to me. When I heard the two of them through the bedroom door—at least, she kept talking like there were two of them—I couldn't believe it. She was even giving him instructions, telling him what she liked. That's why it sounded so real, because that's what she usually did with me. She could be very specific with her instructions. I didn't see any ghost. I didn't see anything but my poor, dead wife."

"Has anything odd happened recently? Did she exhibit any strange behavior before the night you blew her away? Had she started taking any new medications, for example?"

Jacobson sat there for a minute and then said, "Yeah, now that you mention it. She sometimes had depression. A friend of hers told her about a new medicine, and there was some experiment going on where they were giving it to people with depression to see if it worked. I think they called it a clinical trial. Anyhow, she signed up, they sent her some pills, and she started taking them a couple of weeks ago. She keeps the pills in her medicine cabinet in our apartment. Do you think that has anything to do with what happened? Have you ever had a case where a ghost was involved in an affair with someone's wife?"

Jason didn't want to reveal his theory about these strange deaths until he was sure. "I seriously doubt that the pills had anything to do with it. That would be really unusual. I just thought I'd ask. As to ghosts, I saw a movie once where a ghost was forcing himself on random women, and maybe that's what happened with your wife, although there's no way to know for sure. Ghosts can be pretty sneaky. If it was a ghost, from what you heard from your wife, he must really know what he's doing in the bedroom. If a ghost does turns up, please give me a call. Maybe he could give me a few suggestions I could share with my wife. Well, thanks for your time. I wish you all the best and hope that the jury goes easy on you."

• • •

Jason got Jacobson's address from him during his interview and headed for the guy's apartment to retrieve the pills. When he arrived, he had to wait for a tenant to come along with a pass key so he could follow her into the building.

"That was easy," he mumbled as he walked through the door behind a twenty-something woman with her hands full with two bags of groceries. After they were inside, he asked, "Would you like some help with your groceries?"

"Get away from me, you creep. I've got a taser and I know how to use it."

"No problem," he said, putting his hands up in the universal signal that he meant no harm.

He unwisely decided to take the stairs and was winded by the time he reached the fourth-floor apartment. "Need more exercise," he chastised himself in a quiet mumble while gasping for breath. Then he said, "Damn. There's still police tape on the door. Oh well, what the hell. A fearless PI wouldn't let a little thing like some tape slow him down." He pulled off the tape and got out his lock picks.

An hour and a half later, he finally heard the lock give way. "It's a good thing it's the middle of the day, everyone's at work and there were no distractions. Otherwise, this might have taken me a long time."

Jason entered and looked around. It was a small, one-bedroom apartment with a combined kitchen and dining area, a small living room, and a bathroom off the short hallway that led to the bedroom.

"I should probably take a quick look at the crime scene," he said as he walked toward the bedroom. "I'll just take a peak." He opened the bedroom door, and said, "Oh my God, that's a lot of blood." Next thing he knew, he was waking up on the floor, having passed out from the sight of the murder scene. "Well, that was a nice nap," he said as he looked up at the ceiling. "I feel refreshed. I should take naps more often." It never dawned on him that maybe he wasn't cut out for this line of work.

He got up, walked back up the hall to the bathroom, and opened the medicine cabinet. "Well, Jacobson was right. Here's a bottle of Happiness, just like the others. Damn, I'm good." He took down a large bottle of pills marked *Investigational Drug, Happiness, Dose: 200 mg; CureStuff Pharmaceuticals* and put it in his pocket before heading back to the red rocket and driving to CureStuff Pharmaceuticals for one last visit.

CHAPTER 21

Jason arrived at CureStuff as planned. On his way up to Dick Littlething's office, he kept his eyes out for that little black dress. He was thinking, to himself for a change. He hoped to run into Dr. Grayson and was searching for a reason to interview her again. *No way in this world could a woman that looks like that be a murderer, but she might have harmed Wendy Thompkins and Joanne Shipley because she was jealous of their relationships with Lance Harden. But why on earth would she want to kill random people like a construction worker, a NASCAR driver, an old lady, or a Starbucks barista?* He failed to note that none of his other suspects, including doctors Littlething and Harden, had any obvious motive for killing those random people either, but why sweat the small stuff? They weren't all that hot and didn't fit into his midlife fantasies.

As Jason exited the elevator on Littlething's floor, he thought he glimpsed a set of sleek, sexy legs, entering the adjacent elevator just before the doors closed. "Could that have been the lovely Dr. Grayson?" he mumbled to himself. "Would have been nice to get one more look, but that's not why I'm here. A good PI would focus on the job, not on the anatomy of a woman that's not even a suspect. Damn it, Jason, get it together." Then he couldn't help but push the elevator button to hold the doors open just in case those sleek legs had just entered. "Sorry," he mumbled to the impatient, professionally dressed men and women in the elevator.

Dick Littlething's administrative assistant showed Jason into the CEO's office as soon as he arrived. Apparently, Littlething was anxious to please. *This must be driving old Dick here crazy. He still thinks my visits have something to do with their upcoming drug license application. Oh well. It seems to be working in my favor.*

Littlething stood to shake Jason's hand, and then Jason once again sat down in one of the low guest chairs in front of the president and CEO's desk. As before, Jason was eye level with Littlething. "Thank you for seeing me again, Dr. Littlething. I just have a couple more questions before I conclude my investigation, so I can eliminate you as a suspect."

"Best to clear that up as soon as possible. Don't want the FDA thinking I'm a criminal when we send you guys our application for a license for Happiness, our new antidepressant drug. Go ahead, ask your questions."

"The last time I was here, you told me that you had bedded Wendy Thompkins and Joanne Shipley, that they had both willingly had affairs with you, and then you dumped them. However, when I spoke with each of them, they categorically denied this to be the case. They both said they refused your advances. And when I spoke with Tanya Grayson, she confirmed what Wendy and Joanne told me and said that you also tried to hit on her and she shut you down too. I want to believe that you're innocent, but I need to know the truth. Did you or did you not sleep with these women? The answer to this question speaks to whether or not you had a motive to harm them."

Littlething looked shocked at the bluntness of the question. He took a sip from the cup of coffee and realized that Jason had nothing to drink, and used this to try to deflect the question. "Would you like a cup of coffee, Detective Longfellow? I could have my assistant get you a cup."

Jason responded, forcefully, "No, thank you. Please, answer the question."

Littlething paused, then started to get agitated, visibly sweating, his hand shaking as he tried to take another sip of coffee. He looked Jason square in the eye.

"Damn, you're a good-looking woman. How long's it been since anyone satisfied you sexually? I'd like to give it a try. How about it? There's no one here but the two of us."

"Why, thank you. So, you did sleep with . . . hey . . . what? I'm a good-looking what?"

Littlething climbed down from his chair, walked around his desk to where Jason was sitting, put his hands on Jason's shoulders and began to massage. "Such beautiful shoulders, and your neck, it looks delicious. I don't know whether to lick, bite or suck on it. I want you. I want you bad, you sexy thing."

Jason was still struggling with the turn that this interrogation had taken.

"Wow, that feels really good. You have strong hands. Wait, what the hell? Get your pervy hands off me." Then it hit him. "You've been drugged! Someone slipped you the drug, and you're hallucinating. I'm not a woman, you idiot. I'm Detective Jason Longfellow. Get off me!"

But Littlething was clearly under the influence of the same drug that must have been given to Thompkins, Shipley, and the others. The effects had kicked in big-time. Littlething began to stroke Jason's hair while whispering sweet nothings in his ear. Jason stood up, hoping that his superior height would put a stop to this insane assault. He faced Littlething and said, "Doc, get a grip. You're under the influence of a drug. Someone must have slipped it into your coffee. I'm not a woman, and I'm definitely not going to have sex with you. Back off, or I'm going to hit you in the head with one of these stupid little chairs of yours." Jason gave Littlething a shove, but the little guy turned out to be stronger than Jason anticipated.

Littlething kept saying, "I want you. I want you bad. You are soooo hot." He lunged at Jason, grabbed his right leg and began to hump it.

Jason, totally shocked by this, looked down at his leg. "Hey, that doesn't feel half bad . . . I mean, get the hell off of me. You look like my neighbor's full-sized poodle, Ralph. That little bastard humps everything in sight. He got that same leg once, so it's not exactly virgin territory." Jason lifted his leg and shook it, trying to get Littlething off of him, but the man clung for dear life.

Littlething kept humping away, saying, "Oh man, that's good. Baby, you're so hot. I'm gonna take you to heaven, and me along with you." He humped faster and faster.

Jason finally reached over the top of Littlething's desk, grabbed his cordless keyboard and beat the humping man over the head with it. Littlething just kept humping.

"Damn, man, your head must be hard as hell. I thought for sure that would stop you."

Jason dropped the keyboard, shook his leg as hard as he could, gave Littlething a huge shove, and was finally able to dislodge him. Littlething fell down, never taking his eyes off of Jason's leg. He sprung back up, quick as a cat, and headed for Jason again, saying, "Oh baby. Don't be that way. I want to pleasure you so bad!"

At the last moment, Jason grabbed one of the chairs, jumped onto Littlething's giant wooden desk, and used the chair to fend him off. Jason said, "Did you just growl at me? I could have sworn you just growled at me." Then he yelled, "Help! Help! There's a mad man in here, attacking my leg like a horny pit bull."

Littlething's administrative assistant dashed into the room. She saw Jason standing on Littlething's desk, using a chair to fend off her boss. Littlething was saying, "Oh babe. Please, let me have it. I need it, bad. Please. Please. Give it to me!" She turned and ran back out of the office.

Jason yelled after her, "Call security! Dial 911."

A few minutes later, security arrived, and one of the officers tasered Littlething. The police and the EMTs showed up about the same time, and they took Littlething away in an ambulance.

"Damn. Dr. Littlething really lost it," one of the security guards told a policeman. "I never seen anything like that. He wanted that guy's leg bad. Once we got here and restrained Dr. Littlething, the guy got down from the desk, and Littlething went nuts, broke away from us, and started humping his leg all over again. It took three of us to pull him off. I'm thinking the doctor had some sort of mental breakdown—either that or that tall guy had one hell of a good leg for humping. Craziest thing I've ever seen."

Jason still didn't want to reveal his theory regarding the murders and the CureStuff drug until he was absolutely sure, so he told the police, "I don't know what happened. I went into Littlething's office, sat down, started asking him questions, and next thing I knew he ran around his desk and started humping my leg. Best I could tell, he thought he was a dog, and my leg was handy so he went after it. I've seen a dog go after a person's leg, but this is the first time I've ever seen a people go after a person's leg. Maybe he went off his meds. His company is apparently in danger of going bankrupt if their latest drug fails, so maybe he just cracked under the pressure. Studies have shown that when a company goes bankrupt, the president and CEO often goes off his rocker and starts humping someone's leg. If there's no more questions, I've got to drive home to Northern Virginia this evening, where my wife is probably going to kill me."

CHAPTER 22

Jason got home late Monday night. He was as quiet as possible, so he didn't wake Chelsea or the kids. He didn't want to interrupt Chelsea's sleep because she had to go to work in the morning, so he slept on the couch.

"Who am I kidding?" he mumbled very quietly. "I want to put off getting my ass handed to me until tomorrow, and if I go to work before she gets up, maybe she'll forget she's pissed at me by tomorrow night."

So Jason, macho man that he was, took the brave way out. He set his alarm for four, got up well before Chelsea and the girls, and left for work. He told himself as he fired up the red rocket for his commute, "I know she's mad at me, but I have the right to do what I want, and I really want to be a private eye. If she gives me any crap tonight, I'll just have to put her in her place." He knew this was just false bravado, but it made him feel better for the moment.

When he got to work, he waited until nine and called Joanne Shipley on her office phone. "Hi, Joanne. Jason here. How are you? I hope you're doing better."

She answered, "Hello, Jason. Thanks. I'm doing much better,

although I'm not ready to start carpooling with you. I don't know what happened to me that morning, and I'm not ready to trust anyone yet. Have you had any luck with the case? My husband is disappointed that we haven't heard anything from you."

They were talking on a government phone, so Jason figured it was most likely being tapped by at least twelve different government agencies. He wanted to be discreet, so he said, "I have a favor to ask. I've made progress in solving the case, and I need to meet with you. How about we have lunch together so we can talk. Say noon at Ruby Tuesday?"

She sounded suspicious and embarrassed. "Why do you want to have lunch with me, alone? Can't we just talk on the phone? I'm not ready to talk to you face-to-face."

"Please, Joanne. I've got something that I need to show you, so we have to meet in person. You might have to smell, touch, and taste it in order for you to give me what I need. Besides, I've forgotten all about your sexual escapades on our way to work a while back; you know, where you went crazy, unbuttoned your blouse and started rubbing my junk." Jason still had some work to do on his people skills, but he really needed for her to identify the pills that he had collected from the victims to make sure they were the investigational drug Happiness.

Joanne almost hung up on him, but she was intrigued that he had made some progress on the case. *Besides, what can he possibly do to me in the middle of a busy restaurant?*

"Okay. If you insist. But I get to pick the seats. I'll see you at Ruby Tuesday at noon."

• • •

Jason walked to the restaurant since it was only three blocks from his office. It was a warm spring day, in the low 80s, and he was sweating by the time he got there. Joanne was already seated at a table in the center of the room. She was wearing a dark-blue head scarf, dark glasses and a long trench coat, presumably to prevent anyone from recognizing her.

"Hello, Joanne. Good to almost see you."

"I know I'm a little overdressed, but I'm still not comfortable out in public. I don't know what happened to me in your car that morning, but my shrink tells me it gave me PTSD, post-traumatic sexual dysfunction. I freak out every time a man looks at me, and my sex life with my husband is in the tank. So, what do you need?"

"Well, first of all, too much information. Second, I'm sorry you're having problems, but you were the one that attacked me that morning. I should be the one with PTSD. And third, I'm one of the good guys, trying to figure out what happened to you, so please chill."

She raised her eyes and looked at him sheepishly. "Sorry. I'm pretty sure you didn't do anything wrong. I'm just so scared and frustrated. Since I have no idea what happened to me, I'm terrified that it might happen again, and in public would be horrible. Please tell me you have some answers."

"It's a long story, but I'll cut to the chase. I think that somehow, someone slipped you pills that caused that . . . well . . . hypersexual reaction. And I think there's a connection to your previous employer, CureStuff Pharmaceuticals."

"What? How can that be? The company's in North Carolina, and I'm here."

"I realize that. All I can tell you is that I interrogated several people at CureStuff and found there's a clinical trial going on for a new drug called Happiness, for treatment of depression. I also discovered that there've been several deaths in North Carolina attributed to strange symptoms, ranging from those similar to yours to extreme sexual hallucinations. I visited families and friends of several of those victims, searched their homes, and in all cases I found bottles of pills that were marked as an investigational drug called Happiness with CureStuff Pharmaceutical's name and logo on the label. I also discovered that you and Wendy Thompkins, the other CureStuff employee who experienced perpetual happy endings, both worked on that project at some point."

Joanne looked surprised. "Of course I worked on the Happiness project. Half of the company was assigned to that drug. It's supposed to be the savior of the company, worth millions. I don't know about Wendy, but I was never a patient in those clinical trials. Until our infamous carpool ride, I have never been depressed a day in my life. And, to my knowledge, Happiness may have some side effects, but are you suggesting that unending spontaneous orgasms is one of them? I doubt any drug company would want that on the label or in a TV commercial, at least not when it's uncontrollable and can lead to death. What would the warning say? If you experience orgasms for more than four hours, go to your doctor? Oh my God."

"Calm down," Jason said. "I don't know about any side effects with Happiness, but someone at the company did tell me about an earlier antidepressant drug called Pleasuria that failed. One of the lab techs told me about a side effect of that drug in the rat studies—she called it hyper-humping—that was only found at the high dose and conveniently left out of the licensing application. I may be way off track here, but I brought with me a bottle of the pills labeled Happiness that I found at the home of one of the murder victims, and I was hoping you could confirm that they are actually the right pills. Would you be able to tell?"

"Yes, I think so. They were small, red, triangular pills with a large *H* stamped on the front and the CureStuff logo stamped on the back."

Jason took the bottle of pills out of his pants pocket and handed it to Joanne.

"So, based on your description, these are not Happiness pills in this bottle."

"These pills are round, blue, and the only identifying mark is the *200* imprinted on the front. Jason, these are definitely not Happiness pills. I think these pills are actually Pleasuria. The *P* is missing from the front, and the CureStuff logo should be imprinted on the back along with the dose, in this case 200 mg, but Pleasuria was a round, blue pill of this size. Dear God. If this is the high dose, 200 mg, it's no wonder bad things have happened to anyone exposed to them. You're right. I worked on the Pleasuria project, and the high dose in that study caused rats to hump themselves to death. That's why Wendy Thompkins refused to give the high dose to the patients in the clinical studies. It was CureStuff's darkest secret. But how the hell did the Happiness meds get replaced by the old Pleasuria pills? More to the point, why did all of these victims have access to the pills in the first place? Happiness is an investigational drug, and only people participating in the clinical trial should have access."

A light suddenly went on in Jason's head, and it was so bright that his eyes crossed for a moment. "Holy shit! Maybe that's what these victims have in common. They were all depressed, and they signed up for the Happiness clinical trial. If that's the case, I wonder how they all found out about it."

"CureStuff would have listed the clinical trial on a government website, and they may have run an ad campaign to announce the clinical trial to the public," Joanne said. "That's how they usually get patients for these trials, that and talking to a series of doctors that they have on their payroll as clinical trial consultants. So, theoretically the patients would have either contacted the company through the information provided on the website, in the advertisement, or been referred by one of the consulting docs."

"Okay, but why would someone want to kill the patients in this clinical trial, and how the hell would they have managed to switch the pills? Also, since you weren't part of the clinical trial and presumably Wendy Thompkins wasn't either, how and why were you slipped Pleasuria pills? Have you been back to CureStuff since you left several months ago? Did anyone from your old company give you any pills recently?"

Joanne held up her hand. "Slow down. To answer all your questions, I don't know. I don't know, no, and not to my knowledge."

"So, you don't know why anyone would want to kill the patients in the clinical trial, or how someone managed to switch the pills. You don't know why someone might have slipped you Pleasuria pills. You have not been back to CureStuff, and to your knowledge no one has given you any pills. Is that correct?"

Joanne, looking like she was about to run out of the restaurant, said, "Yes. That's what I just said. You suck as a detective. You're just like all men; you don't listen. I have no idea what's going on. All I know is I'm terrified that whatever happened to me will happen again. I can tell you that it starts out pretty good, great actually, but whatever it is builds a head of steam and gets out of control pretty fast. You saw the state I was in when you took me to the ER. If they hadn't given me a heavy sedative, I don't know what would have happened. I'm not sure my heart could have taken much more. There really is too much of a good thing. Who'd have thought that too much pleasure could kill you, but I'm here to tell you it can. Oh God. Oh God."

Jason looked at her, fear in his eyes. "Are you okay?"

"Don't be stupid. That was not the I'm-gonna-have-an-orgasm Oh God; that was a this-is-really-frustrating-and-terrifying Oh God. You're an idiot. How does your wife put up with you?"

That reminded Jason that he still had to face the wrath of Chelsea, which put him in an even worse mood. As he walked away, he mumbled, "Oh God is right. When Chelsea gets through with me, I'm gonna be saying 'Oh God, oh God,' and not in a good way. Murder, humping rats, serious midlife crisis, all these good-looking women, and a fucking convertible sports car so small I can't put the top up so I drive around in the rain. What in the hell was I thinking? I'm an FDA lab rat, not a PI."

CHAPTER 23

That night after work, Jason dodged another bullet. Chelsea had to work late, so he fed the kids, helped with their homework and put them to bed. She still wasn't home by nine, so he went downstairs to his home office, got out his whiteboard, and looked at his current diagram of the case. He kept switching between thinking and talking out loud because talking to himself always helped him to think more clearly and hardly ever led to an argument.

His gut told him that Dick Littlething was innocent. He just didn't have the stones to kill anyone, although Jason was surprised at the little fellow's strength when hanging onto his leg. The fact that someone tried to kill him with the drug probably cleared him as a suspect. Jason didn't think Littlething faked the hallucination in his office, unless he really did just fall crazy in love with Jason's right leg. *Ah, who am I kidding? He's not the killer.* Jason put a line through Dick Littlething's name on the whiteboard.

What about Lance Harden? *I don't think he's the killer, either.* He developed Happiness in his lab and seemed to genuinely want the clinical trial to succeed. That would be difficult if half the patients were murdered. *Studies have shown that clinical trials usually fail if half of the patients are murdered during the trial.* Jason drew a line through Harden's name.

Based on her current state of paranoia brought on by the attack of hypersexual stimulation, Jason also ruled out Joanne Shipley as the killer. She seemed to be suffering from serious trauma. She knew about the side effects of Pleasuria in the rats, and she would have been concerned about how the drug would affect humans, so he doubted that she took the pills to deflect suspicion. He crossed her name off the whiteboard. Same went for Wendy Thompkins. She also worked on the Pleasuria project and knew the side effects. Jealousy didn't seem to be a strong enough motive for either of these women to have risked taking these pills to deflect suspicion. Lucy Chang had no motive whatsoever for harming anyone, either. According to Littlething, she had nothing to do with the Happiness clinical trial, and she wasn't involved with him or Harden.

Jason looked at the whiteboard, and he had crossed out the names of all of his suspects, with the exception of Tanya Grayson, VP, Toxicology.

"No freakin' way," he said, a little too loudly, and then winced, afraid he might wake the children. He listened, but all was still quiet upstairs. He looked at the stick figure with breasts labeled *Tanya Grayson* and said, "The woman is drop-dead gorgeous, dresses to the nines, smells real nice and is very friendly. And oh, that little black dress. I really liked the little black dress. She just can't be the killer. Studies have shown that only about one percent of hot, sexy women are serial killers."

Jason heard from behind him, "What little black dress is that, dear? And what hot, sexy women?" Chelsea had come home, found the girls in bed and gone looking for him.

Jason turned around and saw his wife standing there in her nurse's outfit. He said, sheepishly, "Hello dear. You finally got home. Busy day? How do you manage to look so beautiful after working such long hours?" He thought it was worth a try. "Why are you wearing your nurse's uniform? You work in administration now."

Chelsea responded, irritated, "Nice try, Jason. There was a bad accident on the south Beltway, and the ER was bombarded with injured commuters. A tractor-trailer hit a bus full of tourists. There were two deaths and a whole lot of contusions, abrasions, and broken bones. Since I still work in the ER once in a while to keep up my nursing skills, I was called in to help. That's why I got home so late. I didn't call because there wasn't a second of free time to dial my cell phone. I'm wasted. I've been on my feet for ten hours straight, running around like a chicken with its head cut off . . . So, what little black dress?"

Damn. She's not going to let go of this. I'm already in the doghouse. He said, pointing to his whiteboard, "I'm just looking over my outline of the case I'm currently investigating. It's a difficult one."

Chelsea interrupted. "You mean the one where you brought your carpooler into the ER after she suffered multiple magical orgasms? Are you making progress on that case? Was it really attempted murder? Sounds more like a party to me. And what little black dress?"

He gulped. "She didn't actually have multiple orgasms. Well, she kinda did, but they were spontaneous, not man-made. Crap. I mean . . . as it turns out, it appears to have been the effect of a drug that places a person in a perpetual state of sexual arousal and orgasm until they finally pass out or die. I believe someone at a drug company called CureStuff Pharmaceuticals is slipping these pills to people in an attempt to kill them. There have already been two attempted murders, one of them my carpooler, and at least three successful murders in North Carolina in the same area where this company is located. All the victims had similar symptoms. I've also discovered that most of the victims are patients in a clinical study of a drug for treatment of depression being run by this same company. And my carpooler, Joanne, used to work for them."

"That's interesting, Jason. You seem to be enjoying your gig as Jason Longfellow, Private Eye, but WHAT ABOUT THE FUCKING LITTLE BLACK DRESS?"

Jason ducked reflexively when he heard this blast from Chelsea. "Please calm down, dear. You're gonna blow a gasket. The little black dress is no big deal. It's just that I've eliminated all of my suspects but one, Dr. Tanya Grayson, the vice president of toxicology for CureStuff." He hesitated.

Chelsea said, threateningly, "And?"

Finally, Jason said, "And the last time I saw her, interrogated her, she was wearing a little black dress. She is very good looking, smart, friendly, and I just can't believe that she would do anything like murder people. It's true that one of the other employees of the company that I interviewed, a Lucy Chang, told me that Tanya . . . uh . . . Dr. Grayson had a thing for the scientist, Dr. Lance Harden, who developed their new antidepressant drug, Happiness. Dr. Harden was dating Wendy Thompkins at the time, and he had also dated Joanne Shipley."

"You mean your carpooler, Dr. Orgasm?"

Jason choked. "Yes, my carpooler that I brought to the ER. If I hadn't gotten her there when I did, she would have probably died. I keep telling you, I didn't have anything to do with what happened to her. I think someone slipped her a drug that caused her orgasms, some sort of hyper-sexual response, trying to kill her. Why is that so difficult to believe?"

Chelsea laughed, more like an insane screeching sound, and said, "So you were attracted to this doctor, what was her name, Grayson? Is this the hot, sexy woman? You liked the way she filled out her little black dress, and you don't think she could be guilty of murder because she's good looking, smart, and friendly. You really are an idiot. I'm beginning to think all men are idiots. You're in the middle of some midlife crisis, risking your government job to play private detective with no experience at all, and your family is going to starve to death. Your carpooler has multiple orgasms in YOUR car while you are driving her to work, and now you are running around pretending to solve a case that probably isn't even a crime, while chasing after women in little black dresses. Do I look stupid enough to believe this bullshit? It's men. You're all nuts. One of my friends at work has a husband who just ran off to Hawaii with his administrative assistant and left her high and dry with four children. And I just found out at work today that one of the docs has been screwing most of the nurses in the ER, four of them women and one a man. I'm going to bed. I'm exhausted from taking care of the kids by myself while you've been off in North Carolina playing private eye and from working late tonight. This isn't over. We'll discuss it further tomorrow, when I'm awake and have more energy."

Jason, his ears burning from the tongue lashing, thought, *Damn, that was brutal. Hate to see what happens when she has more energy.* "Goodnight, dear. I'm going to work on the case a little longer. I'll be up in a while."

Jason shook off his wife's barrage and refocused on the case. He needed to solve it to show Chelsea he was serious about this PI thing. If he found the murderer, at least his wife would know his being a PI wasn't just a cover to run around and cheat. *Focus, Jason, focus.*

He thought about Lucy Chang, who had told him that Tanya Grayson had a thing for Lance Harden, and Tanya would've probably been jealous of both Wendy Thompkins and his carpool buddy, Joanne Shipley. But why kill patients in the Happiness clinical trial? *Besides, Tanya's hot, smart, witty, very friendly, smells good, and that little black dress. I gotta stop thinking about that little black dress.* But he knew there was little chance of that, at least until Chelsea killed him. *Studies have shown that attractive women in little black dresses can be fatal to married men.*

Jason looked at his watch; it was midnight. *I'd better get some sleep,* he thought, *I need to go back to North Carolina one more time, to interrogate Tanya Grayson. But that's not going to happen. If I miss another day of work, and especially if Chelsea finds out that I have seen Tanya again now that she knows about her, I'm gonna die. I'd rather avoid that. Maybe there's some way that I can convince Tanya Grayson to come to me.*

He slept on the couch just to be safe.

CHAPTER 24

Jason needed to interview Tanya Grayson one more time. He thought, *I hope she's not the killer. That's not the way I want this story to end. I wish the killer was that idiot Littlething. He ruined my pants.*

The next day, Jason spoke with Joanne Shipley again. He walked over to her office at work, knocked on her open door, stuck his head in, and said, "Hey, Joanne. I hope you're doing better today. I need a favor."

She looked up from her desk and said, "Hi, Jason. I'm doing a little better. Come on in and sit. What can I do for you?"

He took a seat in front of her desk and said, "I need to interrogate Tanya Grayson again, and I need her to come to me this time, without my wife, Chelsea, finding out. Chelsea's worried I'm going to lose my job if I keep taking time off work to travel to North Carolina to investigate. Also, I may have accidentally mentioned something about Tanya Grayson and a little black dress, so I can't go back to North Carolina anytime soon or someone's going to be investigating my murder. If I die, first clue, look to my wife. So, is there any way you can convince Tanya to come up here to visit you? It's my understanding that you were friends at CureStuff. Can you make up a reason to invite her for a visit? Then I could think of an excuse to show up, and ask her some questions while she's here."

"We were friends when I worked at CureStuff, but we haven't kept in touch since I left. I can't think of any reason to invite her to come to Northern Virginia. What about you? Did the two of you get along? You might invite her to come for a visit. You could get a hotel room and meet her there. From what I remember, Tanya wasn't very picky about the guys she'd sleep with. She pretty much worked her way through the whole male staff at CureStuff, with the exception of Dr. Littlething. I'm guessing if there was any attraction between the two of you, she'd be willing to hook up."

"I'm married. I can't do that."

"Yeah, that's not a problem for Tanya. She seemed to prefer them married. Prevents any thoughts of something more permanent developing."

"So, I use my alluring ways to entice Tanya up here to Northern Virginia to meet me in a hotel room for sex? Then I interrogate the hell out of her, get to the truth and solve the case? Sounds like a good plan, except that if Chelsea finds out, I'll die. Okay, I'm down."

"My advice, Jason? Just don't mention anything about the case when you invite her to come for a visit. If she is the killer, she might make you her next victim. In fact, based on what you've told me, Tanya and your wife will probably team up to put you down. Don't say anything to Tanya that might make her think you are inviting her for anything other than wild, kinky sex. The Tanya that I knew was into that sort of thing."

Jason's eyes went blank as he zoned out for a minute, thinking about that little black dress and wild, kinky sex. He shook his head hard to clear his thoughts.

"Thanks Joanne, good advice. I'll stick to the kinky sex stuff, and won't mention that I plan to interrogate her. There was some sexual tension between us when I talked to her at CureStuff, so this might actually work." Somewhere deep in the recesses of his mind an alarm was going off. *Idiot. You're gonna die!* But Jason really wanted to solve his first case, so he went back to his office and dialed the phone.

"Tanya Grayson, VP, Toxicology."

He said, in his deepest, sexiest voice, "Hello, Dr. Grayson . . . Tanya. Jason Longfellow here. I realize we don't know each other very well, but when I first met you at CureStuff, I sensed something between us, a sexual tension. I'm hoping you felt it too."

"Hello, PI Longfellow . . . Jason. It's good to hear from you. I was hoping you'd call. What can I do for you?"

Jason gulped. "I was hoping I could see all of you . . . I mean, see you, again. I can't get away at the moment because I have too much work at the office. I was wondering if you might be willing to come to Northern Virginia for a meet. I could get you a room at a Marriott in Herndon and come over for a visit, for drinks and whatever. Maybe you could wear that little black dress you wore last time I saw you."

"Let me get this straight. You want me to come all the way to Northern Virginia to hook up with you in a hotel room, and we barely know each other? I must admit, I felt a certain attraction to you, but aren't you married? What kind of a girl do you think I am? And, more to the point, when, and which Marriott?"

Jason, now more confident, said, "How about this Friday, the Marriott out by Dulles Airport? I'll text you the address. I'll take the afternoon off and meet you in the room around one thirty." He mumbled to himself, "Damn, I'm good. I'm really getting the hang of this PI stuff."

"What? I didn't hear you."

Shit, I said that out loud. "Sorry. I said that it will be great to see you and hang with you for a while. Don't forget the little black dress."

"No worries. I'll bring it. But I don't expect to have it on for very long. Don't you disappoint me. I'll see you Friday."

Jason found himself feeling a little dizzy. *Jesus, am I really going through with this?*

Tanya was his only remaining suspect. He had no choice. She might have jealousy as a motive for trying to kill Wendy Thompkins and Joanne Shipley; they both hooked up with Dr. Harden. But why would she want to murder a pilot, a construction worker, a NASCAR driver, and a Starbucks barista? It just didn't make any sense. Even if it has something to do with CureStuff, why would she want to kill depressed patients in her own company's clinical trial? *I've got to go through with this. But Chelsea can NEVER find out what I've been up to.*

CHAPTER 25

Chelsea was busy at work, and she and Jason didn't have a chance to talk for the next couple of days, which was fine with him. Come that fateful Friday morning, he went off to work with plans to meet Tanya Grayson. He was confused and full of doubt. As he drove to work, visions of Tanya floating through his mind, he thought, *I have to assume that Tanya's the murderer. She's my only remaining suspect.* But maybe he had missed something. He forced the vision out of his head, and then said to the windshield, "I need to get her to confess, and I'll do whatever it takes, just so long as I stay faithful to Chelsea. Who am I trying to kid? If Chelsea ever finds out about this, she'll run me over in the driveway for meeting this woman in a hotel room, even if it is critical to my investigation and nothing actually happens."

At noon, he got a call from Tanya on his cell phone.

"Hello Jason. I'm here at the Marriott, room 444. I ordered champagne and am about to take a long, hot bath and put on the little black dress. We still on for one thirty?"

"Hey, Tanya. Glad you could make it. Yes, we are most definitely on. I cleared my calendar and took the afternoon off. I'll actually try to get there a little early, depending on traffic, say about one? I haven't had lunch, and I'm starving. Hold off on the bath and the little black dress, and I'll take you out to lunch before we 'get together' in the room, if you know what I mean."

"How about I order room service?"

Jason was desperate to stall. He was hoping to get a confession from her without any kinky sex stuff. *How would I explain that to Chelsea?* "I'd rather take you out somewhere. We can grab a quick bite, and then back to the room for kinky sex. I'll pick you up at one. See you soon."

"Okay. If that's what you want. I do like the idea of kinky sex. I'm into that."

He disconnected the call, and a wave of anxiety washed over him. Fearful thoughts pummeled him as an inner struggle played out in his office. He mumble-argued with himself.

"What the hell? I'm no detective. I don't have a clue what I'm doing." Maybe if he took her out to lunch first, he could trip her up and get a confession. If that didn't work, then he would take her back to the room and ply her with lots of champagne. *That's it, Plan B is I'll get her drunk. I'll get us both drunk. Good idea. That should work. But what if Chelsea finds out?* He was not trying to be unfaithful to his wife, just catch a murderer. *Would she understand?* "If she runs over me, I hope she uses her car. My little red rocket wouldn't kill me, probably just maim me." He felt dizzy, broke out in a cold sweat and had to sit at his desk for a few minutes to clear his head.

• • •

Jason surprised himself by finding the courage to leave the office at twelve thirty, and by one he was knocking on the door to room 444. Tanya opened the door wearing one of the robes that came with the room, handed him a glass of champagne, and kissed him gently on the lips, apparently not enthusiastic about the idea of going out for lunch.

"Hello, big boy," she said, her voice deep and sultry. "I hope you're feeling energetic. I went ahead and took a hot bath, I've already had a couple of glasses of the bubbly, and I'm ready to rock and roll. You wanted me in the little black dress, but how's this?" She flung open the robe to reveal bare breasts, a smooth, flat stomach, and not an inch of fabric covering anything below.

Jason felt faint, his knees going weak, his mind filled with desire to take her naked body in his arms, but a vision of Chelsea in her nurse's uniform, a deranged look on her face and a scalpel in her hand, stopped him. He collected himself.

"I want you . . . I mean, I want food. I'm really hungry. Besides, you promised me we could start with you in that little black dress. I really like that little black dress. I want to tear it off of you with my teeth. Let's go get some lunch first, then back to the room for more bubbly, the dress, and some major sexual activity."

Looking disappointed, she said, "Man, you really are hung up on that little black dress. And you're hungry, for food, at a time like this? I don't understand men. Give me a minute to get dressed, and we can get some lunch. But then it's back here for the main event, and you'd better not disappoint me. I traveled a long way for this."

She came out of the bathroom dressed in a short, dark-blue skirt and sheer white blouse unbuttoned a couple of buttons lower than necessary to show Jason what he was missing by insisting on lunch first. Jason said to her breasts, "Nice blouse. Not the little black dress, but not bad at all."

The red rocket was parked in the lot in front of the hotel, the top down as always. As they approached the car, Tanya said, "That's a really cute car, but isn't it a little small for you? How do you drive it? How do you even get in it?"

Jason looked up at the sky, saw storm clouds on the horizon, noted that it smelled like rain, and said as they got into the car, "This is part of my midlife crisis, my little red rocket. It's an awesome car, with just a couple of minor issues, like I can't put the top up, my knee hits the steering wheel when I use the clutch, and I've developed a slight limp in my left leg as the result. No worries though. We should get to McDonald's long before the rain hits."

Tanya, having trouble processing all the things that were wrong with that statement, said, "Can you drive this car safely? I didn't come all the way up here to die in a car crash. And McDonald's? You're taking me to McDonald's for lunch? I assumed we were going somewhere nice, with plates and silverware, where we could get some good food and a couple of stiff drinks to loosen up for the afternoon's gymnastics. McDonald's? Are you shitting me?"

Jason gallantly opened the passenger door for her, and then struggled getting his large frame into the driver's seat. As he pulled out into traffic, he mumbled, "She's beginning to sound like Chelsea."

"What did you say? I can barely hear you over the force of the wind trying to rip my head off."

He realized he had done it again, and said, trying to recover, "I said, do you like the sound of the engine? This baby really purrs. As to McDonald's, I thought it would be quick, so we can get back to the hotel. Also, I'm a private detective, and my first client hasn't paid me yet, so I'm a little strapped for cash at the moment. The hotel room pretty much cleaned me out. And I sure as hell don't want a midday Marriott rental to appear on one of my credit cards. I'm afraid my wife would take exception to that."

Tanya was still having difficulty hearing him over the roar of the wind, and then there was the periodic rolling thunder that was now also drowning out his voice. "Don't you still work for the government? I thought you were an FDA reviewer, at least that was Dick Littlething's impression."

"Yes, I still work for the feds, but not for long. I'm planning to tell my wife that I'm quitting my government job this weekend. Then I'll only have my PI salary. She's gonna be pissed."

"Not half as pissed as if she finds out you're screwing a hot blonde at the local Marriott. Sure you want to take me to McDonald's?"

Jason still needed some work on his detecting skills; he completely missed her thinly veiled threat to tell Chelsea. "Dear God, Chelsea can never find out about this. She's a nurse, she knows a lot about human anatomy, and I don't even want to think of all the ways she could hurt me. I know neither of us will tell her, but we have to be careful no one sees us."

In the spirit of trying to get Tanya to confess before he had to have sex with her, he asked, "So, while we're on our way to McDonald's, just for the sake of conversation, do you happen to know anything about what happened to doctors Thompkins and Shipley? You didn't have anything to do with trying to poison them, did you? I'm just asking because it would be good to know if you're a murderer before we go back to the hotel for an afternoon of wild sex."

"What? I can barely hear a word you're saying above all that thunder. All I heard was 'wild sex.' I already told you, I'm looking forward to that. Maybe you should put up the top. I think it's going to rain."

Jason realized that he had probably made a mistake by taking Tanya out in public in his red rocket, since the top was permanently down and they were both in plain sight. They were driving on a four-lane road, only two blocks from McDonald's, when they passed a Ruby Tuesday, and Jason said, "Hey, that's my wife's favorite restaurant. Sometimes she goes there for lunch with some of the girls from work. Oh shit! That's her car, parked on the street. Tanya, duck down in case she's looking out the window." He put his right hand on the top of Tanya's head and tried to push her down in the seat, but the car was so small there was no place for her to go.

At that moment, the universe decided to send a loud thunderclap to announce his presence to his wife, probably looking out the window of the restaurant as he approached. Then it started to rain. At this point, Jason's nerves were shot. He said, "Damn, it's raining so hard I can barely see. I've got the windshield wipers on high, but it's not doing any good."

Just then, another loud thunderclap hit, and Jason reflexively yanked the steering wheel to the right. The car jumped the curb and entered the sidewalk. Tanya screamed as they drove up the sidewalk in front of Ruby Tuesday, people with umbrellas scattering in all directions. Jason said, "This is nice. Studies have shown that sometimes the sidewalk is the safest place to drive, but maybe I should try to get us back onto the street, just for the hell of it."

Tanya screamed again.

Jason managed to drive the car back onto the road, miraculously avoiding colliding with parking meters, electric poles, parked cars, or pedestrians. He looked at Tanya, sitting next to him, soaking wet, and said, "Oh my, we'll have to eat in the car. You can't go into McDonald's looking like that. You don't have a bra on. I like it."

Tanya screamed again, but this time actual words came out. "Take me back to the hotel, NOW. I'm soaking wet, I want a hot bath, and if you want sex, you are going to order two bottles of their best champagne and a couple of New York strips from room service. You are going to ply with me steak and bubbly, get me warm and drunk, and only then can you have your way with me."

Jason started to say, "But—"

"Don't say a word. Just shut the fuck up and drive back to the hotel. We're going to salvage this afternoon if it kills me, or you."

Jason mumbled, "Damn, she really is starting to sound like Chelsea. Why do women treat me this way? It can't be me."

CHAPTER 26

When they finally got back to the hotel room, Tanya took another hot bath while Jason ordered the steaks and bubbly. She wore the cloth robe again while they ate. After several more glasses of champagne, she put on the little black dress. She stood next to the bed, sipping, and he walked over to her. He took in her wavy blonde hair, her delicious full lips and perfect features, and then focused on the enticingly bountiful cleavage. He had to tear his eyes away to force them to continue on down to her long, silky legs and perfect, rounded butt, also mostly exposed by the short dress. When he smelled her perfume, *l'air du couchez avec moi*, his knees went weak, and he was immediately confused as to why he was there.

"Plan B, plan B," he mumbled.

"I won't need Plan B, Jason. I'm on birth control. Now get on with it. I'm fed, buzzed, and ready. No more interruptions. What do I need to do to get you going?"

"That dress is plenty. God, you look good." He was losing his focus again, strongly tempted by her overwhelming beauty, sexual allure, and willingness to do kinky things with him. He envisioned slapping himself in the face to clear his head, pictured Chelsea running over him with his car some more, and he mumbled, "Jason, get hold of yourself. Stick with the mission."

Tanya look confused. "What? Sorry, what did you say? You talkin' dirty, nasty boy?"

"Sorry, the sight of you in that dress overwhelmed me for a second. I said that I can't wait to get hold of you."

"So, let's get to it. I'm ready to go." She started to peel the dress up over her thighs.

"Uh, leave the dress on for now. You look spectacular. Just let me sit here for a few minutes, gaze upon your incredible body, and then I'll help you remove it, with my teeth."

Tanya giggled. "That'll work. Sounds like fun."

Jason thought, *I need to bring the conversation around to the murders; need to get her into the right position to effectively interrogate her. Yes, the right position.* "I'm feeling kind of kinky this afternoon. It's been a while since I did anything over-the-top in the bedroom. How about I tie you up and take the dress off of you myself? Maybe I'll cut it off."

She giggled. "I like it. If that's what it takes to get you going, let's do it."

"I need something to tie you up. The complimentary bathrobes have cloth ties for the waist. I can use those."

"I'll pour us some more champagne while you look in the closet. I hung my robe in there, next to the other one. Hurry. I'm ready to play."

He walked over to the closet doors, just outside the bathroom and directly across from a sink with a full mirror. As he opened one of the doors, he glimpsed Tanya in the mirror over the sink, and what he saw put things in a whole new light.

Oh shit. She's dumping a blue powder into one of the glasses. She must know what I'm up to. I might suck as a detective, but it don't take no Jessica Fletcher to figure out that the blue powder is probably ground-up pills, methinks Pleasuria? But his male ego had not quite given up. *Or maybe she's just trying to roofie me."*

He removed the waist ties from the two bathrobes, closed the closet door and said, "Here I come, ready or not. Let's get kinky."

The two full champagne glasses sat side by side on the dresser next to the TV. Since he had seen her add the powder through the mirror, which reversed images, he wasn't sure which one contained the drug. "How about we finish up these glasses of champagne, and then I'll tie your wrists to the bedposts," he said.

He had the advantage; he knew she had spiked one of the champagne glasses, and she didn't know that he knew.

"Which glass is mine?" he asked. "I want to finish the bottle and get to the good stuff."

Jason purposefully stood an arm's length away, waiting for her to hand him one of the glasses. As she reached for the glass that she intended to give him, before she could pick it up he swooped in behind her and put his arms around her, kissing her on the back of the neck.

"Oooh," she squealed with feigned delight. He continued to kiss the back of her neck and nibble on her ear, managing to turn her away from the dresser. She was so sexy, she smelled so good, and he was getting tipsy; his eyes glossed over as he got lost in the thought of kinky sex, and nibbling turned into gentle biting.

"Easy, PI Longfellow. You're going to leave marks," she giggled.

To bring himself back from the abyss once more, he focused on a single thought: *Chelsea'll kill me. Chelsea, kill me. Hurt me, bad, real bad.*

When her back was to the dresser, he stopped nibbling, took one of the glasses and handed it to her. "Let's drink to this afternoon," he said, as he raised the remaining glass in the air.

She was an excellent actress, but he saw just the slightest look of concern as she also raised her glass; had he pulled a double switcheroo? She had to drink or give herself away. She said, "To this afternoon. If you don't make a move soon, it's going to be tomorrow." They both took a sip.

Then he said, "To unbridled passion, and kinky stuff." With that, he emptied his glass in a single gulp, indicating that she should do the same.

She reluctantly finished off her champagne. She said, more concern than passion in her voice, "Yes. To the kinky stuff."

He kept pouring until both bottles were completely empty. His plan B, to get them both drunk, was working, at least on him. The champagne and that damned little black dress were scrambling his brain again. Stalling for more time, trying to figure out how to get her to confess, he took her in his arms, and then shoved her onto the bed.

"Lie back and give me your *wrrishts . . .* wrists." *Crap, slurring my words,* he thought. He tied her wrists to the bedposts, clumsily fumbling as he made knots. *Plan B sucks. She holds her liquor better than I do.*

"Yes, Jason. Make me your slave. Take me. Ravage me. I'm helpless in your hands." She went along, confident that he had been the one to drink the spiked champagne. She was willing to go as far as necessary to give the drug time to take effect.

Tanya knew a lot about Pleasuria; she had worked with Lance Harden to carry out some rather illegal experiments with the drug on human subjects. The drug was intended to be very specific, to counteract depression with no side effects, which was supposed to be its greatest advantage. However, it didn't turn out to be all that specific, and the side effects were very unusual, especially at the higher doses. Pleasuria affected men and women differently. Men suffered extreme sexual hallucinations that were dangerous under certain circumstances. The warning label should read, *Do not take Pleasuria while driving, working with dangerous machinery, cooking, bathing, doing anything in public, or doing pretty much anything at all. Side effects include hallucinations and humping whatever is within reach.* Women experienced hypersexual arousal that led to multiple spontaneous orgasms, each one stronger than the last, that came more and more frequently until it all ended in one final, never-ending explosion of lethal pleasure. That warning label should read, *Do not take Pleasuria unless you want to die from extreme pleasure. Side effects include perpetual orgasm and an exploding heart.*

After Jason had her securely tied her to the bed, he said confidently, his speech still occasionally slurred from too much champagne, "Okay, now that you're *comferble . . .* comfortable. I have a few questions."

She looked surprised. "Questions? What the hell? You are supposed to brutally ravage me, not talk me to death. I didn't come all this way to talk. We could have done that on the phone. Now take me, Detective. Cut this damned dress off and have your way with me."

His eyes glossed over, and he started to tear off the dress with his teeth to ravage her, but that vision of Chelsea running over him repeatedly with his car showed up again. *Damned vision.* He put his teeth away and said, "Tanya. You are my *lasht* . . . last remaining suspect for the attempted murders of Wendy Thompkins and Joanne Shipley. Did you try to kill them? Did you *shlip* . . . slip them something to cause a hypersexual-arousal response?"

Tanya said, quite convincingly, "What the hell are you talking about?" She knew how long it should take for the Pleasuria to take effect, and she was sure that it would happen soon. So far, he had just slurred his words a little, a response to the champagne.

Jason persisted. "I get why you might want to harm two of them women . . . them two women. They both hooked up with Hard . . . Lance Harden . . . and you wanted him for yourself. Isn't that so?"

"Jason, have you gone mad? I don't know what you're talking about. I like Wendy and Joanne. I worked with both of them, and we were friends. I thought you and I were going to meet this afternoon for wild, kinky sex. You obviously lied to me. What a bummer. And you can't hold your liquor worth a damn. You're getting drunk. I doubt you could even get it up."

"Hey, I'm not drunk. You're drunk. I'm just very, very relaxed. Champagne always makes me tipsy, and just because I slur a couple of words doesn't mean I'm drunk. You have to be the one that tried to kill Wendy and Joanne. I've ruled out all my other suspects. But I can't figure out why you would want to kill a pilot, construction worker, NASCAR driver and a Starbucks burrito . . . I mean barista. That makes no sense. Please enlighten me. The way you look in that little black dress, I would very much like to believe you are innocent. No one that looks that good should ever be arrested." Again he mumbled to himself, "Pull it together, Jason. She's right. You are a little tipsy. Solve the crime, and remember your wife . . . Chelshea. Yes, Chelshea. Her name is Chelshea."

When he had called Tanya, she'd suspected that he was onto her. She had gone along with his plan to meet in a hotel room, but not for a hook-up; she planned to get rid of the pesky PI before he figured it all out and she ended up in jail.

"I have no reason to harm Wendy or Joanne, and I don't know any pilots, construction workers, or . . . what did you say? NASCAR drivers? Don't be absurd. Are you on drugs?" She was not about to admit to anything; this wasn't the brightest man she had ever met—an idiot, really. He was obviously a little drunk, and she thought there was hope as long as he continued to talk directly to her cleavage. She might get out of this yet.

She sounded convincing, and she could hold her liquor better than Jason. He mumbled, "I wonder if I made a *mishtake* . . . mistake. She met me in the hotel room and let me tie her up. Maybe I'm wrong about her. Maybe she was just looking for a good time. I certainly hope so."

She heard his mumbling, and her confidence grew. She said, "Yes, you have made a mistake. I just want to have sex with you. I'm all about the sex."

"What? Oh shit! Did I say that out loud again? I've got to stop thinking out loud . . . Are you sure you don't know any pilots, construction workers, or NASCAR drivers? Someone has been killing them in North Carolina, their symptoms were similar to Wendy and Joanne, and you are my only remaining suspect."

"I don't know any such people. And I must say, I'm disappointed as hell. I was looking forward to a wild afternoon, and all you really wanted was to ask me stupid questions about some case you're working on and take me to McDonald's." She sounded indignant. "Now untie me. I want to get out of here if you're just going to talk me to death."

Jason began to feel bad. She was very convincing, he wanted her to be innocent, and the champagne and dress were making it hard for him to think straight, at least harder than normal. He had a sudden change of heart.

"Okay, Tanya. I'm sorry. I guess I'm a worse detective than I thought. I believe you. I don't suppose we could just forget that I tied you up and questioned you, and go back to the kinky sex thing. You look incredible in that little black dress." He tried to release her, but he had difficulty untying the knot he had so expertly tied before finishing the last bottle of champagne.

In his mind, he heard a little voice. *Jason, you're an idiot. You know you can't have sex with her. Chelsea will kill you to death, completely to death. And you've blown it with Tanya anyway. And what about the blue powder? Oh, crap, the blue powder. She was trying to kill you. That could get in the way of having sex with her.* He had another change of heart and stopped his hopeless attempt at untying her.

"This is definitely not my finest hour, and I don't have a lot of experience at this private-detective thing. When I went over the case, I eliminated everyone as a suspect but you." He was a little dizzy, but he had always metabolized alcohol quickly, had made sure that Tanya drank most of the bubbly, and he could already feel the effects wearing off.

"I needed to interrogate you again, and this was my plan, my plan B. Obviously not a good plan, but a plan. I thought if I got us both drunk, I might get you to confess. But you look so good in that damned dress, you smell so good, and I can't stop having kinky sex thoughts. And you hold your alcohol even better than I do, and I'm big. My plan isn't working. I need help. Do you have any suggestions as to how I might get you to confess? I'd ask someone else, but you're the only other person here."

Tanya started to struggle against her bonds. She was getting impatient for the Pleasuria to take its effect on him, and he was babbling like an idiot, but apparently not from the drug. Enough time had passed that he should be freaking out any minute with wild sexual hallucinations.

Frustrated and certain that she would be in control soon, she said, "Jason, you need to untie me. Are you feeling anything, starting to feel strange? I slipped a drug into your champagne while you were looking in the closet. Soon, you should start having wild sexual hallucinations, and I'll be forced to protect myself by shooting you with the .380 Beretta that I have stashed in my purse. I'll tell the police that you insisted on meeting here in the hotel, under the pretense of asking me questions about other suspects in the CureStuff Pharmaceuticals case. Then, you attacked me, and I had to defend myself. That should solve all my problems, including ruining your credibility as a detective and deflecting any suspicion from me regarding the murders."

"No worries. I don't have any credibility, just a PI license I printed off the internet thingy. Wait, a gun? You've got a gun? You were going to shoot me? Can I see your gun? I like guns." He went to her purse and took out the little Beretta. "What a cute little gun. Not very big. Is this just for shooting little people?" He accidentally pushed the magazine release, the magazine fell under the bed, and he tossed the gun aside. "This thing's useless. I just want the truth. So, are you admitting that you committed the murders? Why would you want to kill the pilot, construction worker, and the others? I get it with Wendy and Joanne, but why the others?"

"I really don't know what you're talking about. Why aren't you feeling strange? You should be hallucinating by now. What the hell?"

"Tanya, I'm not as dumb as I look. I saw you in the mirror dumping blue powder into my champagne. I guessed it was ground up Pleasuria and you were trying to kill me. You must have caught on that I suspected you in the murders. So, I switched the glasses. At least I think I did. It's you that should start feeling strange soon. If you confess to the murders and tell me why you killed all these people, I'll untie you and take you to the ER so they can give you a sedative to counteract the effects of the drug. What do you say? Talk, or you're going to die, of pure pleasure." Still a little tipsy, he actually giggled when he said this. "That's funny. Die of pure pleasure."

"First of all, I'd rather die from pure pleasure than have you talk me to death. And second, you're so full of it. You didn't switch anything. Once you start hallucinating, I'm going to blow you away. And you thought you were going to get me out of my little black dress. Take a long, hard look because that's all you're going to get, that and a bullet. You really suck as a private eye."

Then her eyes glossed over, her body tensed and she said, "Ooooh. That feels really good. Do that some more." Then, lucid again, she said to Jason, "Damn you. What did you do? Take me to the emergency room, immediately! Oh God, that feels so good. Make it stop. No, don't make it stop. I want it to go all the way. Ooooh."

When Jason heard this, he knew he had done it, he had her, and what happened next was very important, but he was a little disappointed that this sex thing was happening without any help from him. "Tanya, you need to tell me the truth. Did you murder all those people, and why? Tell me, and I'll take you to the ER."

She kept slipping in and out of a state of hyperarousal, first lucid, then all, "Ooooh. More. Please do that some more. Don't stop." In another moment of clarity, she said, "All right. I'll tell you. Just get me to the ER." Then she started babbling, focusing as best she could, as the tension between her legs continued to build toward an explosion of sexual release.

Jason said, momentarily forgetting the imminent threat of death by wife, "It's not fair. I was getting into that kinky stuff. Why did you have to be the killer? Talk, woman. Confess!"

She babbled, "Okay. Okay. Harold Jennings, pilot. Dated my college roommate at UVA. She was my best friend, my only friend. I was overweight and unpopular freshman back then. Couldn't even get into a sorority. Jennings was older, out of school. He used to make fun of me, mean to me, tormented me. He got her pregnant, stole her away from me, and later dumped her. I wanted revenge. . . . Oh my God. Oh my God. Aaaahh!" Her body went rigid with her first orgasm.

"Wait. What? You were overweight in college? Not possible. So you knew him in college and he was mean to you and pissed you off?

You wanted revenge? So, you decided to kill him? That seems kind of extreme. And why now, after all these years?"

"Whoa, here we go again. Ooooh, that's so damned good. Make it stop. No, I don't want it to stop. Best sex I've ever had. And no man needed. Wow, this would be great if it didn't kill a person." Then, to Jason, "Yes, damnit, Jennings hurt me, so I killed him. Todd DeMarco, weed-smoking creep, I went to high school with his sister. He and his sister bullied me. He grew up to work construction. I took him down too." Then, "Oh God. Here we go again. I'm gonna come. So good." She screamed, "Yes, oh yes! Aaaahh!" Another orgasm; this one seemed stronger than the last. When it was over, she had another lucid moment in which she said, "Take me to the ER. Now! Or I'm done for!"

"What about the others?" Jason pressed.

"Oh God. It's building again, faster and stronger. It's so good, it's overwhelming. I don't know how much more of this I can take. Make it stop. Oooooh. No. Don't make it stop. That feels incredible! I'm gonna die. Oh, that's so good."

Jason repeated, "What about the others? Mary Hutchinson?"

Tanya said, "Oooooh. God. Soooo good. Mary Hutchinson. My high school gym teacher. Bullied me. Made me climb the rope. Oh yes. I'm gonna come again."

Jason said, more firmly, "What about Mary Hutchinson?"

"High school gym teacher. I didn't want to climb the damned rope, but she made me. Fell and broke my arm, the bitch! Oooooh. Oh yes, yes!" She had her third happy ending. "Oh God! Oh God! Aaaahh!" Then, "Jason, please take me to the ER. I can't take any more of this. Oh, wow. Never mind, don't take me anywhere. Just let this go on, forever."

Jason was getting worried. He didn't know how much more she could take, but he was recording her on his cell phone and needed her full confession. "Go on, Tanya. What about Jenny Jacobson and Jimmy Jeb Johansen, the NASCAR driver?"

"Oh God. This one's going to kill me. They just keep getting stronger and stronger. Oh yes, yes! Damned Jenny Jacobson. A fucking barista at the Starbucks around the corner from my house. Got my order wrong, and then spilled hot coffee on me. Had to pay her back. Jimmy Jeb, next-door neighbor when I was a kid. He used to torment me and beat me up. On my list. Got him back, too."

"List? What list? Is this about some list you put together of people that harmed you, and you wanted to get revenge? But why? You are so beautiful, and so hot and curvy, and you smell so good."

"I didn't always look like this. Kind of overweight and plain as a kid, was tormented and bullied a lot, guess it really pissed me off. Father was also a bully, slapped me around some. I've always had anger issues but kept them to myself. Ooooh God! I'm gonna go again."

Then Jason remembered his young daughters, each of whom had a list of bad things he had done to them—spilling ice tea on the older one on her birthday, spilling Pepsi on the younger one at the movies, also on her birthday, having to work the day one of them had gum surgery and not being there for her. They each had a list, and they repeated their lists to him from time to time, especially when they were angry. He thought, *Yikes! I'm gonna apologize to my daughters as soon as I get home, before they grow up and take me out! Who am I trying to kid? After this, Chelsea will beat them to it by a mile.*

He said to Tanya, "So, this is about a list? Am I on your list? You tried to spike my champagne with that lethal drug. How do I get off of your list? I'm gonna be on Chelsea's list too if she ever finds out about this. What can I do to get you to take me off of your list?" He really didn't want to die yet.

Tanya screamed, "Oh my God. Aaaaaaahh!" as she had yet another orgasm. Jason thought the top was going to blow off of her head. "Yes, goddammit. It's about a list. Those sons of bitches, all of them hurt me, bullied me, screwed me over. Needed to get them back. Yes, you can consider yourself to be on my list, too. If you want to get off the list, take me to the ER. Gonna stroke out or have a heart attack if I don't get something to stop this. Oooooh. Not again. Oh, yes, again. Please, again, and again, and again, don't stop!"

Jason knew he should get her to the ER soon, but he needed to get all the facts, a full confession. If she was in jail, it wouldn't matter if he was on her list. She was reasonably young, and he thought she could hang in there a little longer. "So, Tanya, how did you manage to get all these people to take Pleasuria? That is what you did, isn't it? But how?"

"Aaaaahh! Here we go again. Oh God, that's good, so intense. My head's going to explode. Each one stronger and stronger. Don't want it to stop. Please make it stop. Damn you. Saw my chance with the extreme Pleasuria side effects. Sent information to all of them about the Happiness clinical trial. Most of them were depressed and signed up. Then, I switched their pills. I'm friends with docs running the trial and had no problem getting access to the meds." Her body stiffened again, and she screamed, "Aaaaahh! Oh my God! Oh my God! That was a whole new level of orgasm. Over the top. Please make it stop. No, just one more."

"Tanya, we're almost there."

"Almost there, hell, I've been there five times already. Get me to the ER. Now!"

"Just one more thing. What about Wendy and Joanne? Did you try to kill them too? And how?"

Tanya's eyes crossed for a moment, her whole body shook, a big smile came across her face, and she said, "Yes, damn you. Was pissed at Wendy. She hooked up with Lance, and I wanted him, but he wasn't interested in me that way. Can you believe it? Look at me! So I slipped some of the drug into her coffee that morning at work. No one had any idea what was going on. She really freaked everyone out at the meeting. I guess I didn't give her enough to kill her. Oh no! Oh God. The wave is building, and building, and building. I'm gonna drown this time!"

"Okay. I'll dial 911 and get the ambulance here. Just tell me about Joanne. How did you get to her when she was in Northern Virginia?"

"Aaaaaaaahh!" Tanya's eyes crossed, her body went rigid, and the smile on her face was enormous. Her wrists were still tied to the bedposts, so she was in no danger of harming herself, other than maybe her heart giving out.

"Wow. That must have been a good one. So what about Joanne?"

"Oh my God. I can't take any more. Always thought multiple orgasms a good thing, but this is . . . Aaaahh. Oh my, that's very, very good. Building, building, rising, rising. Don't know if I can survive this one. Joanne, that bitch. She dated Harden before Wendy, but I couldn't get to her. She worked in another building. One day she had a headache. I loaned her a bottle of pills for treating migraines. They actually contained Pleasuria pills mixed in. Figured at some point she'd take enough to affect her. She had frequent migraines; must have had a doozy after she moved to Northern Virginia, took some of the pills, and ended up in the ER. Just my luck she had to be carpooling with you, and you turned out to be a PI. Oooooooh! Here it comes! Aaaaahh! Oh God!" Her eyes crossed again and her body went rigid for a long time. She screamed the entire time, "Aaaaahh! Oh. My. God!" Then she said, "Please, get me to the ER. This is way, way, way too much of a good thing."

Jason had everything he needed to have her arrested, and he needed for her to go to jail. *Oh God, I'm on her list now.* "Hang in there, Tanya, I'm dialing 911. They should be here soon."

He untied her and put her shoes on her feet so she would be ready when the paramedics arrived. She was still on the bed moaning and panting. The paramedics asked Jason what had happened, and he said, "She took something, some kind of pill that induces repeated orgasms that get stronger and stronger. The same thing happened to my carpooler a couple of weeks ago. In that case, someone slipped her pills without her knowing it."

One of the paramedics said, suspiciously, "Are you sure you didn't roofie her? That's illegal, you know."

"No, I didn't do anything. I'm a private detective, and we were supposed to meet to discuss my latest case. But she took something, and then this mess started. She's been having spontaneous orgasm after orgasm for the past forty-five minutes, and she can't seem to make it stop. How do you think I feel? I felt kind of left out being in a hotel room with a woman that looks like that with her having all that awesome sex without me. It's very disturbing. I think I need a couple of tranquilizers myself. I'll probably end up with PTSD."

The paramedics put her on a gurney and wheeled her down to the ambulance as she moaned and screamed louder and louder with each new orgasm. Jason asked the paramedic, "Can I travel in the ambulance with her? I'm the one that was questioning her when this happened, and I would like to make sure she's okay."

The paramedic said, "This is the strangest one I've ever seen. I've picked up couples having extramarital affairs that have hurt themselves in the throes of passion, older married couples that have overdone it in the bedroom, injuries due to improper use of sex toys, all kinds of strange things. But this is the first time I've rescued someone in a hotel room, where only one of the participants was hurt having sex with herself without anyone doing anything." He looked at Jason with a combination of pity and disdain and said, "Sure, get in."

Jason couldn't think of anything to say, so he just smiled sheepishly, shrugged, and got into the back of the ambulance with Tanya, and they headed for the ER, siren blazing. Then it hit him; he was in an ambulance, on the way to the ER, again, with a woman that looked like Tanya, wearing a little black dress, and having uncontrollable spontaneous multiple orgasms. He asked the paramedic, already knowing the answer, "What hospital are we headed for?"

The young man answered, "Inova Fairfax Hospital in Falls Church."

As Jason passed out and slid from his seat onto the ambulance floor, he mumbled out loud to no one in particular, "Oh God, oh God, Chelsea."

ACKNOWLEDGMENTS

My heartfelt thank you goes out to my wife for her patience, love and support in reading various drafts of my manuscript and providing helpful input while tolerating my sometimes silly sense of humor, and to my loving youngest daughter, Jackie, for her early edits that eliminated redundancy and improved the flow of the story. I would also like to thank my local Lake Writers group for their early input, and a special thanks goes out to the editors at Koehler Books for their excellent work and for teaching me about throwaway sentences and editing a book for the reader rather than the author.